THE KING AGAINST
ANNE BICKERTON

Borgo Press Books by S. Fowler Wright

Arresting Delia: An Inspector Cleveland Classic Crime Novel
The Attic Murder: An Inspector Combridge & Mr. Jellipot Classic Crime Novel
The Bell Street Murders: An Inspector Combridge & Mr. Jellipot Classic Crime Novel
Beyond the Rim: A Lost Race Fantasy
Black Widow: A Classic Crime Novel
The Capone Caper: Mr. Jellipot vs. the King of Crime: A Classic Crime Novel
Crime & Co.: An Inspector Cleveland Classic Crime Novel
Dawn: A Novel of Global Warming
Dead by Saturday: An Inspector Cleveland Classic Crime Novel
Dream; or, The Simian Maid: A Fantasy of Prehistory (Marguerite Cranleigh #1)
Elfwin: An Historical Novel of Anglo-Saxon Times
The End of the Mildew Gang: An Inspector Cauldron Classic Crime Novel (Mildew Gang #3)
Four Callers in Razor Street: An Inspector Combridge & Mr. Jellipot Classic Crime Novel
The Hanging of Constance Hillier: An Inspector Cleveland Classic Crime Novel
The Hidden Tribe: A Lost Race Fantasy
The Jordans Murder: An Inspector Combridge & Mr. Jellipot Classic Crime Novel
The King Against Anne Bickerton: A Classic Crime Novel
The Mildew Gang: An Inspector Cauldron Classic Crime Novel (Mildew Gang #1)
Murder in Bethnal Square: An Inspector Combridge & Mr. Jellipot Classic Crime Novel
The Police and the Public: Some Thoughts on the British System of Justice
Post-Mortem Evidence: An Inspector Combridge & Mr. Jellipot Classic Crime Novel
The Return of the Mildew Gang: An Inspector Cauldron Classic Crime Novel (Mildew Gang #2)
The Rissole Mystery: An Inspector Combridge & Mr. Jellipot Classic Crime Novel
The Screaming Lake: A Lost Race Fantasy
The Secret of the Screen: An Inspector Combridge & Mr. Jellipot Classic Crime Novel
Spiders' War: A Novel of the Far Future (Marguerite Cranleigh #3)
Three Witnesses: A Classic Crime Novel
Too Much for Mr. Jellipot: An Inspector Combridge & Mr. Jellipot Classic Crime Novel
The Vengeance of Gwa: A Fantasy of Prehistory (Marguerite Cranleigh #2)
Was Murder Done? A Classic Crime Novel
Who Murdered Reynard? A Classic Crime Novel
The Wills of Jane Kanwhistle: An Inspector Combridge & Mr. Jellipot Classic Crime Novel
With Cause Enough?: An Inspector Combridge & Mr. Jellipot Classic Crime Novel

THE KING AGAINST ANNE BICKERTON

A Classic Crime Novel

by

S. Fowler Wright

Writing as "Sydney Fowler"

The Borgo Press

An Imprint of Wildside Press LLC

MMIX

CONTENTS

BOOK ONE: THE INQUEST

BOOK TWO: THE TRIAL

BOOK ONE

THE INQUEST

CHAPTER I.

IT was about five o'clock when Mr. Hackett returned to the Nelson's Head, in Tithebarn Street, and informed the reception clerk, as he passed in, that he would be staying the night, and might possibly require his room for a day or two longer.

He had arrived in Liverpool at midday, and had gone straight to this hotel, where he was accustomed to put up, but had then been uncertain whether he would be staying for more than a few hours.

The clerk observed that Mr. Hackett was in exceptionally good spirits, joking with him as he signed the book. He was halfway along the corridor that led to the commercial room before the clerk remembered the telegram that had been delivered half an hour earlier.

"Mr. Hackett," he called, "there's a wire for you, sir."

Mr. Hackett came back, tore off the envelope, and read the telegram with an evident annoyance.

He began, "I shan't want that room after all. Oh, I don't know."

He stood uncertain, looking aggrieved rather than troubled, and then went on to the commercial room.

While he waited for the meal he had ordered he read the telegram again, muttering angrily, and then threw it into the empty grate.

When he had finished the meal he wrote a letter which he addressed to Mrs. Bruton Hackett, The Firs, Holyhead Road, West Bromwich, and which he gave to the boots to post. Then he went out to spend the evening at His Majesty's Theatre, and to be mildly amused by a provincial revival of *The Lyons Mail*.

After he left the commercial room the waiter, being without occupation (for it was the August Bank Holiday week, and the hotel was almost empty), took the telegram from the grate and read this:

> Come back at once I am much worse since you left
> this morning. BELLE.

The next morning Mr. Hackett got up rather late. He came down to breakfast at 9:45. He found two letters beside his plate, and, having read these with some care, he asked for his bill, saying that he had decided to leave that morning, and would catch the 10:40 for Birmingham, but might be back in a day or two, and any letter that might come in his absence was to be kept till they heard further from him.

Half an hour after he had gone another telegram arrived at the hotel, which said:

Do come Belle really ill most anxious. ANNE.

But this telegram never came into his hands, and was first read by Inspector Taverton when he called a few days later to inquire concerning Mr. Hackett's movements, and, in particular, whether it was quite certain that he had actually spent the night of Thursday, August 8th, in the hotel bedroom which he had booked for that purpose.

CHAPTER II.

IT would be easy to follow Mr. Hackett to his home in Holy-head Road; to hear his conversation with Rose Dorling, the "lady help" who, in addition to a variety of household duties, had the care of his two young children; to overlook the interview with his dying wife; to observe the subsequent conversation—or shall we call it a skirmish?—with his sister-in-law, Anne; to be puzzled by the delay before he phoned Dr. Riggett in response to the urgent message which had been awaiting his return; to overhear a dozen subsequent conversations, which might elucidate or confuse. But if we are to judge this case with open minds, if we are to do justice to coroner, to police-inspector, to principals and witnesses, even to the jury themselves, it is the fairer way to enter the dingy court as they entered it, knowing scarcely more than we know, and hearing the coroner's admonition to put such gossip from their minds, and to be guided in their verdict as to the cause of the death of Mrs. Arabella Hackett solely by the evidence which would be put before them.

"I am afraid, ladies and gentlemen," he added, "that it will be impossible to conclude the inquiry today. We have a number of witnesses to hear, for which purpose I propose to sit today and as late as may be necessary tomorrow, but the circumstances are such that it has been considered advisable that there should be an analysis of certain organs, and without in any way prejudging the evidence which we are about to hear, I am sure that you will agree with me, and that it will be the wish of the relatives themselves that you should have the report of that analysis before you when your verdict is given. Our first witness will be Dr. Riggett."

But at this point the coroner's officer whispered to him that the doctor had telephoned that he had been delayed at the local hospital, and though he was now coming over.

"If it's not more than that I think I will wait," was the coroner's answer. "I should like this evidence first."

So we have three minutes (or it may be four) to glance round the court and observe those on whom the pitiless searchlight of the law is about to fall, and those also who are waiting to strike, if it should pause to indicate a victim among them.

The coroner, Aldwyn Bradson, of Collett, Bradson, and Collett, is an elderly man, with a rather long, grizzled beard. You would say he is probably sixty, but scarcely looking his age. He is, in fact, sixty-eight. He is a sound lawyer and a fair-minded man, logical, impartial, even kindly in a cold-blooded way. He will be patient and diligent in his search for facts, very capable, and, if necessary, quite pitiless in his presentation of them to the jury, when the time arrives for the summing-up.

He has been coroner for thirty years, and has supported the dignity of his office, and his own reputation, for that period without lapse or scandal. On the whole, a man that the innocent should trust, and the guilty fear.

We can leave the jury without more than a passing glance. They are like all juries, looking ill-dressed and self-conscious, and having a freakish aspect, being taken suddenly from their familiar settings. The jury really does not count very much here. A coroner's court does not require a unanimous, but only a majority, verdict. When the time arrives, Mr. Bradson is probably capable of obtaining from them the verdict which the case, in his judgment, will require.

There are five witnesses to be called after Dr. Riggett.

There is James Bruton Hackett, the husband of the dead woman, a dark, rather heavily built man, of about thirty-five years, and sitting next to him on his left there is her sister, Anne Bickerton, with a pale, quiet face, looking very white in contrast to the black she wears.

On James Hackett's right sits his lawyer, Duff-Preedy. Under a manner which is as gravely alert, sympathetic, and reassuring as he can make it, he is inwardly in excellent spirits at being retained in a case which he anticipates (it might be unfair to say "hopes") will be of a dramatic celebrity.

On this other side is the fourth witness, the "lady help," Rose Dorling, a fair-haired girl, looking grave and anxious enough, but with a glance for James, when their eyes met, which caused Duff-Preedy to lean a little forward, so that it might be intercepted as quickly as possible and (he hoped) escape the notice of the jury (which would be unfortunate), or of the coroner (which might be much more so).

11

It is by his contriving that he sits thus between Miss Dorling and her employer. There might be certain facts which could not be concealed, which it might be best to admit with an aspect of unfearing frankness, but that was no reason why the jury should have opportunities of observation, which may be so much more convincing than the spoken word, especially to unimaginative minds.

Next beyond Miss Dorling there is the ponderous, blue-jowled form of Russell-Welch, K.C., ready to cross-examine on behalf of the police such witnesses as the coroner may call, showing that the Home Office is stirring, though it may take no decisive step till the present inquiry is concluded. Beside him is Chief Inspector Taverton, whose presence also shows that the Chief Constable has called on the resources of Scotland Yard.

The fifth witness is Mr. Price Glasbrook, a public analyst from Birmingham, who will have evidence to give which is of decisive importance, though it may not occupy the court for more than two or three minutes.

There will be another witness, Dr. Thomas Elgood, who like Dr. Riggett, has not yet reached the court.

The reporters present have overflowed their allotted table, and the public have crowded in so thickly that it is requiring the energetic piloting of two uniformed constables to clear the way for Dr. Riggett—who has just arrived—to reach the witness-box on the right hand of the coroner.

The doctor having been sworn in the usual way, the coroner proceeded to elicit evidence, with the nature of which he was himself already familiar, by a series of questions which continued for some time without interruption even from Mr. Russell-Welch. The K.C. took notes with some diligence, glancing up between then at the little doctor with shrewd, penetrating eyes under heavy blows, or engaging in hurried whisperings with the Chief Inspector, or with the solicitor from whom he had received his instructions, and who was seated behind him.

It will be necessary to follow the doctor's evidence rather closely.

"I think, Dr. Riggett," the coroner commenced, "that I am correct in stating that it was about nine o'clock on the morning of August the 8th—of the 8th instant—that you were first summoned to attend Mrs. Hackett?"

"Yes—that is, on this occasion. I had attended her previously."

"At what interval?"

"My last visit had been in January of this year."

"So far as you know, she had not been ill in the meantime?"

"I believe that she had consulted Dr. Elgood during that interval."

"Well, we shall have Dr. Elgood's own account of that. At what hour did you first see Mrs. Hackett on this occasion?"

"About twelve—or possibly a few minutes later."

"Then may the jury understand that the first summons was not of a very urgent character?"

For the first time the doctor hesitated for a second before he replied.

"I should not like to imply that it was not urgently worded. I did not regard it as of so pressing a nature that I should take it out of its place on my round. I had other calls that morning which were at least equally serious."

"I am not questioning your discretion, Dr. Riggett," the coroner answered soothingly. "I am only trying to place the facts as accurately as is possible before the jury, because in a case of this kind it is difficult to say in advance that any one, however trivial it may seem, may not ultimately prove important. Can you say from whom the summons was received, and how it was worded? Did you take it personally?"

"It was from Miss Bickerton. My wife took it, and repeated it to me as it came over the phone. I was at breakfast at the time. It said that Mrs. Hackett was in bed with an attack of muscular rheumatism. She was also unable to eat, and in very severe pain from an attack of what was suggested to be gastric catarrh. I replied that I would be round as early as possible."

"Was any further message received?"

"I believe that Miss Bickerton rang up twice again in the interval before I called."

"Will you tell the jury in non-technical language how you found the patient when you called at midday, and what opinion you formed on that occasion?"

"I formed the opinion that there was nothing seriously wrong. The pulse was rather rapid, but the temperature was normal. There was an absence of disquieting symptoms of any serious kind. I learned from Miss Bickerton that Mr. Hackett had insisted on leaving for a business journey, although his wife had protested that she was too ill to be left, and that she had refused food since his departure that morning."

"Then you formed the opinion that she was not dangerously ill at that time?"

"Yes, I did."

"Have you since altered or modified that opinion in the light of subsequent events?"

"No, I cannot say that I have."

"Did you tell Mrs. Hackett that you did not regard her illness seriously?"

"No. I prescribed rest and light food. I gave a prescription for a tonic, and promised to look in again in the evening.

"Did you say anything to Miss Bickerton before leaving?"

"Yes. I saw her downstairs, and reassured her as to her sister's condition."

"Reassured her? Then you had formed the opinion that she was unduly anxious? Can you recollect your conversation with her on that occasion?"

The doctor paused again, and then said, with a careful precision: "I am anxious not to confuse what I may have said or thought on that occasion with any event which occurred subsequently. Of course, I did not regard the matter then as having any special importance. I think I was aware of a certain tension in the atmosphere of the house. It is a condition which we medical men must often observe, and of which we must appear unconscious unless our attention is directed to it by those who have called us in. I had gained the impression that Miss Bickerton was half in a somewhat emotional state, and that she was over-anxious—genuinely anxious—about her sister's condition. I think I tried to reassure her. I remember that I said that I would give a sleeping-draught when I came in the evening if it should seem desirable, but that it might be avoided if she could keep her patient quiet and get her to take some food. She asked what she might have, and I said anything she fancied which may be taken to show that I had satisfied myself that there was no gastric disorder at that time."

"After that will you tell us the course of events in your own words?"

"I was called out after lunch to a confinement case, and did not get back till nearly six o'clock. I then learned that Miss Bickerton had telephoned for me again during the early part of the afternoon. I called about 6:20 P.M. and saw Mrs. Hackett, who appeared to be in a similar condition to that of the morning, but more agitated. There was some rise in temperature, but not more than might have been anticipated at that hour.

"She told me that she had taken no food since the morning, which her sister afterwards confirmed. The tonic which I had prescribed had been made up, but had not been taken. I was told in explanation that it had only just come from the chemist's, which I subsequently learned was untrue."

"But it had not been taken?"

"No. It was still full at the time of Mrs. Hackett's death."

"Did you understand that she had taken no nourishment at all?"

"She had water beside her bed, of which I understood that she drank freely. Her sister told me that she had had a cup of tea during the afternoon."

"If at that time she had taken anything of a harmful nature—in plain words, if she had taken poison at that time—there was no development of any adverse symptoms which your skill could detect?"

"No. Not at that time."

"Did she appear to be alarmed at her own condition?"

"It is not easy to answer that. She was anxious that I should say that she was so seriously ill that her husband ought to be summoned home. She asked me to write to him myself to that effect, which I declined. She told me that she had wired for his return, and she was then writing a letter to the same purpose. She asked me several times whether I thought she were dying."

"And, in spite of that, you remained of the opinion that there was nothing seriously wrong?"

"Yes. I thought she was shamming."

"And will you tell the jury what opinion you have since formed, in the light of subsequent events, as to what her condition then was—I mean at the time of this second visit, as distinct from that of the first?"

"I still think she was shamming."

"Even though it should subsequently appear that she had actually taken a fatal dose of poison at that time? You would still be of that opinion?"

"Yes, certainly. On the assumption you mention the poison had not had any adverse physical effects at that time."

"Supposing—the jury will understand that it is no more than a hypothesis—that such a dose had been taken, was not her anxiety as to her condition, and her repeated questions as to whether she were about to die, consistent with her knowledge or suspicion of such a circumstance?"

"No, I don't think so. I don't think she was in any real anxiety. I regarded it merely as a pose to attract attention and sympathy."

"Do you think she was of a temperament, or was at that time in an abnormal condition, such as might incline her to the taking of her own life?"

Dr. Riggett paused for a long moment, and then said with deliberation, "No, I feel sure she was not. "

Mr. Duff-Preedy interposed. "Would it surprise you, Doctor, to know that she had threatened to take her life many times—that this tendency or obsession was common knowledge among her relatives and friends?"

The doctor thought again, and said with the same deliberation, "No, not at all. "

Mr. Duff-Preedy, an adroit man in the finessing of evidence sat down at once when he had obtained this answer, but the coroner said, "I don't want us to get upon ground which is better discussed, if at all, when the whole of the evidence is before us, but I think it may be well for you to reconcile those two replies, Doctor, in a way that will be clear to the lay mind."

"I think, sir," the doctor answered, "that any psychologist would accept my replies as consistent with, or even complementary to, each other. Many people talk of committing suicide at one time or another, and there may or may not be any serious purpose behind the words. Usually there is none. But of all people, those who talk frequently of taking such a step are the least likely to do it. That is what would be expected on psychological grounds, and it is borne out by general experience."

"Very well," said the coroner, "then I will ask you one further question before you go forward to the events of the next day. Was Mrs. Hackett in such a physical condition that afternoon that she could have gone downstairs and returned to her own room without the assistance or knowledge of those who were in the house with her?"

"That is another question which is difficult to answer in a word. I should say that the muscular rheumatism of which she had first complained when she took to her bed had a real physical basis—it was an affection of which she had severe intermittent attacks, for which I had prescribed for her previously—and that its natural effect would be to make the passage of stairs a slow and somewhat painful process, but it was certainly possible; under a sufficient nervous stimulus, such as an alarm of fire, she would have done it quite easily. But she was professing to be incapable of rising at all. I should say that she was theoretically capable of such exertion, that it was doubtful how far she was aware of having this capacity, and that it

16

was exceedingly improbable that she would have made such an attempt."

"But you cannot entirely exclude such a possibility?"

"Not in theory. Actually I am quite sure that it did not happen."

Mr. Duff-Preedy rose again. "But, if I may suggest such a distinction, it would not be inaccurate to say that, as a medical man—as an expert—you say it was possible; it is only as a personal opinion that you discredit such a consideration."

"Yes," the doctor replied, "you may put it that way if you like."

"And after that, Doctor?" said the coroner.

"I was summoned again during the night. About three o'clock Miss Bickerton rang me up, and I must own that I was reluctant to go. I had had a very tiring day, and I thought that there was probably being called up for no adequate reason. I said I would look in during the morning. Then there was another voice—that of Miss Dorling, as I afterwards learned—saying that Mrs. Hackett was really seriously ill. She had been violently sick, and they were alarmed by her condition. I got up and went round at once."

"How soon were you there?"

"Within ten minutes. I walked round, as the houses are not more than three minutes apart. I found Dr. Elgood's car at the door, and hesitated whether to go in, but I thought I had better have a word with him, as I had been called. When I went in he asked me to stay."

"What was Mrs. Hackett's condition at that time?"

"On consultation with Dr. Elgood we agreed that her symptoms were those of acute arsenical poisoning."

"You naturally inquired as to what food, if any, she had taken since your previous visit?"

"Yes. It appeared that she had roused her sister, who had been sleeping in the same room, about 1:00 A.M., saying that she felt hungry, and asking her to cook a meal for her. Miss Bickerton told me that she had gone down to the kitchen and fried a chop, and served it with some potatoes which had been previously cooked, and which she warmed. Her sister had only eaten a few mouthfuls when she was violently sick, and other symptoms which are indicative of arsenical poisoning rapidly developed."

"In your opinion could these symptoms have been caused by anything in the meal which she had commenced to eat?"

"No. The symptoms are such as would be caused by the taking of food some hours after a dose—probably a large dose—of arsenic had been swallowed."

"Did you make any inquiries as to how such a dose might have been taken, either accidentally or otherwise?"

"Yes. In conjunction with Dr. Elgood I made very close inquiries as to such possibilities. Miss Bickerton appeared certain that she had had nothing during the day except water, and the cup of tea which she herself had made during the afternoon. We asked to see both the cup and the pot in which the tea had been made."

"Were they readily produced?"

Again the doctor paused for a moment, as though to choose his words, before he replied: "I think Miss Bickerton thought that they would have been washed, and that it would be useless to make any inquiry about them."

Russell-Welch, K.C., interposed for the first time.

"If I may suggest it, Mr. Coroner, it might be better for the witness to tell us what Miss Bickerton said and did—or declined to do—instead of what he thinks she thought."

His heavy figure half rose from his seat as he spoke, and subsided again before the sentence was finished. His manner was faintly contemptuous in a good-humoured, sardonic way. He had made no imputation upon Miss Bickerton, but it was as though the searchlight of the law had passed over her, and had paused for one sinister instant upon her head.

For the first time the jury looked on her curiously. The general gaze of the court was directed upon her. She must have had some consciousness of this, for a faint colour rose in the whiteness of her face, though she did not move or look up.

Mr. Bradson might have liked to say that he was quite capable of directing the evidence of witnesses without the assistance of the K.C., but he was far too capable a man to let any sign of annoyance appear as he answered: "I think Dr. Riggett's meaning was clear, though the phraseology may not have been exactly that which would have been selected by a legal mind. Go on, Doctor, please."

"As we were not satisfied to leave it in doubt, Dr. Elgood and myself went down to the kitchen together. We found that the teapot had been washed, but the cup and saucer and spoon had been put on a shelf with other unwashed crockery. The cup was not quite empty."

"How were you able to know that it was the actual cup which had been taken to Mrs. Hackett's room?"

"Miss Bickerton identified it."

"And I think you took possession of these articles, and they have since been in the hands of the public analyst?"

18

"Yes."

The coroner turned to the jury to explain that the evidence of the analyst would be brought before them.

Dr. Riggett went on to narrate how he had spoken to Mr. Hackett on the telephone about 3:00 P.M., and had obtained his consent to the calling in of a specialist from Birmingham. He gave the further medical experience of the case up to the time when Mrs. Hackett, having become steadily worse in spite of all that could be done, had died about midnight.

Dr. Elgood had agreed that it would be impossible for either of them to sign a death certificate, and he had reported the matter to the coroner accordingly.

Neither Mr. Russell-Welch nor Mr. Duff-Preedy desired to ask the doctor any questions at this stage, though the latter gentleman said he might have to ask the coroner to recall him later, and he left the box.

As Dr. Elgood was still absent, the evidence of Price Glasbrook, the analyst, was interposed at this point. It was brief, definite, and unchallenged. The dregs of tea in the cup had shown arsenious oxide to be present in such quantity that a cupful of tea of a similar composition must have contained from four to five times such a dose as is usually fatal. There were also traces of powdered weed killer on the spoon, appearing to show the form in which the poison had been introduced.

"Do you mean," the coroner asked, "that the spoon was dry? Could these grains have remained clinging to the spoon after it had been used to stir the tea?"

"No. The spoon had not been in any liquid since it had been in contact with the powder which I found upon it."

"You are sure of that?"

"Oh, yes. Quite."

Again there were no questions asked by the legal gentlemen present.

The coroner now addressed Mr. Duff-Preedy: "I understand that you appear for the relatives of the deceased, and also for Miss Dorling, and that they desire to give evidence. I need scarcely say that I shall welcome all the assistance which they can give to the court, but I am sure that you will appreciate the serious nature—and the possible implications—of the evidence which we have just heard. The cause of death cannot be definitely determined until the results of the post-mortem are before us, but in the meantime I think you

19

should make it clear to your clients that none of them is under obligation to give evidence unless he or she elects to do so."

Mr. Duff-Preedy did not consult any of his clients on receiving this hint. Probably it was a matter which had been discussed already.

He rose at once, saying, "I fully appreciate the position Mr. Coroner, and thank you for what you have said. But my clients wish to assist the court to the full extent of their ability. They are most anxious that the doubt—or mystery—of the case should be cleared up, and they will be glad to give evidence."

The coroner only nodded in reply. He did not exclude other possibilities, but it appeared almost certain that there was a poisoner among the three, and there might be guilty knowledge or connivance on the part of one or both of the others. He expected that if they all three entered the witness-box he would know where the guilt lay before they left it. But it was Mr. Preedy's responsibility, and it was the best course in the interests of justice, though less certainly so in those of his own clients.

His impassive face gave no sign of his thoughts, but Russell-Welch glanced up at Duff-Preedy with an expression of admiration, wonder, and puzzlement, which was noticed by some of the jury, and did much to discount the effect of the solicitor's attitude.

"Very well," said the coroner; "then it may be convenient if I call the witnesses in this order; Mr. Hackett first, then Miss Dorling, and then Miss Bickerton; after which Inspector Taverton will give his evidence, that of Dr. Elgood being interposed when he may be able to reach the court conveniently. I understand that it is very difficult for him to attend today, and I am letting him know that I can excuse him, if necessary, until tomorrow."

Mr. Bruton Hackett entered the witness-box.

CHAPTER III.

THE examination of Mr. Hackett was first undertaken by the coroner himself, as is the common practice at these inquiries.

He said that his name was James Bruton Hackett, that he was thirty-six years old, and had been married nearly seven years. He had two children—a boy and a girl. He was an engineer by profession, specializing in bridge construction. For the past eighteen months he had been occupied as the commercial representative of the Lepard-Watts Construction Company, and it was on their business that he had gone to Liverpool on the day of his wife's illness.

So far the witness's answers had been readily and clearly given, though his manner had already impressed the spectators somewhat unfavourably. He appeared to be ill at ease, and he spoke without lifting his eyes and with the aspect of one who, if not conscious of any actual guilt, was ashamed or embarrassed by the ordeal through which he was passing.

From this point the examination proceeded: "When you left home on the Thursday morning, it has been suggested, Mrs. Hackett had expressed a feeling that she was too ill to be left, and had asked you to stay with her."

"She was always like that."

"Do you mean that she was always afraid to be left?"

"She used to say so."

"Did you think she was afraid of others, or of anything that she might do to herself?"

"I didn't think either."

"Had you heard her threaten to take her own life?"

"Yes."

"Often?"

"About twice a week."

"When was the last occasion?"

"Oh, I don't know. It might have been that morning. She was always saying it."

"Mr. Hackett," the coroner said, with some severity, "you must please take my questions more seriously. You can surely recollect if there were such a conversation before you left."

The witness did not respond to this rebuke or lift his eyes as he answered: "Well, then, no. I shouldn't say that she did."

"Had you any special reason for thinking that she might be likely to take her life at this time? Please answer carefully."

"Nothing particular."

"Never mind whether it was anything particular. Had you any reason at all?"

"Well, it must have been she or Anne, mustn't it?"

There was a murmur of excitement in the court at this startling answer, which died away as the coroner glanced round with severity.

Miss Bickerton raised her eyes to the witness, and her face flushed angrily.

Mr. Duff-Preedy, who had been making notes somewhat voluminously as the examination proceeded, allowed himself no expression whatever.

Russell-Welch, making notes also, but confining them to an occasional word or a cryptic sign which would be meaningless except to himself, surveyed the witness, with a pleasure of anticipation, as something come to life such as a K.C. can only hope to meet in his dreams.

The coroner, having obtained the silence which he considered that the dignity of his court required, addressed the witness again: "Mr. Hackett, I must ask you once more to direct your mind to the questions I ask, and to answer them with the intelligence which I am sure you have. I did not ask you to speculate who might or might not have poisoned your wife. In strict fact, until we have the result of the autopsy, we have no proof that she was poisoned at all. I have asked you twice, and I ask again, whether you had any reason to think that your wife might attempt to take her life during your absence on this occasion. I must warn you that you are doing yourself no good by the way in which you are answering."

"I'm not trying to do myself any good."

"Answer the question."

"Then I'll say no."

"Were you on good terms with your wife when you left that morning?"

"Well, she didn't want me to go."

"That may be. But such a wish might arise from various motives. I am asking you to say—and I urge you in your own interest to answer this with care and frankness—whether there was no dissension between your wife and yourself on that occasion?"

"There was nothing worth talking about. There was always something or other."

The coroner paused, considering the witness, while he stroked his beard. Surprisingly he let the point drop, or appeared to do so.

"During the afternoon you received a telegram from your wife. Did you keep it?"

"No."

"Well, we have the original. Did it not say, 'Come back at once. I am much worse since you left. Belle'?"

"Yes, I expect it did."

"What did you do when you received that telegram?"

"I didn't believe it. I wrote to say that I'd be back as soon as I could."

"Why didn't you believe it?"

"I'd had some before."

"Is this the letter you wrote?"

The witness took the note which the coroner passed to him, and handed it back with scarcely a glance.

"Yes, that's it."

The coroner read it aloud:

DEAR BELLE,

I'm sorry you're so unwell. I've got to stay here a day or two—I'm not sure how long yet—but I'll be back as soon as I can. I've got a chance of an order that I can't leave.

Give my love to Anne, and ask her to stay with you if she can till I get back.

Love as ever,

JAMES

"After writing that letter you stayed the night, but in the morning you came back. Why was that? Was your business concluded?"

"No. But I had letters in the morning."

"Can you produce them?"

"No. I burned them."

"Who were they from?"

"My wife and Miss Bickerton."

"I have something here which appears to be a draft of your wife's letter. Will you read it and say whether it is substantially the letter which you received?"

The coroner handed him a sheet of paper which had been torn across, and on which pencilled words had been erased and altered. The writing, however, was still clearly legible.

It read:

DEAREST JAMES,

I'm sorry about this morning, but I'm really dreadfully poorly and can't eat anything. The pain's like a knife.

Do come home when you get this. You know I can't sleep when you're away. I should think you'd see that business can't matter when I'm so ill. I think a wife ought to come first.

I want you to give Rose notice when you come back. I'm too nervous after what's happened, and if you do it she'll know you didn't mean anything. But I should like to be there.

Your own

BELLE

James Hackett read this over, and handed it back with the words, "That's about it."

"And do you mean to say that the wire of the day before had no effect, but that you were induced to return at once by reading this letter?"

"I've told you I had two letters. Here, you'd better see the other, as you've got that."

He pulled a handful of soiled papers from his jacket-pocket, searched among them, and passed one to the coroner, who was roused for once from his usual cold urbanity.

"Do you mean that this is the letter which you swore that you had burned not five minutes ago?"

"Well, I didn't want them read. I wasn't likely to. They're no one's business but mine."

"You had better give me your wife's letter."

"I can't do that. It's burned."

"Mr. Hackett, I must give you a final warning that the consequences of perjury may be serious—very serious indeed. There is also such a thing as being committed for contempt of court. I direct you to produce the other letter without further evasion."

"I can't do that. It's burned. It really is."

"Mr. Preedy, I'm sorry to have to say that the first witness you have offered me is not of a character which enables me to believe anything he says. I presume that this really is Miss Bickerton's letter."

The coroner proceeded to read it in silence, but looked up sharply as James Hackett, hoping that his ordeal was over, was leaving the box. "No, don't go yet. I think I had better read this:

DEAR JAMES,

I sent you a telegram from Belle this afternoon, and hope you may now be on the way back, but I'm writing this in case you have not come.

I want you to know that Belle is *really ill*, and I think it was *most cruel* of you to go as you did. Dr. Elgood has been here this afternoon, and Dr. Riggett has been in since, but they don't seem able to do much. Belle is in an *absolutely distracted* state, and if you don't come back at once I can't say what may happen.

I don't think it's fair to leave me with her like this. If you had any decency you'd know how intolerable it must be, with Rose's insolence on the top of everything else. Of course, I'm not speaking to her. I think that Belle has behaved splendidly, and I think she'd overlook it now if you came back at once and turned her out of the house, as you know you ought.

If you don't come back in the morning, *I won't be responsible for anything that may happen*. The business can't be so important. You know you never really do anything worthwhile.

ANNE

The coroner read this letter carefully and slowly, and then turned to the witness, who may have already regretted the sullen impulse which had caused him to produce it.

"Do you still say, after hearing these letters read, that you had had no serious difference with your wife before leaving, nor any special reason for anxiety concerning her?"

"Well, I came back. It was just women's fuss."

"Is it 'women's fuss'," the coroner asked, with an unusual sternness in his voice, "that your wife is dead?"

"I wasn't talking about that."

The coroner looked reflectively at his notes, then at the flushed and sullen face of the witness. He turned to Mr. Russell-Welch.

"Have you any questions to ask?"

The barrister, who had been engaged in a whispered conversation with Inspector Taverton, said that he had.

He took a glance at his notes, and rose with a heavy deliberation.

"Mr. Hackett," he said slowly, and with an emphasis which gave an importance to the query which the words would not otherwise have conveyed, "how do you live?"

Mr. Duff-Preedy rose at once. He had watched while his client made a fool of himself to the coroner, ready to interpose at any moment, but seeing no opportunity when he might not have made matters worse rather than better. His time would come.

But he had no intention of letting the K.C. have a clear run. It is only on such occasions as these that a solicitor who has a good practice and reputation in the magistrates' and county courts can cross swords with a K.C. on an equal footing.

"Mr. Hackett," he said quietly, "has already given that information."

The coroner confirmed this, with a glance at his notes.

"He stated that he is an engineer, and is employed by the Lepard-Watts Construction Company as a commercial representative. Do you challenge that statement?"

Mr. Russell-Welch shook his head. "Oh, no. We know that that is quite true. But I should just like him to give some account of his financial position in his own way."

"Very well," said the coroner, "if you think it will assist our inquiry."

Mr. Russell-Welch repeated his question, but the witness made no answer.

26

The barrister showed no annoyance, nor did he press for a reply. He said, "Perhaps I had better be more explicit. Just tell the court the amount of the salary which you have received during the last twelve months."

"You know I've not had any salary."

"Never mind what I know. You've had no salary. Have you had any allowance for travelling expenses?"

"No. I didn't want to be paid in that way."

"No? Now will you tell the court as exactly as possible what commission you have received during this period?"

"I haven't had any yet. It was the arrangement I proposed my-self—"

"Oh, yes? No salary. No expenses. No commission. And that has gone on for twelve months—or longer?"

"Yes, but in our business—"

"Never mind the explanations just yet. I've no doubt my friend Mr. Duff-Preedy will help to put these matters in the best light he can when his turn comes. All *I* want is the facts. What other source of income have you had during the last year?"

"I haven't had any other income."

"I see. No salary. No expenses. No commission. No other source of income. Now just tell the court who kept your home, and where you got the money from to go travelling on that Thursday morning when your wife said she was too ill to be left."

"My wife had plenty of money. I drew some from the bank the afternoon before."

"From your wife's account?"

"We had the same account. We could both draw on it."

"You mean you could draw on hers. She put all the money in, but you drew most of it out?"

"No, I didn't."

"Well, we may have to look into that. Anyway, you went off with her money in your pocket on this holiday week, because it was so urgent to do some business for the firm that valued your services so highly that it never paid you at all. Are orders for bridge con-struction particularly easy to get in that week of the year? *Did you really do any business at all?*"

For the first time James Hackett lifted his eyes and looked straight at his tormentor. He said, "No, I got no orders at all."

He seemed to take an actual pleasure in the reply, so that Rus-sell-Welch, who had one of the shrewdest intellects at the Bar, had an instinctive apprehension of something in his mind which he could

27

not reach, and with habitual caution of the unknown he changed the subject of the next question.

"Can you tell the court how you will be affected financially by your wife's death?"

"It won't make much difference one way or other."

"How is that, if you and your children have been supported by her entirely? Do you suppose that you inherit all that she left?"

"If you want to know, she has left most of it in trust for the children, as I asked her to do."

"Don't answer like that. I don't want to know. I know as much as you, and perhaps more. I want you to tell the court. Your wife made wills rather frequently, didn't she?"

"Yes. She liked making wills. The last was about three months ago. I've told you what's in it. Mr. Preedy's got it, if you want to see what it says."

"Then you don't know that your wife made a will a week before she died?"

"No, I don't; and I don't believe it. She wouldn't have done that without telling me."

He was plainly startled, and looked at Mr. Duff-Preedy, as though asking him to confirm or deny it.

That gentleman rose, and said, "I have a will dated May the 3rd last, which is substantially as Mr. Hackett has said, and which I am about to prove. Mrs. Hackett did change her mind rather frequently, and seemed to enjoy executing these documents, but I should think it very unlikely that she would have made a later one without my knowledge."

Mr. Russell-Welch turned to the coroner, and said with the full deliberation which he reserved for the dramatic moments which he knew so well how to develop:

"My instructions are that Mrs. Hackett executed a will on August the 7th—the 7th instant—at the offices of Messrs. Ashton and Cross, leaving all her property absolutely to her sister, Anne Bickerton, and that Miss Bickerton was present when the will was signed. I propose, with your permission, Mr. Coroner, to call Mr. Tomkinson, of that firm, to give evidence as to the facts, and to produce the document."

He sat down, having said this, without another glance at the witness. He bent forward across the front of Miss Dorling's slim figure to whisper audibly, "I shouldn't waste any money proving that will, Preedy, if I were you."

He was satisfied that James Hackett had not been aware of the existence of the latest will, which had been the point he had been anxious to ascertain.

Inspector Taverton made a remark to him which Miss Dorling (whose ears were good, and whose quietness had absorbed and would retain almost every word of the morning's drama) failed to hear entirely, though she understood that it was in disparagement of the witness, who stood uncertain whether he might at last retire from his uncomfortable publicity; but she heard the reply, "Oh, I wouldn't say that—he's straighter than most." And then she was aware that the coroner, who had been engaged for a long minute on his notes, looked up to ask, "No more questions, Mr. Russell-Welch?"

The K.C. shook his head. "It's your turn," he said to Mr. Preedy, with the geniality which his opponents had learned to dread.

For once Mr. Duff-Preedy felt scarcely ready. But his adroitness did not fail him.

"There are a few questions that I should like to put to Mr. Hackett, if you will kindly allow him to be recalled after the luncheon interval, Mr. Coroner."

The coroner took the hint. He observed that it was already ten minutes after one. He adjourned the court for forty-five minutes.

CHAPTER IV.

MR. DUFF-PREEDY'S mind was accustomed to work at high pressure when its owner called upon it for such exertions, but it was seldom required to perform such a feat of intellectual agility as on this occasion, between the time when he filed with his three clients—two before and one behind him—out of the row of seats they had occupied, and the moment when he halted at the top of the five stone steps that descended to the pavement of the West Bromwich High Street.

He had already calculated that, unless the jury should deliver a verdict of suicide, which he thought unlikely—and we must remember that he had the advantage of having prepared the evidence of both Miss Bickerton and Miss Dorling, which we have yet to hear, and that he knew a good deal also of the nature of the investigations that Inspector Taverton had been making—their minds would be directed almost inevitably to a verdict of wilful murder against one or other of his clients, and he was inclining to the opinion that it was one of the ladies who would be required to defend herself from this accusation. Up to ten minutes ago he had regarded Miss Dorling (for reasons which have as yet been only partially indicated) as the more likely to be the defendant in the trial which he foresaw, but he recognized that this tale of the new will (of the truth of which he had little doubt), while it did not directly reduce the weight of the circumstantial evidence that Miss Dorling might have to meet, did very materially increase that with which Miss Bickerton might be confronted, as it supplied a motive, which had previously seemed to be entirely lacking.

He had already felt the difficulty of jointly representing his three clients; but while he had anticipated that Miss Dorling would be nominated as the central figure for the principal act, he had not felt this difficulty to be insuperable. He had regarded James Hackett as the only one of the three with any financial resources whatever, even deferred or potential, and he had already taken the precaution of obtaining his signature to a general retainer, but if this will should stand, it might be that Miss Bickerton was destined not only to be the central figure in the approaching drama, but the only one who would be able to supply the somewhat substantial funds which lawyers consider appropriate for such occasions. Yet he considered shrewdly that such a will might not stand—might at least be contested, so that its benefits would not be promptly available for the defence of one who should be accused of murdering her sister and benefactor to secure them—and he was influenced somewhat (being human) by resentment at the fact that Miss Bickerton had not informed him of its existence.

"Mr. Hackett, "he said, pausing at the top step, "I want a few words with you about your evidence. If you'll come over to my office I'll have some sandwiches brought in. I expect the ladies will like something more comfortable. It won't matter if either of you is a bit late back—but you shouldn't be after 2:15, Miss Dorling, as I expect you'll be called next. You'll find there's nothing to worry about if you answer the questions quietly and just keep to the facts. Don't let Russell-Welch hustle you. You'll find the Monitor Restaurant the best place for a quick lunch. You can get a private room upstairs, if you like."

"Oh, I'm not worrying, Mr. Preedy. We've got to go through with it, so what's the use? Of course, I'm very sorry about it all, and it's been hateful for Mr. Hackett."

Saying this, Rose Dorling turned away, with a cool and pleasant smile for the clicking cameras that confronted her as she descended the steps.

She did not wait for Miss Bickerton. The two women had ignored each other's existence as they came down the corridor, and were little likely to go anywhere to lunch together.

Miss Bickerton also answered Mr. Preedy's remark, but in a somewhat different spirit. Her voice trembled with a suppressed excitement, which might be that of anger, indignation, or fear.

"No, Mr. Preedy, I shan't be late back. If I'm to be accused of poisoning Belle to get her money I'd like to be there to hear what's said."

"I don't think anyone has gone that far—"

"Oh, yes, he has." She looked at James Hackett, with a dislike which she made no effort to hide. "He said if Belle hadn't committed suicide, I must have poisoned her, and he knows quite well she wouldn't do that."

"Well," said Mr. Preedy, reasonably enough, "you'd better not quarrel here unless you want to see yourselves doing it in the picture papers tomorrow."

He took Mr. Hackett's arm, and hurried him through the curious crowd to the shelter of his office on the other side of the street.

CHAPTER V.

MR. DUFF-PREEDY declined to talk until his guest had completed the demolition of the sandwiches which he had provided. Then he said briskly: "Now, Mr. Hackett, we've got a clear ten minutes, and we've got to make up our minds what line we're going to take. We've got to face facts here. We knew most of them before, but we've got another now, and it gets everything into different proportions, though, of course, they mayn't be true ones.

"It mayn't be strictly proved yet, but we must take it as a fact that your wife died of arsenical poisoning, and there's no doubt as to where the poison came from.

"Anyway, the jury won't have much doubt when they've heard Miss Dorling's evidence.

"Now that means either accident or suicide or that she was poisoned by someone, and in this case 'someone' means Miss Bickerton or Miss Dorling or yourself."

"Me? I wasn't there."

"Well, you might have instigated it or contrived it somehow, if you weren't there. I'm mentioning everything possible. Now we can rule accident out. None of you seems to think that suicide was a likely thing. I can't say I do myself. Still, something unlikely must have happened, so we won't rule that out. We leave it in.

"Now between the two ladies it seemed to me this morning that there was very little to choose, and that they might, so to speak, save each other. If anything, the chance seemed to be against Miss Dorling, because you can make out a motive—"

"Miss Dorling's utterly—"

"Yes. I know. We all are. I'm only talking of what a jury might be persuaded to think. But when I went into court this morning I was aiming at an open verdict of death by poison or, at the worst, of murder, but that there was not sufficient evidence to make an accusation against anyone.

33

"But now it's all changed. I should say it's three to one against Miss Bickerton, whatever we do, but if you want to save her—I don't know whether you do or not—there's only one way. We've got to go all out for suicide. Unless you're willing for that, I don't think I can go on representing both her and you."

"I don't think it was suicide."

"Nor do I. But it must have been something. Look here, Mr. Hackett, let us have it plain. Do you want to shield Miss Bickerton if she murdered your wife?"

"I don't know what to say. I can't think that she did. Anyway, Belle wouldn't want her sister hanged. It's too late to do any good. It's a family matter. We don't want strangers interfering. That's how Belle would feel."

"Do you think that your wife would have kept to this new will if she had lived?"

"No, not a week. She'd told me the first time we were friends again, and made another next morning."

"And Miss Bickerton would know that as well as you?"

"Yes, I've no doubt she would."

"And she has no income of her own?"

"She has her salary at Tucker and Thomson's. I don't think she's got anything else."

"Well, we must go now. I shan't ask you much. You've done rather well, as it is."

"I must have looked a fool."

"You might have done worse than that. Russell-Welch let you down rather easily. I wish I knew why, though I can guess well enough."

"The man's a cad."

"Well, he was a good cad to you. He might have baited you about Miss Dorling and other things in the letters. But he's after Miss Bickerton, or so it looks to me. We shall know more when Miss Dorling has given her evidence."

They were walking over to the court as this conversation concluded, Mr. Preedy asking again as they entered the building, "Are we all out for suicide, or not? If not, I'll tell Miss Bickerton to go to Ashton and Cross—she knows the way there already."

"I'll leave that to you. Whatever's happened, it's a case of the less fuss the better. Even the police ought to see that, but I suppose they're paid to make trouble."

Mr. Duff-Preedy did not allow his mind to be diverted to discuss the true function of the police.

He said, "I suppose you see that if Miss Bickerton comes clear it means that the will stands? I don't say it wouldn't stand anyway. It's hard to say till we know more than we do now. But it would leave you and the children without anything."

"I wouldn't quite say that. I expect it's meant for the children, but it's to give Anne control, instead of me. It's to knock out Rose, really. I can look after myself."

"Very well. I'll go for suicide. It may be the best way, all round. You mustn't be surprised at any questions I ask. Just answer them in your own way."

The coroner had already taken his seat as they turned in, and both Miss Bickerton and Miss Dorling had arrived, and were sitting some distance apart. Mr. Duff-Preedy placed himself between them, and James Hackett returned to the ordeal of the witness-box.

As Mr. Preedy settled himself into his place he found time to say to Miss Bickerton, in a low voice: "I've been talking things over with Mr. Hackett, and we have decided that suicide is the only possible explanation that will fit all the facts. I wish you would consider it from that point of view, before you give your own evidence. I don't suppose you'll be called till tomorrow."

Miss Bickerton answered, "It's very good of James to say that." He could not be sure whether she were sarcastic or grateful, but the coroner was looking at him, and the court was waiting.

"Mr. Coroner," he said, "there have been certain questions raised about Mr. Hackett's occupation and income that may not be strictly relevant to this inquiry—that is a matter for your ruling—but as they have been raised, I should like to clear up some possible misconceptions which might arise from the interrogations and answers as they now stand."

"You know, Mr. Preedy," the coroner answered, "I always try to keep these inquiries within as narrow bounds as I can, bur it is impossible to say that anything which throws light on the characters and relations of a household may not prove to be relevant in such a case as the present. By all means let us have any further facts or explanations which your client can furnish."

Mr. Preedy then proceeded to take his client in some detail, which we need not follow, through his professional training and business career up to the point, four years ago, when he had been offered and had accepted an appointment in Brazil, for which he had resigned a position which he then occupied.

He continued, "Why did you not take up this appointment?"

"My wife changed her mind at the last moment. She had been told that the people were not educated, and—"

"Do you mean that the people of Brazil are not educated?" the coroner interposed in some surprise.

"It was what some silly woman told her. You know what fools women are." ("She was told by friends," the coroner translated, half aloud, as he entered it on his notes.) "Anyway, she wouldn't come, and she didn't want me to go alone."

"So you gave that up," the solicitor continued, "and after that you were offered your present appointment by the same firm. Will you tell the court why you took it on terms which may be considered somewhat unusual?"

"Because it isn't like selling cheese. I wanted to be free to pull off a big deal when I could, and I didn't want to be rowed if I didn't do anything for twelve months, nor to lose the job. Besides, I can get a bigger commission this way. And we weren't needing money in a hurry. We'd got enough to go on with."

"When you went away on this Thursday, August the 8th, was it for pleasure, or had you any definite business in prospect?"

"That's my business "

"Exactly. It was your business, not your pleasure, which would have kept you in Liverpool?"

"Yes, of course."

"Was your wife rather difficult to live with at times?"

"Off and on. I suppose all women are."

"Changeable?"

"Yes, you could reckon on that."

"Would you describe her as unbalanced?"

"No, I shouldn't say that."

"But there might be a good deal of trouble if she didn't get her own way?"

"Well, she jibbed a bit now and then."

"I think that's all, Mr. Hackett," Mr. Preedy concluded as he sat down, and the coroner added:

"I suppose we all like our own way. But tell me this, Mr. Hackett. Did you live happily with your wife as a rule? What I want to know is how far the incidents of these days may have been of an exceptional character." The witness was not quick to answer, and Mr. Bradson went on, "Were your relations generally of an affectionate character?"

"Yes, of course."

"Did your wife usually make it a trouble that you should go away for a few days?"

"Well, when I got to the hotel there was usually a wire for me to go back."

"She couldn't do that, unless she knew where you would be staying?"

"Oh, yes, she could. Once she wired to every hotel in Newcastle."

"Really? I wish you would appreciate the importance of accuracy, Mr. Hackett. I suppose you mean she wired to several?"

"No, I don't. She wired to every hotel in the Trade Directory."

"It must have cost a good deal."

"So it did, but she wouldn't mind that. She never counted her change."

"One thing more, Mr. Hackett. It is clear from the correspondence which has been read that there had been some trouble regarding Miss Dorling, and that your wife had some feeling of jealousy in that direction. I am sorry to have to ask you, but it is necessary—had you given any serious cause for such feeling?"

"No, I don't think so. Nothing that she knew of. Nothing serious. Nothing like you think, anyway."

"Could you swear that you were fond of your wife, and that your affection had not changed?"

"Yes, you could say that."

"And that you are sincerely grieved by her death?"

"I'm not going to talk about my feelings here."

The coroner had a moment of contemplation, stroking his beard, as his way was. He had shown no sign of being aware of the brusqueness of the witness's answers at this afternoon examination. He looked at Russell-Welch. "Any more questions? Thank you, Mr. Hackett, you may go now. You will please continue to attend the sittings till the inquiry is concluded. I think we will take Miss Dorling's evidence next."

CHAPTER VI.

THERE was a stir of freshly excited interest, in a court which had not been drowsy before, as Miss Dorling rose and made her way to the witness stand.

The eyes of all were concentrated upon her, even the reporters pausing with lifted pencils, which would be busy a moment later in describing her appearance, dress, and manners for the avid appetites of a million readers.

The *Daily Catch* would be particularly florid next morning. It had reason for a special flutter in the fact that its artist had succeeded in making a sketch of "Rose Dorling in the Witness-Box," which was against a rule of elementary decency the coroner enforced as far as he was able, and had smuggled it out of court without detection. It said:

> The next witness, Miss Rose Dorling, is a tall, fair-haired girl, who gave her evidence with an air of quiet self-possession which remained unruffled even under the ordeal of the searching cross-examination of Mr. Russell-Welch. She has regular features, rather large grey eyes, and a particularly attractive smile, though it was natural that it was not often to be observed on this occasion. She has a rather low and pleasant voice, which could be heard without difficulty in all parts of the court. She wore....

But we have had enough of the *Daily Catch*. Does it matter what she wore? She was not likely to be in mourning for an employer whom she had only known for three weeks. She wore white, and looked cool in a hot and crowded court. She had made up her mind not to be hurried, and if she felt less cool than she looked—well, that was natural enough.

She said that her age was twenty-eight (the *Daily Catch* commented that she looked younger), that she was a B.A. (Sheffield), and a games mistress by profession. She had seen an advertisement a few weeks ago for a "lady help" who would also undertake the care of two young children, giving them elementary lessons. She had answered this, being unemployed at the time, and thinking that she would try what such a post would be like. She had called on Mrs. Hackett, who had engaged her at the first interview.

"Subject to references, I suppose?" the coroner asked.

"I offered references, but she said she liked to judge people for herself. So I agreed to go for a month on trial on both sides. I went in the next day."

"Then you had been in the house less than three weeks when the death occurred. There is, as you know, some evidence that Mrs. Hackett, whether with or without cause, was jealous of some attention which Mr. Hackett had paid to you. Were you aware of this?"

"Yes. Miss Bickerton told me the first day she came. That would be Friday, August the 2nd. After that things were very uncomfortable."

"Do you think it was wise to stay under such circumstances?"

"I thought it might be open to misconstruction if I left before the month was completed. Besides, Mrs. Hackett asked me to stay. She said I had no right to go and leave her stranded."

"Then you had discussed the matter with Mrs. Hackett?"

"Yes, twice. I had it over on the day that Miss Bickerton first mentioned it to me, and again on the afternoon of August the 8th."

Mr. Russell-Welch looked up sharply at this. He was evidently surprised. He made one of his rapid hieroglyphic notes.

"That was on the afternoon of the day that Mr. Hackett had left—the afternoon before the day on which she died?"

"Yes."

"Where did you see her?"

"In her bedroom."

"Alone?"

"Yes."

"How came you to go there?"

"She called me in."

"We have understood that her sister was constantly with her during that day."

"It was while Miss Bickerton was downstairs making the tea."

"I should like to know—but," the coroner checked himself, "it may be best to take the events of that afternoon in the order in which they occurred. Will you tell us, Miss Dorling, how you were occupied from lunchtime, and generally all that occurred as far as it came within your experience or observation. I need not emphasize the importance of accuracy."

"I had lunch with the two children in the nursery. It was rather earlier than usual, because Gladys was going out—"

"Gladys Forman is the maidservant?"

"Yes. She went out as soon as lunch was over, after I had helped her with the washing up so that she could get off. She was going to the West Bromwich Fair."

"She was out for the rest of the day?"

"Yes. She came in about eleven or half-past."

"I believe Inspector Taverton has verified that Gladys Forman was seen at the fair by several people who knew her during the afternoon and evening. Is not that so, Inspector?"

"Yes, sir. That's quite clear," the Inspector answered.

"Very well. Go on, Miss Dorling. Who would be left in the house when the maid had gone out?"

"There was no one except Mrs. Hackett and Miss Bickerton and myself, and the two children. I got the children ready, and sent them to play in the next-door garden with a neighbour's child. I was going to use some weed killer on the garden paths, and I thought they were best out of the way."

"Was it part of your regular duties to attend to the garden?"

"No, but I am fond of gardening, and I found that both Mr. and Mrs. Hackett were pleased for me to do it."

"From where did you get the weed killer?"

"Mr. Hackett had bought it for me a few days before."

"At whose suggestion?"

"At mine. It was the only possible way to deal with the paths. They were green from side to side."

"Did you understand that weed killer had been used previously?"

"No. I shouldn't think it had, by the state of the paths."

"Is it a large garden?"

"Yes. It must be nearly an acre, and most of it is quite uncultivated. Of course, I couldn't do much, but I thought I could get the front a bit tidier than it was."

"So you proposed to Mr. Hackett that he should get some weed killer, and he bought a tin for you. When was that?"

"About a week earlier."

Inspector Taverton rose again.

"It was purchased by Mr. Hackett on the afternoon of Saturday, August the 3rd, at Blatch and Pritchard's."

He produced the tin, which he handed up to the coroner, by whom it was passed on to the jury, who gazed upon it with great solemnity, one after another, though it is difficult to suppose that they could learn anything of importance from the inspection.

"It was bought quite openly?"

"Oh, yes, sir. Mr. Hackett is a regular customer at the shop."

"Very well, Inspector. Please go on, Miss Dorling. Can you identify this tin as the one which Mr. Hackett bought for your use?"

"Yes. It looks like it. I've no doubt that's the one."

"What did you do when you had sent the children away?"

"I got the tin down—it was on a high shelf in the scullery—and mixed the watering can full. When I'd emptied it on the paths I came back and mixed another can. I did this several times."

"Where did you leave the tin while you were away?"

"On the copper or on the sink. I think it was on the copper most of the time, if not all."

"This was the first time it had been used?"

"Yes. It was the first chance I had had."

"Was the tin opened previously?"

"No I opened it then."

"You are quite sure of that?"

"Yes. Quite."

"Did Miss Bickerton know how you were occupied?"

"Yes. I told her before lunch I should be having a go at the weeds during the afternoon."

"Well, go on."

"While I was watering the paths there came a few spots of rain. Only a few, but very large spots. They stopped after a minute, but the sky was very black at one side, as though a heavy storm were coming, and I remembered that the children had only their thin summer clothes on, so I put the can down, and ran upstairs to get some wraps for them, and I put on a raincoat myself."

"But if they were only in the next garden wouldn't it have been quicker to call them in at once?"

"No, I don't think so. I had better explain. The children are young—the boy five, and the girl three. The house next to The Firs is a very old one, and it's been empty for years. It has a large garden, which has been neglected for I don't know how long, and there's an old orchard beyond that. I've been nearly half an hour finding them there before now. If they'd been sheltering from the

41

rain I should have got them soaked bringing them in, if I hadn't had their waterproofs to put over them."

"Very well. Then you ran upstairs. Had you seen Miss Bickerton during the afternoon, up to this point?"

"Yes, I may have done. I think she'd been in and out of the kitchen once or twice, but I'm not sure. We passed each other on the stairs as I went up."

"And then?"

"I had got the wraps and was on the landing, just coming down, when Mrs. Hackett called me into her room. She said that her sister had gone down to make her a cup of tea, and she didn't like being left alone. I suppose she really wanted to talk. There wasn't very much said. I told her what I wanted to do, and she said of course she mustn't keep me, but she did, just from minute to minute—it wasn't actually raining then—and then the rain came very heavily, and I got away, and ran down."

"Can you recall the conversation?"

"Not very clearly, because I was trying not to seem unkind, and yet to get away, all the time. It was mostly about how ill she was, and how cruel everyone was to her, and why didn't the doctor come?"

"Did she mention this trouble about you and her husband in any way?"

The witness paused for the first time before she answered, and then said:

"Not exactly. She asked me if I would wire Mr. Hackett to come home. She said he would come if he had a wire from me. But I don't think she meant it at all."

"Did she say anything about your leaving?"

"She said she wanted me to stay. But I don't think she meant that either. She said it at first as if she meant it, and then said, wouldn't I stay for Mr. Hackett's sake? It wasn't always easy to tell what she meant."

"Did you promise to stay?"

"I said I would think it over. I was only trying to get away without saying anything which would make more trouble."

"And after that you went out to fetch the children? Did you see Miss Bickerton again before you went out?"

"Yes. We passed again in the passage. She was carrying up the cup of tea on a tray."

"Not the pot—only the cup?"

"Yes, I think so. I didn't notice particularly. But I feel sure the pot wasn't taken up. It wasn't on the tray, anyway, when it came down."

"Was anything said?"

"Miss Bickerton asked me, 'How did she seem?' or something like that. I suppose she had heard us talking. And I said, 'She seems rather worried,' or something like that. I didn't think she was really ill. Then I went out and found the children, and brought them in."

"Where was the tin of weed killer during this time?"

"I put it back on the top scullery-shelf as I went out to fetch the children."

"Then it was standing open in the scullery while you were upstairs? Did you notice whether it had been moved at all during that time?"

"No. I mean I didn't notice. I might have done if it had. So far as I recollect, it was standing on the side of the copper against the wall. I don't think it had been moved at all."

"Was all this before Dr. Elgood's visit in the latter part of the afternoon?"

"Yes. Because I saw him in the hall, and I remember that I was careful to pass without touching him, because I was so drenched."

"Now I am sure you will answer this very carefully. Do you know, or can you suggest, any way by which a quantity of that weed killer, however small, could have got into the pot, or the cup, or the saucer or spoon, in which the tea was served to Mrs. Hackett that afternoon?

There was a dead silence in the court as the coroner put this question with more than his usual deliberation.

"No. I can't imagine how it could have happened at all. The more we talk it over," she added, "the more puzzling it seems. But I'm sure there was nothing wrong with the pot."

"How can you be sure of that?"

"Because I had a cup from it myself after I changed. I felt chilled, and the pot was standing on the side table by the gas stove, and I made myself a cup from it. It was while Dr. Elgood was upstairs."

"Did you see anything more of Mrs. Hackett that evening?"

"No. I put the children to bed, and after that I was reading most of the time in my own room. I knew Dr. Riggett came, and after that I asked Miss Bickerton how she was, and she said she seemed rather better, and she was trying to persuade her to have a meal. Then I went to bed, and was waked by hearing Miss Bickerton go down to the kitchen. I think I went to sleep again, and was waked by her calling me to get up at once, as Mrs. Hackett was very ill, and she didn't know what to do. I went and did what I could, and helped her phone the doctors. We rang up Dr. Riggett first, and then Dr. Elgood, because we weren't sure that Dr. Riggett meant to come."

"Did Miss Bickerton seem very distressed by her sister's condition?"

"Yes, she seemed distracted."

"Were they generally on affectionate terms?"

"Yes, very."

The coroner paused at this point to glance over his notes and then up at the clock.

"I think that will do, Miss Dorling, unless Mr. Russell-Welch would like to ask any questions. Yes? Well, if you think you will take more than a few minutes I think we can conveniently adjourn at this stage."

But Mr. Russell-Welch said that he would not take more than ten minutes, and as he evidently wished to go on the coroner signified his assent.

"You have told us, Miss Dorling," the K.C. began, with a delusive suavity, "that you are a games mistress by profession, and that you hold a B.A. degree. Can you tell the court what induced you to apply for such a position as this—that of a lady help and nursery governess?"

"I had been out of employment for a term, and thought I would try it."

"Nothing else?"

"No."

"Miss Dorling, please answer this carefully, in your own interest. *When did you first meet Mr. Hackett?*"

"About seven years ago, when I was staying at Staines."

The reply was given quietly and readily, but its effect was immediate on the listening court. There was a murmur of voices, which drew a sharp rebuke from the coroner, and which only stilled itself lest it should miss the continuation of this unexpected development.

"You were on rather intimate terms with Mr. Hackett at that time?"

"We were friends for a short time—nothing more."

"Never engaged?"

"No."

"And so you enter his house seven years later, in the capacity which you have told us, without informing his wife of this previous relation?"

"I did not know who it was till I met him on the second day of my engagement."

"Miss Dorling! Don't you think that is stretching our credulity rather far? I must suggest to you a very different explanation. I must suggest that you would not have taken such a position at all had you not been attracted by the opportunity of renewing this acquaintance."

"You overlook the fact that I answered an anonymous advertisement."

"Not at all. I suggest that it was one to which your attention had been directed by Mr. Hackett as furnishing the opportunity which you desired."

"You are utterly wrong."

"Then will you seriously tell the court that even the name of Mrs. Hackett—Mrs. James Bruton Hackett—meant nothing to you when first you heard it?"

"It meant nothing at all. When I knew Mr. Hackett we used to call him Tony. I suppose it was a nickname, but I don't really know. I never heard him called James till I went there."

"Then you wish it to be believed that it was by a pure coincidence that you entered this house, in this almost menial capacity, and met the man you had known, we will say as a friend, before his marriage, seven years ago?"

"That is what it was."

"And having entered his house in this way, you resumed the relations with him—whatever they were—which you had had previously?"

The girl looked at the K.C. with a self-control that she would not relinquish.

"Will you please be more definite? I should like to know what you mean by 'resume relations,' before I reply."

"You would like me to be more definite. Well, Miss Dorling, I don't think I will. We will just leave it as a question which you decline to answer. Can you tell how it was that the teapot was washed, but the cup wasn't?"

Even this abrupt transition did not disturb the cool poise with which the witness faced the ordeal of the examination.

"Yes, I can. I had washed the pot myself, because Gladys was out, and I thought it might be needed later in the evening. Mrs.

Hackett sometimes had tea very frequently. I told Gladys when she came in that she could leave the washing up till the morning, as it was so late. I expect Miss Bickerton thought she had done it."

"Well, so much for that. Then perhaps you can say also how Miss Bickerton was able to identify the cup she had used, as you told the court that you had also made a cup for yourself, and I suppose there may have been others which had been used and were left unwashed?"

"Yes, I can tell you that. Mrs. Hackett always had her tea served in a cup from the best service, which was not generally used."

Mr. Russell-Welch sat down.

Mr. Duff-Preedy rose.

"I should like to re-examine the witness, but, as you have intimated that you are closing the court, I will defer it till tomorrow, Mr. Coroner, with your permission."

Mr. Duff-Preedy gained the interval which he valued as highly as Mr. Russell-Welch the advantage of the unexpected attack.

CHAPTER VII.

CHIEF INSPECTOR TAVERTON was a man of simple tastes, and one whose moderate income was easily absorbed by his some- what numerous family. Even when he could debit his expenses to the nation which he served, his meals were rarely of a higher cost than eighteen pence or two shillings. When he left the court he spent nine pence and fewer minutes in the branch of the ubiquitous Lyons which is in West Bromwich High Street, and then got on the tram which would take him to Birmingham in little more than an hour, and so enable him to catch the 6:00 P.M. from Snow Hill to Pad- dington. He dispatched a telegram from the Birmingham station to Scotland Yard, and when he arrived there at 8:30 P.M. he found his chief awaiting his arrival and prepared to hear his report.

"You don't think it's suicide?" the Assistant Commissioner asked, when he had concluded his narrative.

"No, sir, I'm almost certain it isn't. It's one of the plainest cases of murder that I've ever met. The trouble is that there's so much evi- dence against both of them, but for the other. The question is which to pick."

"We can't have a mistake this time, Taverton. I don't want any miscarriage of justice, and for that reason I want you to be quite sure which it is before you apply for a warrant. You must bear in mind that when you *have* made an arrest you must carry it through. After the Foote case we can't afford to fail again. Of course, if you arrest on a coroner's warrant that's a different matter. But you ought to agree with Bradson who it's to be before he sums up, or whether an open verdict would suit you best.

"But you know, Taverton, watching the witnesses as you can, there oughtn't to be any doubt. It's not like reading over the evi- dence here. I suppose the women can't be in collusion and shielding each other?"

"No. I don't think it's possible. They hate each other about equally. I expect I shall know who did it when I've heard Miss Bickerton's evidence tomorrow. I rather hope it's her. The other one's too cool to be easily caught, and she's too pretty for most juries to hang her. We may have a hard fight to get a verdict if we pick her. But there's plenty of evidence against either.

"Of course, it would have been easy enough if this inquest hadn't queered the pitch."

He thought regretfully of the "voluntary" statements which he could have extracted separately from each of the inhabitants of The Firs, and of the endless hours of questioning to which he could have subjected them, without the disconcerting presence of their own solicitors, or of any impartial shorthand writer to take down what was said without his judicious phrasing to give it the tone at which he aimed.

Well, he must make the best of the facts as he had to face them. He must decide which of the two women was the murderer before tomorrow was over, and after that there must be no looking back. Guilty or innocent, she had got to hang. But the thought did not perturb him. He had too great a confidence in his own ability.

When he decided that a woman was guilty—well, she was. It was his job to see that a jury said so, and if he failed in that he wasn't fit to keep it.

"Miss Bickerton lives at Shrewsbury, sir," he went on. "She's a cashier with a firm of builders' merchants. Quite a good firm. She was spending her holiday with her sister, which she usually did— and most weekends. I wish you'd have some inquiries made there, and have anything wired to me that might be useful during the day."

He went home to a short night's rest and slept soundly, with a consciousness of duty done.

CHAPTER VIII.

THE day had been warm, but there was a change of wind, which became cool in the evening, with a drizzle of chilling rain. It was not enough to disperse the crowd which gathered outside The Firs to gaze at the stone pillars and the iron gate of the drive, and at the grey shoulder of the house, as it showed through the thick leafage of the summer trees.

They made it easy for the people on the tram-tops to know when they passed the house, and these had an advantage of height, so that they could see some of the bedroom windows and a part of the tangled garden as they stared and pointed.

But they could not see into the shadowing gloom of the low-ceiled dining-room, where the three protagonists of this sudden tragedy sat at supper together, and none cared to switch on the lights as the evening closed.

There had been constraint enough before the inquest opened, but there was none of the three who had not learned new facts during the day, against one or another, to anger or alienate further, or to change or deepen the suspicions of carelessness or crime which barred any freedom of intercourse and increased the distance which had separated them in the past. Those days which were now over had seemed wretched enough at the time, but two, at least, of those at the table would have given almost anything in life to regain them, and to wake to find that the present had been a nightmare dream.

Each of them had hesitated whether to be present at the meal, but James had something to say which he felt he could do more easily to both at once, and Anne had felt—as she had felt at the inquest—that she would like to hear anything that was said. She was not going to leave James and Miss Dorling alone to discuss her and make their plans, and perhaps evolve new theories to make the case look darker against herself.

As to Miss Dorling, she seemed to have a habit of facing that which came without overmuch perturbation, but whether that is to be taken as a courage of innocence or a coolness of criminality, whether it be her natural manner or a calculated pose with which to disarm suspicion, we may prefer to reserve opinion, at any rate till we have seen how Miss Bickerton will survive the ordeal of the witness-box, which her two companions have already experienced, and have the advantage of Chief Inspector Taverton's expert decision.

Miss Bickerton broke the long silence which had followed a request from Miss Dorling that she should pass the pepper—Anne was seated at the head of the table, with James on her left and Miss Dorling on her right—by saying: "I shall go back to Shrewsbury tomorrow if it's over in time for me to get a train. I suppose you won't stay here, Miss Dorling, by yourself?"

Rose looked at her as though hesitating whether to make any reply, and then said, "Probably not." She turned her eyes to James. "I've been trying to persuade Gladys to stay, but it's no good. I'm afraid she'll go when she gets her wages tomorrow, whatever we say."

Gladys had declared that she "wouldn't stay, miss; no, not for a million pounds." She was, in fact, staying for the £3 6s. 8d. which would be due to her tomorrow night, but she was not good at arithmetic.

"Lor', miss," she said, "every time I looks at that shelf it gives me such a turn as never was."

So much for Gladys.

Rose went on, "I don't think I can stay longer when the inquest's over, but I don't like to think of you being left all alone, if Miss Bickerton's going too."

James said, "I shan't stay here alone. I might go to the Mercers' for a few days, but I wish you could have kept on with the children—"

Then he stopped, for he saw his sister-in-law's expression, and he realized that she might have something to say later on that point—unless she were otherwise occupied.

The children had been sent to stay with some friends in Birmingham, and it was there that he thought he might find a few days' asylum also from the shadows of that deserted house.

Thinking of future arrangements for the children reminded him of the will of which he had heard a few hours earlier. It did not decrease the coldness with which he habitually regarded his sister-in-law, or the doubt of her innocence, which he had never been able to stifle entirely.

He had no gift of finesse, as we may have observed.

He said, "Aren't you staying to scoop the loot?"

Miss Bickerton seemed on the edge of an angry or indignant answer, but checked herself to say only, "You mean Belle's will? I thought those things had to be proved, before anyone could do anything."

"Well," he said, "you can watch the pot till it boils—but perhaps you've thought that a watched pot never does." He was dimly conscious of implications here which he would have been incapable of intending.

So, perhaps, was she. She made no answer at all.

He went on, "But I wanted to talk to you both about what Preedy said at lunch.

"He says that what our evidence, taking it in bulk, amounts to is just this: we're sure it wasn't accident, and we're sure it wasn't suicide, and we didn't do it ourselves, and there was no one else in the house. Now if it turns out that Belle wasn't poisoned, as we hope it will, that's all right; but if not, we're saying what *can't* be true, and if we don't want it to end in a criminal trial, we've got to put our heads together, and go all out for suicide. He thought you ought to think of this, Anne, before you give your evidence tomorrow."

"And if I don't say that Belle might have committed suicide, I suppose I'm to be the criminal?"

"He didn't say that. But you have got to look at this. If it was suicide you've got to have some possible explanation of how the arsenic got on the spoon, when the spoon hadn't been in the tea."

"There's no difficulty about that. Belle didn't take sugar. You know that as well as I do; and you know that we had to take a spoon and the sugar up just the same, or she was sure to say that she wanted it that time, and it meant another journey to fetch them."

"That doesn't explain the arsenic on the spoon."

"No, but there are ways it might happen. Someone might have known that she'd taken some of the poison, and then put it on the spoon."

"But you were alone when the tea was made. No one could have done that but you."

"Yes, they could. They could have put it on the spoon any time during the evening if they wanted to make out that I'd poisoned Belle."

"But there was arsenic in the dregs of the tea."

"Well, they could have put that there too."

"Are you making this fantastic accusation against Miss Dorling or me?"

"I'm not accusing anyone. I'm only showing you that you should leave me alone."

"But I don't want to interfere. I only want to let you know what Preedy thinks—that we shall make more trouble for ourselves if we try to make the jury think that it wasn't suicide."

"Well, it wasn't. I know Belle too well to think that, and I'm not going to say so for anyone."

"Then what do you think did happen?"

"I don't know any more than you. Perhaps less."

"Well, I suppose you're not going to suggest that I put anything in the cup when I was in Liverpool at the time."

"No, but you might have known what was being done. After all, you bought the weed killer."

"He only bought it," Miss Dorling interposed, "because I asked him to."

"Yes, I know that quite well—and it was you that got it out that afternoon."

"Look here, Anne," James said, "we're all talking too fast. If you don't think out what you mean a bit better, you'll look as silly as I did when you give evidence tomorrow. I don't quite know what you mean to suggest, but you say that you're certain that Belle didn't commit suicide, and then that Miss Dorling knew she'd done it, and put some arsenic into her teacup so that suspicion might fall on you, and that I knew what she was going to do. That's how it sounds to me, and it's just rot; and if you want to make everyone think you did it yourself you can't go a better way."

After saying which James Hackett, who rarely talked at such length unless he were in a condition of unusual exasperation, got up and left the room.

He switched on a light in the hall, and observed a letter lying on the mat, which had come by the evening delivery.

He read this, and though it would be too much to say that he felt in good spirits, he was conscious of some lifting of the previous misery, as he made his way to his solitary room, where Belle would never vex him again with affectations of illness, or weary him with tales of endless grievances, or tantalize him with inconstant moods, or meet him with swift outbursts of jealousy or passion or penitence. He would never forget Belle…would never cease to feel a sharp pang of regret for that suddenly shortened life. She had loved life in her own way. She had had vivid moments which could never be forgotten by the man to whom she had given all of herself—as far as such women can. In her own way she had loved him well.

Yet good news is good, whatever miseries may be ours when it arrives. He may have slept better for that letter, though he woke early enough to go over the events of the last days with a dull fury of exasperation. He didn't want to think that Anne could have done such a thing, even if there was this will of which he had not heard, and which certainly would not have outlasted the week, had Belle lived to revoke it. He was determined that he would not entertain the thought that Rose could have done it. He knew that Rose had been fond of him years ago. He had left Staines when her preference had proved an embarrassment, for he had been engaged to Belle Bickerton at that time, though she did not know it. He had never been in love with Rose. He wasn't now. He was quite certain of that. But he liked her. He always had. Perhaps he liked her better than he had at Staines. Anyway, he wouldn't admit the possibility that she would do such a thing as that. Then *was* it suicide? He didn't think it was. Was it accident? He didn't see how it could be. Damn it all! Would the truth never be known? Was he sure that he wanted it known? He knew that he would stop the inquest at once if he were able to do so. Such things only made bad worse. It was curiosity more than anything else. There was no consideration for Belle or anyone, living or dead. How Belle would have hated the way in which they discussed her and laid her weaknesses bare! And it could do no good. It could only put the idea of poisoning into other people's minds and tell them how best to do it.

James Hackett went to bed in a bad temper, but he woke up in a worse. Why wouldn't Anne be sensible, and say that it must have been suicide, which she had always rather feared or expected? He couldn't think it was really Anne. Still, there *was* the will.

He read the letter again, and felt that slight lifting of the clouds which he had experienced the night before.

CHAPTER IX.

THE court had been crowded yesterday, but it was worse today. There had been a long queue that waited for admittance hours before it had opened. Now the street was jammed with hundreds who could not enter, but waited to observe the arrival of those from among whom they could already surmise that the law would select its victim.

James had been phoned an hour before by the West Bromwich police station, advising him to bring his party by taxi, rather than to come in on the Birmingham tram that passed his gate. It was arranged that the taxi should be met on its arrival by an adequate force of police, so that its occupants might gain entrance in safety.

As they took their seats in the vehicle—Anne and Miss Dorling side by side (but with some distance between them) and he opposite—James was conscious of some feeling of sympathy for the white-faced figure of his sister-in-law, who had to face the ordeal which he and Rose had already experienced. She looked ill. He knew that she could be hysterical under sufficient provocation. She had not spoken at all this morning, except for answering monosyllables. She had eaten nothing at all. All these things might be consistent with her having poisoned her sister, but he could not think that she had. Still, there was the will. It was not sufficient reply, to his own mind, to say that it seemed unlikely that she would act in such a manner, for he knew that they were faced by some unlikely thing. If she had done it, it must have been on some sudden impulse, for the opportunity had not been of her providing. His powers of apprehension were much greater than his powers of expression, which was partly why he was irritated so easily by the glib legal talkers who seemed to observe so much and to realize so little. If she had done it on such an impulse, he saw that she must be the most wretched among them, and the most needing of sympathy, and would still have been so even though her fellow men might not have been gathering for the pitiless hunt.

On the opening of the court Miss Dorling was at once recalled to the witness-box. Mr. Preedy was about to rise when Russell-Welch asked permission to put a few further questions.

"Miss Dorling," he asked, "did you at any time inform Mrs. Hackett of your acquaintance with her husband?"

"Yes."

"When?"

"When I spoke to her in her bedroom on the afternoon of the 8th of August."

"Was that the first time?"

"I am not sure."

"Not sure? Come, Miss Dorling, do yourself justice. You could not forget a conversation of that kind."

"I have not forgotten."

"Then will you explain what you mean?"

"Yes. At the earlier conversation I tried to tell her more than once, but the sentences were sometimes unfinished. When I tried to explain anything, Mrs. Hackett said it was all too trivial and she didn't want to hear, and then she went on talking. It was rather a one-sided conversation." A faint smile came to her lips at the recollection, which Mr. Russell-Welch found somewhat disconcerting, it being seldom that he observed a witness to be so much at ease when he was cross-examining in this manner. He tried another attack.

"You have said that the conversation on the afternoon of the 8th of August was quite a short one, and that you were only trying to say such things as would avert further trouble, and that you were trying to get away all the time. Do you think it sounds a probable thing that you should have first made such a confession at such a time and under such circumstances?"

"It wasn't a confession: it was an explanation. It was the most natural reply I could give to a remark that Mrs. Hackett made."

"Very well. We will leave it that you did not tell her until that day, so far as you are aware. You were very much in love with Mr. Hackett when you used to meet him in Staines?"

Miss Dorling looked at the K.C. without answering, and the coroner intervened.

"I am sorry that it should be necessary to probe into these matters, but I think you should answer. The question is, were you in love with Mr. Hackett when you knew him at Staines years ago?"

"Yes, I was."

Mr. Russell-Welch said quickly, "And you are still?"

She looked at him coolly. "I think you are going too far."

There was a murmur of approval from the crowded court.

"I don't think you should press that question if the witness objects to answer," said the coroner.

"Then I must defer to your ruling." Mr. Russell-Welch sat down.

Mr. Duff-Preedy rose briskly.

"Do you think, Miss Dorling, that Mrs. Hackett was seriously jealous of or distressed by any signs of friendship or intimacy—I don't mean in any serious sense—between Mr. Hackett and yourself before she knew of this previous acquaintance?"

Miss Dorling paused to consider her answer.

"No, not very. She never liked him to talk to anyone except herself. I don't think she was really upset. I think she liked having a grievance."

"Do you mind telling the court exactly what it was to which she took exception? Was it nothing beyond the fact that you talked to her husband too much, or he to you?"

"She said she had seen us kiss."

"Was it true?"

"No."

"But she thought it to be so?"

"She may have done. I cannot say."

"Then I will put this to you, and I want you to answer carefully: If Mrs. Hackett had no serious cause for jealousy, but only what I may describe as a restless doubt or suspicion, may not your conversation on this afternoon of August 8th have had the effect—however unintended by you—of making it suddenly seem a more serious thing; may it not have suddenly appeared to her as something which had been going on for years without her knowledge, and, to one of her exceptional temperament—to one in her physical condition at the time—have had the effect of an unexpected shock?"

Miss Dorling made no haste to reply to this question, and the coroner was the first to speak.

"Of course," he said, "I see what you are driving at. I have had the same thought in my own mind—that this conversation may have originated some sudden impulse of self-destruction. But there is this difficulty: if we are dealing with a case of arsenical poisoning, and if the poison was taken in the cup of tea that Miss Bickerton was bringing up almost at the moment—to which all the evidence so far points—how should Mrs. Hackett have put it into the tea unless she had already secreted it, and done this during the earlier part of that same afternoon when the tin of weed killer was first opened?"

"I have considered that also," Mr. Duff-Preedy replied, "but I submit that though we have had evidence of when the tea was carried up, we have as yet had none of when it was actually drunk."

"Still," said the coroner, "there would be difficulties. But there may be more evidence to come on this point. It may be better not to discuss it now. Well, Miss Dorling, you heard the question. What do you say?"

"It would be possible."

Mr. Duff-Preedy sat down at once. He realized quickly that Miss Dorling did not accept the suggestion, but she knew that he was aiming at a verdict of suicide, and she would back him up. It was a shrewd reply.

Miss Dorling stepped down, and Miss Bickerton took her place in the witness-box.

CHAPTER X.

IT may have been unfortunate for Anne Bickerton that Miss Dorling had been recalled to the witness-box that morning, so that the jury had the immediate contrast of a witness who gave hesitating and confused replies, who left sentences unfinished, or altered her evidence even in the act of giving it, with one who was sure alike of herself and her facts, and who would hold her position unshaken, even when it was of an inherent improbability.

She said that her name was Anne Bickerton, that she was unmarried, was three years younger than her sister had been, and lived alone in rooms at 17, Raven Close, Shrewsbury.

Of these facts she appeared sure, and she gave them readily, but there was little of her subsequent evidence which had a similar certainty.

"Occupation?" the coroner asked. These routine preliminary questions were necessary, for he must have the identity and status of a witness clearly recorded, but it was routine, all the same.

"I am—was cashier at Tucker and Thomson's."

He looked up from the notes he was taking, slightly puzzled. "'Am' or 'was'?"

"I was—am—at least, I don't know whether I shall go back."

"Thinks she's got the money already?" the Chief Inspector whispered to Russell-Welch, half in jest and half in jest and half in query.

But the K.C. shook his head. "It isn't that. There's something else here. You'd better follow it up."

"I'm having police inquiries made in Shrewsbury this morning. We don't leave much to chance in these cases."

"Good man!" said the K.C. "But just listen to this."

The coroner had settled the point with a characteristic grammatical exactness. "Have been cashier, up to a fortnight ago"—so he directed the shorthand writer to record it. He went on: "You had come to visit your sister during a holiday? Did you often visit her on such occasions?"

"Yes. Not—well, at weekends. It wasn't—"

"Yes, yes," said the coroner. "Wait a minute. I only want to know whether there was any special reason which caused you to come to her at this time?"

The witness paused in an evident confusion before a question to which the coroner had expected no more than a simple negative.

"Well, there was something—I did want to see her particularly—"

The coroner looked at her keenly, and with an expression which was not without sympathy, though it showed some impatience also.

"Tell me this, Miss Bickerton: did you visit your sister in response to any special request from her, or because you had any reason—any special reason—to think that she might need you, or that things were not going happily with her?"

"No—nothing special."

"Very well. And it was the kind of visit that you often paid?"

"Yes—except I couldn't often stay so long, except at Christmas and sometimes at Easter."

"Well, never mind that. It was just an ordinary visit. That's what I want to get at. She was your only sister?"

"Yes."

"Only near relative?"

"Yes—at least, we've a second cousin at Tewkesbury, and abroad there's—"

"Never mind those who are abroad. It was quite natural that you should come to see your sister on your holidays."

"So I always said. It wasn't only her, it was the children—"

"Then was there some objection to your coming so often?"

"Not except James, and Belle always said—"

"Your brother-in-law thought your visits were rather too frequent?"

"James was always nasty to me."

"So that you probably didn't see your sister as often as you otherwise might have done?"

"Oh, no. That didn't make any difference. It wasn't likely—"

"I see. Your sister liked you to visit her as often as possible, although your brother-in-law rather objected, and his objection didn't weigh much with either of you? Well, we needn't go further into that. Not now, anyway. I want you, before we come to the events of the 8th of August, to recall as clearly as you can what happened on the previous days. Which day did your visit commence?"

"On August the 2nd—no, the 1st—no, I'm not sure—on the Friday—the Friday night."

"On the evening of Friday, the 2nd of August. And on the same day you had a conversation with Miss Dorling, of which she has told us something already. Was this conversation at your sister's request, or in consequence of something that you had seen yourself?"

"Belle asked me. She said she was too nervous. Of course, I'd seen."

"Seen what?"

"How they were going on."

"How were they?"

"Talking and laughing, as though they didn't care how ill she was."

"Was that all?"

"I should think it was enough; and they had breakfast without waiting for Belle to come down."

"And without you either?"

"No—yes—I mean, it was before I came."

"Then you don't know that it happened from your own knowledge?"

"No—yes, I do. Belle told me."

"Was that what she asked you to mention to Miss Dorling?"

"Yes, and not to be cruel in other ways."

"What ways?"

"Making her not have her meals, and forgetting how thin she was, and talking to James, and making the children like her more than her, and laughing when she was ill."

"What did Miss Dorling say to all this?"

"She said she'd leave."

"But she didn't leave?"

"No. I told her it just showed what a sort she was to start talking like that and leave Belle stranded."

"So she agreed to stay?"

"Yes—no—till the end of the month, or till Belle got someone else."

"So no doubt you told your sister of this arrangement. Was she satisfied?"

"Who? Belle? Of course not; she said it showed there was something in it, or she wouldn't have stayed, after being accused like that."

"But I understood that you had pressed her to stay till you could get someone else?"

"Yes, of course. Belle didn't want to be stranded; she said it just showed what a sort she was to talk of going off like that."

"Very well. We'll leave that. Suppose we go on to August the 7th. A statement was made in court yesterday that your sister made a will on the afternoon of that day by which she left all her property to you, excluding her husband and her own children entirely, and that you knew of this—that you were with her at the time. Is that true?"

"Yes, I was with her. We always went out together."

"Did her husband know that she was changing her will in this way?"

"Of course not. Belle didn't want any fuss."

"Did you expostulate with her against making a will of such a kind?"

"No. She didn't want Miss Dorling to have them if she died."

"Them?"

"The children, of course."

"Do you mean that the will creates a trust for the children under your control?"

"Yes. I mean, I was to look after the children."

"Does it say so in the will?"

"No. That was what Belle said."

"Did you know that she was not going to her usual solicitor for making this will?"

"Yes."

"Why was that?"

"She didn't want Mr. Preedy to know that she was being nasty to James."

"Do you know how much money she had?"

"Yes—no—at least, Mr. Sledson left her twelve thousand pounds. That was what Belle said was left after they bought the houses, and there were some shares in a screw works."

"What property?"

"The house where they lived and the one that's empty next door."

"So, if she died while that will remained, it would appear that you could take all this considerable estate, including the home in which her husband and children lived?"

"I don't know how much is left. They must have spent a lot."

"Beyond the income?"

"I don't know how much. Belle spent a lot."

"Did you say anything to persuade your sister against making this will?"

"No. Mr. Tomkinson said it would be quite good."

"That was not what I asked. Did *you* think it was 'quite good'?"

"Yes—with that woman in the house."

"But Miss Dorling had offered to go."

"Well, there might be someone else if Belle was dead."

"Did your sister often make wills?"

"No—yes—well, she made some. You have to, if you've got money to leave."

"Had she ever left her property to you before?"

"I don't know."

"As far as you know?"

"No."

"And when she made the next will it would be very likely to be a different one?"

"Yes, if she was being silly with James."

"Well—perhaps we'd better come on to the events of the next day. We have been told that your sister was ill in bed. Was it a sudden attack?"

"No, she'd been very ill all the week."

"But you have told us that she went to the solicitor's office the day before?"

"Well, she wanted to."

"When she was seriously ill? Why didn't the solicitor come to her?"

"We went in a taxi."

"Dr. Riggett has told us that she was suffering the next day from muscular rheumatism."

"Well, it was James making her go out like that that made her so bad."

"Making her go out? I thought you said he didn't know?"

"It was his goings on."

The coroner paused a moment. He looked at the legal gentlemen who had been keen, though silent, observers of this curious evidence.

"Mr. Preedy," he said, "I'm wondering whether Dr. Riggett knew that his patient had been able to go out on the previous afternoon. I think I must recall him on that point. It might be very material."

"I was thinking the same thing," the solicitor answered; "but I think Dr. Riggett gave us a broad hint yesterday." Few could be more skilful than he at gradually building up an impression. He hoped to develop this point of whether Mrs. Hackett could have gone downstairs till the jury would be influenced by the proof of potentiality, almost as though it were a proof of the fact itself.

The coroner resumed his examination.

"In spite of her having gone out with you that afternoon, do you suggest that your sister was seriously ill on the following morning?"

"Yes, of course she was. She told James, and he wouldn't have gone if he hadn't been the brute he is."

"Is your only reason for thinking that she was seriously ill that she said so herself?"

"Yes—no—I know she was ill. She wouldn't have sent for Dr. Riggett, if not."

"Do you mean that she never had a doctor unless she were seriously ill?"

"She might have had Dr. Elgood."

"I'm afraid I don't understand."

"Well, she didn't like Dr. Riggett, but she thought he was a real doctor. She said he wouldn't stand her—any nonsense. She liked Dr. Elgood when she just wanted someone to talk to."

There was a ripple of merriment through the court at this answer.

"Silence, please," said the coroner, with the shadow of a smile on his own lips. The two doctors were known.

"We have heard that your sister took no food during that day—nothing at all till she had a cup of tea in the afternoon. Can you swear to that, definitely, from your own knowledge?"

"Yes, of course."

"Why 'of course'?"

"Well, nothing to talk of. She might have had something in the morning, of course."

"'Might have had'? Did she, or not?"

"You couldn't expect her not to eat anything all day."

"It's not a question of what I expect. I want to know what happened."

"She only had some milk that I took up to her in the morning."

"Anything else?"

"She might have had some biscuits out of the wardrobe."

"Did she to your knowledge?"

"Just a few with the milk."

"She kept food in her room?"

"She had to for when James was cross."

"Do you mean that he wouldn't let her eat when he was cross?"

"Yes—no—of course not. She had to have something when she wasn't eating. Anyone would."

"Very well. Then she had milk and biscuits in the morning. Who put the milk into the glass?"

"I did. It was out of one of the 'Grade A' bottles—the same that the children had. It's no use saying there was anything wrong with the milk."

"And after that she had nothing till you made her the tea in the afternoon. You made this tea yourself?"

"Yes, of course I did. Gladys was out."

"Where did you make it?"

"In the kitchen."

"Tell me just what you did. I am sure, Miss Bickerton, you will see the importance of being as exact as possible. Tell me just what you did from when you entered the kitchen."

"I put the kettle on and laid the tray. Then I made the tea. That was all."

"Tell me this: did you at any time move or do anything to this tin of weed killer that Miss Dorling told us was in the scullery during the time?"

"Of course not. I didn't even know it was there."

"Did you go into the scullery, or were you in the kitchen the whole of the time?"

"Of course I went into the scullery. I had to boil the kettle."

Inspector Taverton rose at this point. "I think, sir," he said, "it may be helpful to explain that the gas cooker is in the scullery. Entering the scullery from the kitchen, there is a small flap-table on the right, which can be lowered against the wall, and the gas cooker is just beyond it. The copper is further on against the opposite wall. The wall to the left—that which is level with the door from the kitchen—is bare, except for odd things standing against it. The sink is against the wall opposite the table, and the door into the garden is beyond the sink on the same side.

"How large is the scullery?"

"Quite small. About ten feet square."

"Very well. You might let me have a plan of the scullery, Inspector. Go on, Miss Bickerton. You boiled the kettle on the gas-cooker in the scullery. I suppose you had filled it from the sink?"

"Yes, of course. No, I think it was full. It may have been half-full and I filled it up."

"From where did you get the teapot?"

"From the kitchen cupboard, of course."

"And the tea?"

"It's kept in a tin on the kitchen mantelpiece."

"And you got it from there?"

"It may have been on the table."

"In the scullery?"

"No, the kitchen table, of course."

"Don't you remember where you found it?"

"Yes. It was where it always is."

"Very well. Now where did you lay the tray? In the kitchen or the scullery?"

"In the kitchen, of course."

"Was the tray never in the scullery at all—are you certain of that?"

"It was in the scullery while I made the tea."

"Now, Miss Bickerton, I want you to answer this question with great care. Can you recall anything that happened while you were laying the tray or making the tea by which any of this weed killer, which, according to Miss Dorling's evidence, was in the scullery at the time, could have got into the kettle, or the teapot, or the cup or saucer, or the spoon?"

"Not while I was there."

"Was there any time when you were not there?"

"I went to the lavatory to wash my hands."

"When?"

"While the tea was drawing. I'd blackened my hands on the kettle. It was no use waiting about."

"Couldn't you have swilled your hands at the sink?"

"Well, I didn't."

"Any other reason?"

"There wouldn't have been a towel there if I had."

"Very well. How long were you away?"

"About five minutes. Not that much. About two or three."

"How far is the lavatory from the kitchen? I think the jury may like a full plan of the house, Inspector, before this case is finished."

The Inspector took the question to himself, as well as the instruction. Doubtless, he was the more competent to give an accurate answer. He rose in his place to reply.

"The lavatory—it's a gentleman's cloakroom really—is at the front of the house. Its door is at the foot of the front stairs. It must be about thirty feet from the kitchen door."

"Very well. Then there was a time after the tray was laid and the tea made when you left them so that anyone coming in from the garden could have had access to them without your knowledge. Is that what you say?"

"Yes, of course they could."

"Where were they exactly at this time?"

"The tray would be on the scullery table, and the teapot by it."

"Now I must ask you three questions, Miss Bickerton, which you must please answer as carefully as you can. Can you swear positively that you did not do anything while you were preparing this tea by which it is possible that it could have been contaminated by the weed killer in any way whatever?"

"Of course I didn't."

"But it is not 'of course' at all. You must recognize, Miss Bickerton, that in some way the arsenic got there—I'm not suggesting that you are necessarily responsible—but there it is."

"Well, I didn't. I didn't know it was there."

"Then I must ask you this. The analysis shows that the dregs of the tea contained arsenious oxide, such as could have originated from contamination by the tin of weed killer. It is natural, therefore, to connect the two, but this is something less than an absolute proof.

"Arsenious oxide can be obtained in different ways and from various substances. Are you aware of any way in which such a poison was, or could have been, introduced, other than from the tin of weed killer, which you say that you did not see?"

"Not except when I wasn't there."

"Then tell me this. While you were in the lavatory could you have heard anyone enter the kitchen, either from the garden or the hall?"

"Yes. I did."

The atmosphere of the court had been of a breathless stillness during the latter part of this examination, but at this answer there was a stir of uncontrollable excitement, which died again into a waiting silence at the coroner's next question.

"From the hall or the garden?"

"I don't know."

"Tell me just what you did hear."

"Just a noise. Someone moving about."

"Could you tell that it was in the kitchen?"

"Well, it sounded that way."

"What kind of noise was it?"

"Just like someone moving about."

"Like footsteps?"

"No. More like people moving something."

"A loud noise?"

"Nothing special."

"It might have been upstairs?"

"No, it wasn't."

"Should you have heard anyone come down?"

"Yes. Unless they were very quiet. No, I mightn't."

"At this time both Mrs. Hackett and Miss Dorling were upstairs. You had come down, leaving Mrs. Hackett in bed, and Miss Dorling has told us how she passed you on the stairs. Do you agree?"

"Yes, I suppose so."

"Do you know as a fact that they were both upstairs at the time?"

"Yes, I suppose so."

"Could either of them have come down during the short time that you were in the lavatory, gone to the kitchen, and returned upstairs without your knowledge?"

"Yes, they might—Miss Dorling might."

"Do you think she did?"

"No, I wouldn't say that."

"The time would have been very short, and anyone coming down in that way must have expected to see you, or at least to be most likely to do so?"

"Yes, I suppose so."

"And would have no object in coming down very quietly unless it were to do it without your knowledge? No one could have foreseen that you would blacken your hand when you lifted the kettle."

"No. I don't say they did."

"Then, if you heard a noise from the direction of the kitchen is it not the more probable that someone had entered from outside?"

"It isn't likely at all."

"Why not?"

"There was no one there."

"That is what we should naturally suppose. But we are searching for some unlikely thing. It appears to me"—and the coroner addressed himself at this point rather to the legal gentlemen before him than to the witness—"it appears to me that anyone might have entered from the garden who had observed Miss Bickerton leave the kitchen, or who might have supposed it to be deserted that afternoon, but that those who were upstairs would have supposed her to be there. Of course, it's all guesswork, and there are improbabilities in every theory that we are yet able to form." He turned back to the witness.

"When you took the tea up did you see Mrs. Hackett drink it?"

"Yes—no—some of it, anyway."

"Did she make any complaint about its taste?"

"She always did."

"Did she on this occasion?"

"Yes, I expect so. Yes, she did—yes, I think so—I'm not sure."

The examination went on from this point to the meal that was prepared in the night, the subsequent sickness, the summoning of medical help, and the final illness, of which we have heard already, and of which it is needless that we should hear more, this being neither a medical treatise nor a poisoner's guide.

The coroner concluded his examination, and adjourned for lunch.

CHAPTER XI.

WHEN Anne Bickerton re-entered the crowded court, after a vain attempt upon a lunch which she badly needed but could not force herself to eat, it was not, as she had expected, to return to the witness-box immediately, but to sit for a quarter of an hour, or perhaps longer, in an atmosphere of silent expectancy, facing the coroner's empty chair.

It was observed that the places of Russell-Welch and Inspector Taverton were also vacant, and Mr. Duff-Preedy, reviewing possibilities in a rapid mind, would have given much to overhear the conversation which (he had no doubt) was proceeding in the coroner's room.

Taking Miss Bickerton's evidence at its worst, he could not think that it would justify any sudden action by the police, such as would bring the present proceedings to an abrupt conclusion. Rather, her assertion that she had been absent from the kitchen, and her evidence of the noise that she had heard, opened the door of a defence which might not have been previously anticipated. Was it possible (he thought) that it was at Miss Dorling that their suspicions had been directed, and that this evidence had supplied the final support that they needed? He looked at her, sitting grave, quiet, and impassive beside him, serious but not seeming over-concerned, and wondered whether she would maintain her poise, should the coroner return to announce that the inquest was indefinitely adjourned, and Inspector Taverton arrest her for the murder of her employer. He did not think it likely, but he anticipated that there would be some unexpected development, which he must be prepared to meet.

He was at least right so far as that the coroner, the K.C., and the police inspector entered the court together. The ponderous form of Russell-Welch was scarcely settled into its place when the coroner spoke.

"Mr. Duff-Preedy," he said, "I have been considering the position, and I think that it may be a convenient course to adjourn at this stage until the result of the autopsy is before us. In any event, Mr. Russell-Welch prefers to reserve his cross-examination of Miss Bickerton until the cause of death has been finally ascertained. I therefore propose to adjourn the court until this day week, when I understand that Sir Lionel Tipshift will be prepared to give his report, and we can then conclude Miss Bickerton's examination and take the evidence of Dr. Elgood and of any further witnesses."

"With your permission, Mr. Coroner," the solicitor answered, "I should like to ask Miss Bickerton one or two questions before the court is adjourned. They will not occupy more than a few minutes."

"If they are matters arising strictly out of this morning's examination which you think should be cleared up—"

"There is really only one point," Mr. Preedy answered. "Beyond that I should prefer to reserve my examination until after Mr. Russell-Welch, in the usual way."

"Very well."

"Miss Bickerton," Mr. Preedy commenced, as soon as she had returned to the witness-box, "you have told us that Mrs. Hackett was seriously ill on the morning of August the 8th, when Mr. Hackett left—"

"So she was," the witness interjected quickly.

"—and that she had been in that condition for several days previously?"

"So she had."

"Yet this illness had not prevented her from going to her solicitor on the previous day, because it appeared to her to be a matter of urgency?"

"She wasn't going to let—"

"Yes. We know that. What I wish to ask you is this: was there any change in her condition between the afternoon of August the 7th and August the 8th which would have rendered her incapable of going out on the later day, if she had had a similar necessity?"

"But she didn't want to at all. She didn't want to get up. She was too ill."

"But suppose she had wanted to very much?"

"I know she didn't mean to get up."

"But that is not what I am asking. Let me put it in this way: suppose she had found it necessary to go to the solicitors' again to complete the will—"

"She'd have got up if she knew she ought. She wouldn't think of herself."

"Very well. We'll put it that way. She would have got up at the call of duty. Now don't you think, Miss Bickerton, if she had had an intention of self-destruction, that would have been a matter of even greater urgency, of greater importance, than the making of a will, for which her solicitor could easily have come to her?"

"She didn't want him in the house while James was there. It wasn't likely she would."

"That is not what I asked you. Do you not think that an impulse of self-destruction would seem as important—?"

"Not to her. She wouldn't do such a thing."

"But if—?"

"Not like making a will."

"Well, Miss Bickerton, that may be your opinion, but I think most of us would think differently." But here the coroner interposed.

"I'm afraid I can't let this go on longer. You are really asking no more than the witness's opinion on a point on which it is of no more value than that of others. Of course, the point itself is quite legitimate; and can be argued at the right time."

Mr. Duff-Preedy sat down, well content.

The coroner adjourned the court with a final admonition to the jury not to discuss the case with others and to maintain open minds, remembering that all the evidence had not yet been heard.

Perhaps we may also observe the wisdom of this advice.

CHAPTER XII.

"You don't believe it?" said the Assistant Commissioner.

"I don't say she didn't go to wash her hands. She may have done that on purpose. Or it may just have happened. And she may have heard a noise, or half a dozen, for that matter. But I say that's nothing to do with the case.

"You know, sir," the Inspector went on, "I'm not often wrong in these cases—not after I've seen the witnesses and made a few inquiries on my own and summed them up. I don't want to boast, but there was the Benson case, and there was almost everyone against me then, and you know how he confessed at last, when he thought it was the only way to save his neck."

"Well," said the Commissioner, "I know you're a safe man, and you've seen the people, and I haven't. Tell me just what you think did happen."

"Well, sir, I had to think first whether it wasn't suicide, and I made up my mind against that, because it wasn't sense. There wasn't much opportunity, for one thing. She couldn't have gone down, even if she'd known the tin of weed killer was open in the scullery—which there's no evidence that she did—without one of the other women knowing. It isn't likely at all. And if they're innocent, as they would be then, why shouldn't they say, if they saw her go?

"Then she wasn't the kind to do it. Dr. Riggett was clear on that, and the facts make it less likely still. If she was jealous of this Dorling girl she wouldn't put herself out of the way to make room for her. She wasn't that kind at all. And if she wasn't really jealous and was just teasing, as you might say, she wouldn't do it for that.

"No, sir, I'm as sure that she meant to live as I sit here."

"I expect you're right, Inspector. But you've got to allow for the fact that she was in bad health at the time."

"Well, sir, perhaps I should, and perhaps I have, but not overmuch. I don't think there was much wrong, and I don't think she thought so herself, though I dare say she'd played at being ill till she herself didn't rightly know what was real and what wasn't, nor the doctors either. I expect it was the same about Miss Dorling too. She was jealous in a way, but she always would be about someone or something. No, sir, it was just her ordinary goings on."

"And the husband?"

"Well, sir, he was away at the time. It's a bit hard to bring him in any way. But he's not the sort. I'd bet half my pension on that. And he was fond of her too. I don't say she didn't lead him a dog's life, but he liked it well enough, in a way. And as to the money, he could have had just what he liked, and he doesn't seem to have taken any worth talking about from first to last."

"Well, there's Miss Dorling."

"Yes, sir, and I'll own that's a tougher bullet to chew. She's a cool piece, and she'd been fond of James Hackett, and there isn't much she wouldn't give to marry him now. I expect she will in the end if we don't hang her. I'll be straight about this, that if she were the only one in the case I should have said it was she, though I don't say I'd have been quite as easy as I should like. Still, I'd have said it was she, though it's against myself to admit it.

"But it's the sort of case that seems strong, but the closer you look the weaker it gets, and that's always a bad sign.

"It's a tall tale about her going there by chance, and it's a fact that she and Mr. Hackett got the weed killer together, and that it was she that had it out that day. That's against her. It might be taken to be against them both. But you've got to consider that it was done as openly as could be. I know she's a cool hand. But she wouldn't have planned it in such a way. She *couldn't* have planned just how it did happen, and you'll notice that she never seems to have come near the cup of tea, from first to last, even if she could have known that it was going to be made while she had the weed killer out.

"Of course, you'll say she might have come downstairs and done it while Miss Bickerton was washing her hands, but how would she have known that she wouldn't have met her going back?

"She'd have made about as simple a case against herself as ever was.

"No, sir; if she'd done it, it would have been cool enough, but quite different from that."

"Still, Inspector, you're not quite as sure as you'd like to be— not as sure as I should like you to be."

"No, sir, you're right in a way. I'm not as sure as I should like to be that it's not Miss Dorling, or, rather, I mightn't be if I wasn't sure of the other, which is just what I am. And there's another point I haven't mentioned. It mayn't be much, but it all points the same way. If Miss Dorling had done it she'd have given something like the right dose. There must have been enough to poison a family in that cup."

"She mightn't have known what the right dose was."

"Oh, yes, sir, she would. She wouldn't take on a thing like that without finding out. And, besides, everyone does. The Sunday papers see to that. There's millions of men and women who wouldn't know how to start killing a sheep if they hadn't had any meat for a week, but if they wanted their mother's money they'd know where to get what they need, and just how much of it to give."

"But is this quite fair to the other woman? Suppose they are both able to read."

"Yes, sir, but you've got to remember that the one isn't a fool, and the other is. You've got to remember, also, that if the one did it, it was a planned thing, and if the other did it, it was more probably an impulse when the chance came, knowing how cornered she was. And then she makes up this tale of going into the lavatory when she's found out."

"Still, Inspector, I shouldn't let this point of the amount of the dose weigh with you too much. There's such a thing as a spoon that slips or a hand that shakes."

"Yes, sir, so it might, but Miss Dorling's wouldn't shake much. Still, I'm not building on that. It was like this.

"I was listening to this Bickerton woman in the box, and I was almost sure it was she, and I tried to keep an open mind, but the time came when I said to myself, 'You're the one,' and I had no doubt at all. So we were walking out of court for lunch, and Russell-Welch came up behind me in the corridor, and he said, 'Well, which is it now?' and I said, 'It's the sister, as sure as Queen Anne's dead, but how we shall get her I don't know,' and then I went on to the station, and there was Shrewsbury on the phone as I went in."

"Yes, it does seem to settle it," said the Commissioner. "It gives the motive you needed. The will didn't seem strong enough by itself. And you say that Russell-Welch and the coroner think the same?"

"Yes. They both thought it was sure. But they thought we'd better not bring it all out then, unless we meant to arrest her before the post-mortem report, and I wasn't sure that you'd think that was quite safe."

"You don't think anything will happen in Shrewsbury to give her the alarm?"

"No, I don't. I think it will be hushed up; and you've got to re-member that she can't hope to deal with it now. Besides, she's watched too closely to get away if she did try it. No, sir, she won't do that: she's too big a fool."

"Very well, Inspector. I expect you're right. Murderers mostly are. But I should keep an open mind till the inquest is over. If you want a warrant you can have it at any time."

CHAPTER XIII.

MR DUFF-PREEDY was hopeful.

"It's no more than we expected," he said, in reference to the post-mortem report, of which he had been informed; "and unless they've got something absolutely fresh—and I can't see what it can be—I think we ought to get an open verdict. We can't hope for a verdict of suicide, but I think I can convince the jury that we can't exclude that possibility, and if so we're really home. You must expect a verdict of 'Death by arsenical poisoning,' but how or by whom administered there is insufficient evidence to say. Something like that.

"Of course, we mustn't halloo till we're out of the wood, and we don't know what the police may do afterwards. But that's how it seems to me."

This was to Mr. Hackett, as they made their way over the street from his office, to be shepherded by the watchful police through the curious, idle crowd into a court which was somewhat less closely packed than a week ago, for admittance had been more strictly regulated on this occasion.

James observed that his sister-in-law, to whom he had not spoken since the last sitting of the court, was in her place, looking, if possible, paler and certainly more ill than a week ago. There, also, was Miss Dorling, looking in excellent health after a week of tennis. He also may have shown some benefit from a few days of quiet kindness from the friends with whom his children were staying. The Firs had been deserted for the past week, except for the morbid crowds that came from West Bromwich and Birmingham to gaze at the padlocked gate, and to be held back from a closer invasion by the patrolling constables.

The coroner went through the necessary preliminaries with an expert rapidity. The jury were in their places. The witnesses were present.

76

He said, "I propose to call Sir Lionel Tipshift, so that we may know the cause of death positively before we proceed further, and so that we may release him as soon as possible, as I understand that he is anxious to return to London. His evidence will not take very long, and we will take yours, Dr. Elgood, immediately afterward."

Sir Lionel Tipshift's evidence may be briefly stated. He had analysed certain organs, or parts of them; he had examined muscles and fingernails. He stated with certainty that death had occurred from acute arsenical poisoning. More—much more—than the minimum fatal dose had been taken within forty-eight hours of death. We may avoid his decimals. The importance of his evidence lay in his assurance that the poison had been taken not less than twenty-four hours nor more than forty-eight hours before death occurred. He gave his reasons.

The coroner's examination being concluded, Mr. Russell-Welch was invited, but declined, to ask anything further.

Mr. Duff-Preedy, with some reluctance, was also silent. He would have liked to ask this very confident man how his evidence would compare with that which had been given by other doctors at similar trials twenty-five years ago, and what assurance there could be that the medical evidence of twenty-five years later would not show similar or greater differences. But to do this would have been to attempt to score where the interests of his clients might not be served in any evident way. The cause of death was too clear. He kept his seat, anticipating that his time would come.

He was silent also during the evidence of Dr. Elgood, which confirmed that of his colleague, as such evidence always does, only making his one point, that Mrs. Hackett had been quite well enough to leave her bed on the afternoon of August the 8th, had she wished to do so. On this Mr. Duff-Preedy scored more easily than he had done previously. Dr. Elgood had no doubt. "She could have got up any time she wished," he said definitely. But on the question of suicide he was less helpful. He would not exclude the possibility, but he did not think that she was of a suicidal type, or that she had been in the mental condition when he saw her that afternoon of one who knew that she had just swallowed a fatal dose of poison, as there seemed no doubt that she had.

This he had said to the coroner, and Mr. Preedy was too wily to give him an opportunity of saying it again. He made the only point that he could, and let the witness go.

The next to give evidence was Inspector Taverton. It was his part to tell how and where the tin of weed killer had been found, where and how it had been bought, of the state of the garden, which certainly justified such a purchase, and of other matters, of which we have heard already from others.

His evidence added little to what the jury already knew: it merely arranged and proved it with the required formality.

He produced plans of the kitchen, of the house itself, and of the surrounding garden, which were passed to the jury-box, and went from hand to hand very frequently for a time, to be laid aside and forgotten as the following witnesses diverted their minds to fresher and more exciting evidence.

Mr. Tomkinson was the next witness. He said that he was the managing clerk of Ashton and Cross. His age was forty-seven. He held a practising certificate. He remembered the two ladies calling upon him. Mrs. Hackett had required a will to be drawn up there and then. She had brushed aside his suggestions of delay or of a second interview being necessary for completion. She had seemed to be quiet and normal, and to know her own mind very well indeed. She had seemed familiar with wills, remarking that it could be a very short document in the form in which she required it.

She had remained with her sister in the room of one of the partners while it had been engrossed, and had executed it in the presence of two of his own clerks. He produced the will.

The coroner perused the document. It was quite short, as Mr. Tomkinson had said, leaving everything without qualification or restriction to her sister, Anne Bickerton.

"I see," he said, "that you are the sole executor, Mr. Tomkinson."

"Yes. I suppose that I need scarcely say that that was not at my suggestion. It was how she wished it to be."

"Well, we needn't go into that now. Was Miss Bickerton present while the instructions were being given?"

"Yes."

"And when the will was executed?"

"Yes."

"Did she make any protest at any time?"

"No."

"Did she appear to be urging her sister to make such a will, or influencing her to execute it at once?"

"No. She seemed to be entirely under the influence of Mrs. Hackett."

"Did Mrs. Hackett appear to be ill?"

"No. It did not occur to me that she was in anything but normal health."

"Did she appear in every way fit to give the instructions for a document of this kind?"

"Yes; or I should have declined to draw it."

"Did she offer any explanation of why she came to you when you had not acted for her previously?"

"It is not quite correct to say that we had not acted for her previously. We had dealt with certain matters before. She did explain, however, that her husband's solicitors (so she described them) had drawn a previous will, but she thought that she ought to have an independent firm in a matter of that kind."

"Have any steps been taken to prove the will?"

"Not yet."

"It is a wise delay," said the coroner, and Mr. Tomkinson looked somewhat disconcerted.

Mr. Duff-Preedy rose. "With your consent, Mr. Coroner, I should like to ask Mr. Tomkinson what was the nature of the business which he had done for Mrs. Hackett previously—or perhaps the question might come better from yourself."

The coroner's face was expressionless as he said, "Will you please tell me that, Mr. Tomkinson?"

It was clear that the question was unwelcome.

"I think I am entitled to decline to reply to that question. I claim privilege."

The coroner looked at him reflectively. His legal powers were wide—in some respects even more so than those of a High Court judge. He was not at all clear that the solicitor was entitled to refuse an answer. He might threaten him with committal. He recalled a recent case at the Birmingham Assizes when a doctor (rightly or wrongly) had refused information on the ground that his professional honour bound him to secrecy, and had then made himself and his profession contemptible by giving it, lest he should be committed to prison. The coroner did not wish to send Mr. Tomkinson to jail. Still less did he wish to see him degrade the profession to which they both belonged by yielding to such a threat after the plea he had made. He thought he knew why Mr. Tomkinson was reluctant to reply, and it made him doubt the good faith of the objection which the solicitor had set up. But if he were right it would come out in other ways.

He said, "Very well, Mr. Tomkinson, I shall not press it. You can stand down," which Mr. Tomkinson very promptly did.

Mr. Russell-Welch had not appeared particularly interested in this episode. His eyes had been upon Miss Bickerton. He thought she looked relieved when the question was left unanswered. He was not surprised.

CHAPTER XIV.

MISS BICKERTON returned to the witness-box.

"Now, Mr. Russell-Welch," said the coroner, and that gentleman rose, with the characteristic adjustment of the gown on his shoulders which was known to indicate that he expected to score a point or to spring a surprise on the court.

"Miss Bickerton," he said quietly, "will you tell us whether you are still employed by Messrs. Tucker and Thomson?"

"Yes."

"But you had been suspended from your employment when you were giving evidence here a week ago?"

The witness made no answer, but Mr. Russell-Welch went on as though she had admitted the fact.

"Will you tell the court why that suspension has been withdrawn?"

"It's no business of yours."

"Answer the question, please."

Mr. Duff-Preedy rose. "I must object to that question. It is obviously outside this inquiry to go into matters of Miss Bickerton's employment at Shrewsbury, which it must be naturally painful to her—and perhaps seriously detrimental—to have publicly discussed here."

Mr. Russell-Welch did not wait for the coroner's ruling upon the propriety of his question. He said at once: "Well, I won't press it. Let me ask you this, Miss Bickerton. You told us a week ago that your sister had inherited about twelve thousand pounds, apart from the amount expended upon the purchase of some property and other securities. *How much of that twelve thousand pounds have you had during the last four years?*"

Miss Bickerton's pale face went whiter still, and then slowly flushed to a deep red. It seemed that she was trying to speak, but no words came. Her eyes were fixed on those of the barrister as though hypnotized by the shock that the question gave.

At last she said something so low that it could not be heard distinctly even by those who were nearest.

"What did you say, Miss Bickerton?" the coroner asked, his quiet and level voice seeming to break the spell which the barrister's question had laid upon her.

"Not a penny," she said more clearly. "I've had nothing at all."

"Really? Then, let us say, how much has Dick Thomson had during that period? How much has gone to him?"

Miss Bickerton did not answer. Her hands clutched the front of the witness stand as though its support were needed to keep her upright.

Miss Dorling rose, turning to Russell-Welch as she did so. "Can't you see she's unfit to go on?"

She did not raise her voice, but the cool, contemptuous words sounded clearly through the silent court. She was halfway to the witness-box when Anne Bickerton let go of the rail and sank, an unconscious heap, to the floor.

The coroner spoke to an attendant, directing that Miss Bickerton should have any necessary attention.

"I think," he said, "it will be convenient, at this stage, if we adjourn for lunch."

CHAPTER XV.

MR DUFF-PREEDY left the court at the luncheon adjournment in a less confident mood than that in which he had entered it three hours earlier.

He saw that he was confronted by some fresh evidence, some new and unexpected thing, such as he had said would be the only danger that he had to fear.

He walked over to his office with James Hackett, asking him to have lunch with him as before, but on this occasion he commenced to talk immediately they were seated, without waiting for the disappearance of the sandwiches and bottled beer on which he was accustomed to nourish himself and any sufficiently favoured client, on such occasions.

He said, "Do you know anything of this, Mr. Hackett? It looks as though some of your wife's money's gone in ways which Miss Bickerton knows more about than most of the rest of us, and I'd stake twenty to one that it was through Ashton and Cross that the business—whatever it is—has been carried through."

"I expect you're right, but it's as much news to me as to you, and I'm surprised that it could have happened without my knowledge. But Belle never valued money, except what she wanted to spend at the moment, and she would have done pretty well anything for Anne if she'd asked her as though she meant it. I thought you looked after any serious business for either of us."

"I thought the money was on deposit in the Northern and Midland. I remember advising you both that better investments were possible, and your wife replying that there was nothing like a bank, and that it was no use having money that you couldn't get at when you wanted."

"Yes, I thought it was there too. I know it was, up to two or three years ago, as I saw the pass-book when I was making some income tax returns. After that Belle said she'd like to make her own separately, and, of course, I didn't mind, though I wondered what they'd look like when the Inspector got them. I've chaffed her about it once or twice since, but she asked me why I always tried to make out that she was a fool, so I said no more."

"No doubt Tomkinson's been doing that for her too."

"Is it going to make much difference this afternoon?"

"It looks like making all the difference in the world. It's too early to say for sure. We don't know all the tale, nor what reply there may be. We must see Miss Bickerton if she's come round. That's why I'm hurrying as I am. But I want to ask you this first. Hadn't I better retire from the case as far as she is concerned, and let Ashton and Cross take it on?

"You see, we know now that your wife was poisoned. There wasn't much doubt before, but still, knowing for certain is rather different from a suspicion, however strong.

"Then there's the question, is Miss Bickerton really innocent? The evidence of the will was bad enough, but we both know that your wife would have her own way in such matters. It gave a motive, but it didn't seem enough to explain anyone poisoning her sister unless she were in great need of the money, or were of a particularly despicable character.

"But now you can see that the police have got something which, as they think, will strengthen the motive, and, till we know more, we can't say how black it will be.

"You've got to face the fact that the police think that your sister-in-law poisoned your wife. Now we know what they are when they've once started on a case, but they do try to pick the real criminal, and they're used to judging the evidence. They don't often start unless they feel sure of a winning finish.

"Now what I want to ask you is this: do you want me to defend her against the charge of poisoning your wife if it should be made, as I think it will?"

James looked miserable and uncertain.

"I don't know what to say. I suppose I ought to say, 'No, of course I don't.' But I can't make up my mind that she did it. Not yet, anyway. I want to hear more. I can't be sure what Belle would wish. It's her matter really, more than mine.

"It seems to me that it isn't fair to Anne if you withdraw now. It looks like saying that you think she's guilty, and it might just turn the scale and get her committed—and suppose she didn't do it, after all?"

"Well," said Mr. Preedy, "I understand how you feel. I dare say I should feel much the same. But we've got to make up our minds sharp.

"Suppose we do this. You shall come back to the court with me now, and we'll see her together. I'll ask her straight if she would rather I go on or let Tomkinson undertake her defence. If she wants me I'll go through this afternoon and do the best I can; and if we can get an open verdict, well and good. If it's against her we can talk it over again, with more time to think, and with all the cards on the table. But if she wants me to go on this afternoon she'll have to tell me everything, and about as quick as she can."

"Yes," said James, "that seems the best way." And they walked back together.

CHAPTER XVI.

MR DUFF-PREEDY left his client in the solicitor's room, which had no other occupant, and came back almost at once with Miss Bickerton and Miss Dorling together.

Miss Bickerton looked better than she had done at any time during the morning, and the two women, to the surprise of both the men (neither of whom was sufficiently old to have outlived surprise at anything which a woman may do), seemed to be on better terms than at any time since they had first met.

"I think," said Miss Dorling, "Miss Bickerton will be all right now. I've got her to take some food, which was what she needed. But what we want to know, Mr. Preedy, is whether you can't stop this going further. It can't be anything to do with how Mrs. Hackett died, and it *ought* to be stopped."

"I'm afraid I can't hope to do that, Miss Dorling. You see, an inquiry of this kind brings in the question of possible motives, and it can be a very wide one in consequence. What I wanted to ask in the first place was whether you would prefer, Miss Bickerton, under the new circumstances that have arisen, that I should retire and that Mr. Tomkinson should undertake your defence?"

The suggestion was ill received.

Rose Dorling looked puzzled. "What good would that do?" she asked.

"I won't have anything to do with Mr. Tomkinson. I don't like him," said Anne.

"If I'm to go on," said Mr. Preedy, "I must know where I am. I can't be kept in the dark."

"I'm sure Miss Bickerton will tell you anything she can. She didn't see that it was anything to do with the case." This was from Miss Dorling.

The solicitor saw that Miss Bickerton had found an unlikely champion.

He looked at his watch. It was three minutes to two. The court would be assembling again.

He said, "You'd better wait here till I come back."

He went out hastily, and returned saying that the coroner had consented to extend the interval until 2:15.

"Now, Miss Bickerton," he said, "please tell me what it is they are trying to get at, and we may be able to put a better construction upon it than they would be likely to do."

"I think," said Miss Dorling, "I'd better do that if Miss Bickerton is willing. She has explained it to me, and there isn't much time."

"Yes," said Anne, "I should be very glad if you would."

CHAPTER XVII.

IT was twenty minutes past two when the coroner resumed his seat, and Mr. Russell-Welch, who had had his turn of waiting, though in somewhat less uncertainty than had been Mr. Duff-Preedy the week before, rose to resume the examination.

"Miss Bickerton," he said, "I must repeat the question which I asked previously. How much of your sister's money has gone into Dick Thomson's pockets?"

Miss Bickerton was ready with her reply on this occasion.

"I don't know the amount. You'd better ask Mr. Tomkinson."

"Would eight thousand pounds be about the figure?"

The coroner interposed: "I think, now that he has heard Miss Bickerton's permission, Mr. Tomkinson might give us this information."

Mr. Tomkinson did not look grateful for the suggestion. It occurred to the coroner (and may have done so to Mr. Tomkinson also), that he could easily say that Miss Bickerton was not the client in whose interest he maintained his silence; but if he thought this he thought it wiser to meet the position without further show of reluctance.

He rose in his place to say, "I believe the total advances made by Mrs. Hackett to Mr. Richard Thomson amount to eight thousand five hundred pounds."

"Interest?" asked the coroner laconically.

"There may be some arrears of interest which should be added to that figure to give the total sum which will be due to Mrs. Hackett's estate."

"Well," said Mr. Russell-Welch, "I will accept this figure. It is a somewhat substantial one. Can you tell me what security was deposited against these advances, or what prospect there is—if there be any—that they will ever be repaid?"

Mr. Duff-Preedy rose again.

"Mr. Coroner, I am bound to protest against both the tone and substance of this examination, which are calculated to create prejudice against the witness in what, I submit, is an absolutely improper way. The position appears to be that Mrs. Hackett made advances through her solicitors, Messrs. Ashton and Cross, to a Mr. Richard Thomson. No doubt it will be found at the proper time that those solicitors have protected her interests in these transactions. But I submit that there is no obligation upon Miss Bickerton to give evidence even if she were competent to do so—as to the securities on which these advances were made."

But the coroner was unsympathetic. "I don't think I can intervene at this stage, Mr. Preedy must rely upon Mr. Russell-Welch not to ask questions which are not reasonably relevant to the inquiry on which we are engaged."

"Then I can only ask that you will take a note of the protest which I have made."

"Yes, if you like," said the coroner, with a slight smile, "but this isn't a trial, Mr. Preedy."

Mr. Duff-Preedy was unperturbed. He knew that his protest had no legal value just as well as the coroner, and he had expected it to fail. But it was worth trying, and his final suggestion had been for the ears of the jury, whose sympathies he must now make every effort to win.

Mr. Russell-Welch gave some ground in recognition of the wakeful energy of his legal opponent. He abandoned his favourite line of attack, that of the sudden dramatic effect, for a more pedestrian but no less deadly advance.

"How long have you known Mr. Richard Thomson?"

"About since—about five years—no, seven. Nearly six."

"That will do. He is a director of the firm by which you have been employed as a cashier?"

"Yes."

The coroner interposed again. "I am anxious that there should be no avoidable introduction of matters which are not strictly relevant to this inquiry, and which may be damaging to those who are not present. I am sure I can rely upon you, Mr. Russell-Welch, to exercise your discretion."

Mr. Russell-Welch was about to reply when Inspector Taverton touched his arm and passed him a telegram, which he read. After a moment's pause he said:

"Perhaps it may be best to mention—it will be public knowledge as early as these proceedings can be reported—that Richard

Thomson was arrested yesterday, and was remanded by the Shrewsbury bench this morning on a charge of embezzlement and falsifica-
tion of the accounts of the firm of Tucker and Thomson, of which he
was a director, and of which Miss Bickerton has told us that she is
the cashier."

"Very well," said the coroner. "Go on."

"Now, Miss Bickerton, is it true that you were asked to take
your holiday at the end of July—that, in plain words, you were suspended from your employment, and told that you must not resume it
unless you had Mr. Abraham Tucker's permission to do so?"

"Yes, but—"

"Never mind the explanations just yet. Their time will come. I
just want the fact. Why were you suspended in this way?"

"They thought I had got the cash wrong, but I'd never taken a
penny at any time."

"I am not questioning that. But you knew that a large sum was
missing, and—to put it on no higher ground—you failed to report it
to the directorate or auditors, as it was your duty to do?"

"I was under Dick—I was under Mr. Richard ever since I went
to the office—and besides, I knew—"

"Wait a moment, Miss Bickerton," the coroner interposed. "I
still feel, Mr. Russell-Welch, that this examination may easily—and
perhaps prejudicially—affect matters into which we are not inquir-
ing, and which may already be *sub judice* elsewhere. Can we not
reach the point at which we are aiming by a shorter route?" Turning
to the witness, he said, "Tell me this. Were these advances which
your sister made to Richard Thomson at your request?"

"Yes."

"Did you know that they were made without her husband's
knowledge?"

"Well, it was her own money."

"But did you know that?"

"Yes. James was always nasty to me."

"Did you ask your sister to make a further advance on this last
visit?"

"No. James was worrying her too much. She wouldn't think of
anything else."

"Did you intend to ask her before your return?"

"I might. Dick had got to have it from somewhere. You see
what a mess it is now."

The coroner looked at Mr. Russell-Welch again. "I think that is
the point you wished to make, and I don't think we ought to take it

further than that. But if there is any other question you wish to put…?"

The K.C. was again conferring with the Inspector, who appeared to be putting forward his views in a whispered urgency, to which he got a nod of assent.

Mr. Russell-Welch rose. "I don't think I will ask anything further."

"Mr. Duff-Preedy?" the coroner asked.

The solicitor rose promptly. He used an easy conversational tone to a witness whose mind was never of a very clear and logical habit, and who was now confused and distracted by the ordeal to which she had been subjected, the sight of the pit into which it seemed that she was about to fall, and perhaps, he thought, by the news of the arrest which Mr. Russell-Welch had announced

"Was your sister," he asked, "ever unwilling to make the advances to Mr. Thomson of which we have heard?"

"No—oh, no—not at all."

"Were they a ways made through her solicitors—through the solicitors whom she appears to have employed particularly for this purpose—Messrs. Ashton and Cross?"

"Yes, I think so. It's so hard to remember now. Yes, always. I'm quite sure."

"Your employers, Messrs. Tucker and Thomson, are an old-established, substantial firm?"

"Yes, of course."

"They do a large business?"

"Yes, of course. It wasn't quite so good last year, but—"

"Never mind comparisons. It has a large turnover?"

"Oh, yes."

"It employs a large number of workpeople?"

"Yes. Over four hundred."

"Quite so. And you knew Mr. Richard Thomson as a director of this firm?"

"Yes."

"And one of the largest shareholders?"

"Yes. He had—I think it was—"

"Never mind the details. He is one of the largest shareholders. Do you claim to be an expert in financial matters?"

"No, of course—yes, I hold a Secretaries' Training College certificate. I don't quite—"

"Never mind. The jury will judge that for themselves. It has been suggested that you would have proposed to your sister that she should make a further advance to Mr. Thomson, and I think you have admitted this possibility. Do you think your sister would have been likely to refuse?"

"No. Why should she? Not if I asked her, of course."

"And if this money had been obtained it might have prevented whatever trouble has since arisen?"

"Yes, of course. Dick could have put everything right."

"Then your sister's death has been of no benefit in this direction? On the contrary, it has prevented what might have been done, and what you were anxious to arrange?"

"Yes, it was James going on as he did, and then this happening all at once, and Mr. Abraham being a brute, and wanting Dick out of the firm."

"Thank you, Miss Bickerton. I think that's all."

"One moment," said the coroner. "I think there is one thing which you should tell us, Miss Bickerton, in your own interest. Had you any reason to regard these amounts which had been lent to Mr. Thomson as lost, or likely to be so?"

"Not if he had them. That was to put things right. It wasn't his fault: it was the horses'."

There was a stir of laughter at this reply, which the coroner checked with a stern word.

He did not pursue the question of security. He said, "Yes, I see. Did your sister know the circumstances under which these large sums were advanced, and what was done with the money?"

"No, not—yes, if I knew I told Belle all I could. I always did. She didn't care, anyway."

Miss Bickerton left the box.

CHAPTER XVIII.

"I THINK," said the coroner, "that that concludes the evidence, and though it may be less than complete or satisfactory, yet it seems unlikely that anything would be gained by a further adjournment.

"I think, Mr. Duff-Preedy, that your questions have indicated a leaning towards the theory of suicide. I will tell you frankly that I can see very little in the evidence to support such a probability, but if you would like to direct the attention of the court to any facts which appear to you to point that way, I should be pleased to hear you before I sum up."

Mr. Duff-Preedy rose.

"Yes, sir, I am of that opinion. I can put the point very shortly.

"If we accept the medical evidence, and agree that the cause of death was arsenical poisoning—and, further, that the tin of weed killer was a probable source, though, of course, not a certain one, from which that poison may have been introduced—we have to recognize that something very improbable has occurred. The objection of improbability is, therefore, less than conclusive, even if it be accepted as applicable.

"But here there is evidence of mental disturbance—not to put it more strongly—and of opportunity, for the suggestion of incapacity to leave the bedroom cannot possibly be sustained after the evidence we have heard, which seems to me to render it impossible to eliminate the suggestion of suicide, especially as there is no alternative which is not more improbable, and of which there is no proof at all."

Mr. Preedy went on to argue his case with some elaboration, which we need not follow. It was not for the benefit of the coroner, who was as capable (as he well knew) of appreciating a short argument as a long one, but for the jury, who might very probably include some of those individuals who are most influenced by the reiteration of fact or contention in twenty varied forms or phrases.

When he had concluded the coroner summed up.

He did this without notes, not hesitating, or failing to express his thoughts in clear, completed sentences, speaking with a cold deliberation of logic and a scrupulous moderation which rarely failed to impress itself upon the juries to which it was directed.

He was a delight to the reporters' table, for his unhurried periods could be taken down without difficulty, and printed without redaction.

"Gentlemen," he said, "I have called you together to consider the death of Mrs. Arabella Hackett, to decide its cause, and to allocate responsibility, if you are able to do so.

"I have already urged upon you that you should put out of your minds anything which you may have heard outside—anything of the hearsay gossip of which there is always too much on such occasions—and give your verdict entirely upon the sworn evidence which has been given here.

"You must remember also that, whatever assistance I may be able to give, the verdict is yours, and the responsibility is yours. You must give your verdict without fear or favour or sympathy for either the living or the dead, on the evidence you have heard, as reasonable men, and as you would decide a question which might arise in your own business, or in the affairs of your private life. I shall require your verdict on two separate issues. There is first the question of the cause of death, which may not present any great difficulty. You may accept the medical evidence that the cause was poison by arsenious oxide. If you decide that, there remains the question of through whom, or under what circumstances, that poison came to be taken.

"In a case of this kind it becomes your duty to entertain every possibility with open minds, and to examine it with scrupulous care.

"The possibilities are these. The deceased may have taken the poison in some way by her own carelessness or mistake. That would be death by misadventure. Or she may have taken it with deliberate purpose. That would be suicide, and the state of her mind at the time—the question of her moral responsibility—would be for you to consider.

"Or the poison may have been introduced by the accident or carelessness of another. That might also be death by misadventure, if such action were of the nature of an excusable mistake or of a degree of carelessness insufficient to be regarded as criminal; but if it were of a degree of carelessness of a gravely culpable kind it would be manslaughter. If it were deliberate, with the intention of causing either death or bodily harm, it would, of course, be murder.

"As to the cause of death, I think you can have little difficulty. There is the medical evidence, which is definite. As to the source of the poison, you will, I think, conclude that it is proved beyond reasonable doubt.

"There is the tin of weed killer, containing a high percentage of arsenious oxide, open in the scullery. There is the teacup and spoon, showing the same poison. There is the fact that the symptoms first developed at a time consistent with the taking of the poison in that cup of tea.

"The connection seems too obvious for any serious doubt to arise, and you will notice that while Mr. Glasbrook found that the cup must have contained much more than a minimum poisonous dose, Sir Lionel Tipshift found similar indications in the organs of the deceased that much more than a minimum dose had been taken.

"The cause of death be agreed, there remains the more difficult question of how the poison came to be there.

"You have heard the arguments for the possibility of suicide very ably and forcibly put by Mr. Duff-Preedy. I cannot tell you that I was greatly impressed by the strength of these arguments, apart from the ability with which they were presented.

"It is evident that Mrs. Hackett was of a somewhat emotional temperament, but you have the clear opinion of her two doctors that she was not suicidal. They both discredit this possibility. So does her husband. So does her sister.

"I do not suggest that these opinions would be conclusive. It happens at times that the most unlikely people commit suicide, though, speaking as a coroner of rather long experience, I have never known a case in which one of Mrs. Hackett's character and temperament and circumstances, as the witnesses have represented them to us, has been known to do so.

"But that is not all. There is the absence of reasonable opportunity. It seems very highly improbable that she could and would have got up from her bed and descended to the scullery and returned after securing the poison, unobserved either by Miss Dorling, who was coming backwards and forwards into the scullery during the afternoon, or by Miss Bickerton, who seems to have been in almost continuous attendance upon her.

"There is no evidence that she knew that the tin had been opened, or, if so, that it was being used in the scullery, and the reasonable presumption is that she had no such knowledge.

"It does not appear from the evidence of Miss Dorling and of Miss Bickerton that there was any possible opportunity for Mrs.

Hackett to have descended unobserved to the kitchen while the tea was being made, and there is no apparent reason why either of them should give inaccurate evidence on this point.

"In my judgment, there is an absence alike of disposition, sufficient motive, and opportunity, to make suicide a reasonable hypothesis, and I am bound to advise you accordingly. At the same time I must say again that the verdict will be yours, not mine, and if the arguments for this solution have impressed you as being stronger than I am able to regard them, you will give it accordingly.

"Then there is the possibility of accident. This must not be eliminated from your consideration, but I have found it very difficult to imagine how such an accident could occur under the circumstances with which we are dealing, and you may consider it significant that no such suggestion has been put forward from any direction.

"Then we have to consider the evidence that Miss Bickerton has given that she was absent from the kitchen for some minutes while the tea was made, but before it was poured into the cup. This evidence is not corroborated in any way, but it is not, in itself, improbable. If we accept it as fact, we have to consider what possibility there may be that the kitchen may have been entered during that time by someone who may have introduced the poison.

"Here we are confronted by two difficulties. The poison was in the cup, and the cup had not been filled at this time. The poison was not in the pot at all, if we accept Miss Dorling's evidence that she subsequently drank a cup from it herself without experiencing any ill effects. Of course, we are not bound to accept that evidence, but if we are accepting the supposition that someone other than Miss Dorling entered the kitchen and introduced the poison, then there is no easily conceivable reason why she should make this statement if it be untrue.

"If the powdered weed killer had been put into an empty cup, is it conceivable that Miss Bickerton would have poured the tea into it without observing its presence?

"There is the rather curious fact that there were traces of the poisonous powder also on the dry spoon, which appears to indicate that it had been the vehicle by which the powder had been taken from the tin, but, beyond that, I cannot suggest that it is a fact of any certain significance.

"But if we overlook this difficulty of procedure there remains the improbability—to my mind, I must say frankly, the overwhelming improbability—that anyone should have been lurking in the garden with such an intention, or of a disposition to take such advantage of such opportunity, and that it should have been presented to them in so remarkably simple a manner. How were they to know certainly for whom the tea was intended? How were they to know that Miss Bickerton had left the kitchen, for such an interval as would enable them to enter it and to retreat unseen? The more we examine such a supposition the more difficult it becomes.

"Some of the same difficulties confront the alternative suggestion that the kitchen may have been entered by another inmate of the house. There were only two. We have the evidence of Miss Dorling that she was engaged in conversation with Mrs. Hackett at the time. Again it is difficult to conceive of any reason she could have for giving such evidence if it be untrue. Neither is it a point on which she could easily make a mistake.

"There remains Miss Dorling herself. It is conceivable that she might have concocted the statement that she had been in conversation with Mrs. Hackett, because she wished to give a plausible account of the time during which she had been descending to the kitchen and returning, unnoticed by Miss Bickerton, to the upper floor. But how could she know—how could she reasonably anticipate—that she would return unseen? Our judgment of the possibility of such a solution must depend in part upon its inherent improbabilities and in part upon what we have seen and heard of Miss Dorling in the witness-box. I will return to her later. But surely, so far as this particular incident is concerned, it might be doubted whether in the whole history of poisoning there has been so crude a risk of exposure as would have been the case had Miss Dorling gone down to put the weed killer into pot or cup and been confronted by Miss Bickerton as she had been leaving the kitchen to return to the upper floor; and you must remember that when they next met—as Miss Dorling has said—and as Miss Bickerton has not denied—Miss Dorling was descending the stairs.

"Still, with all these improbabilities, you must give due consideration to the fact that Miss Bickerton says that she was away from the kitchen after she had made the tea, and that she heard noises—of a somewhat indefinite kind—during that interval. So much for the suggestion of suicide, or accident, or of any outside possibility.

"The inmates of the house were four, besides Mrs. Hackett herself.

"You will probably be able to eliminate the maid-servant, Gladys, without difficulty.

"Apart from the fact that there is no evidence of any animosity against her mistress, or of any motive for such a crime, she was absent for the whole of the period during which it seems certain that the mischief was done. You have heard Inspector Taverton, who is fully satisfied that this was the case. You can eliminate Gladys.

"There remain the three other inmates of the house, whom it may be convenient to consider in the order in which their evidence was taken.

"There is first the husband, James Bruton Hackett, concerning whose demeanour in the witness-box you may agree that it was sometimes lacking in respect to the court, and in appreciation of the gravity of the oath he had taken. I should hesitate to advise you to accept his unsupported testimony on any serious issue. But was that demeanour such as you would expect from a man whose mind was burdened by a guilty knowledge of his wife's death? It is for you to judge.

"So far as the afternoon of August the 8th is concerned, he was certainly in Liverpool, and could have had no actual part in the events which we are considering. There is the possibility that the poison might have been given before he left in the morning. The evidence of Sir Lionel Tipshift does not exclude this possibility, though he regards the afternoon as a much more probable time. But it is a possibility without a shred of supporting evidence, and the condition of the cup and other circumstances may incline you to dismiss it as negligible. Miss Dorling states definitely that the tin of weed killer was first opened in the afternoon. She is 'quite sure.' I will deal with that point again when we come to her.

"It is of course, possible that he might have left the house with a guilty knowledge of something which had been planned to occur while he was away. To estimate this probability, we must consider his relations with Miss Dorling, as they have been suggested to your minds and (in part) admitted by the witnesses themselves. The way in which Miss Dorling enters the house is somewhat singular.

"It is the house of a man whom, as she has frankly admitted, she would have married seven years before, had he asked her to do so. She does not say that her feelings have changed at the present time. She applied for a position which was different from, and would be generally considered to be inferior to, that which she was qualified and accustomed to occupy. She says that she took this position in absolute ignorance, even his wife's name making no suggestion to her mind. As to the truth of that statement, you must judge as you will. If you consider it too improbable for acceptance it does not logically follow that Miss Dorling is a murderess, but it would oblige you to take the question of her motive in entering the house, and of the plot between the husband and herself by which she must have been introduced, into very serious consideration, in the light of what happened subsequently. Mr. Hackett was frequently away from home. They would have had opportunities of unsuspected meetings at little risk of discovery, and under more comfortable conditions than under his own roof. To introduce her thus, under such circumstances, might be held to indicate a depth of infatuation which could not be lightly overlooked in considering the sequel of that introduction.

"But how far is this theory or surmise supported by the sworn evidence which must be our sole consideration? How far is it supported by the demeanour of the witnesses, as we have been able to observe it here?

"I think you may find that the more carefully this evidence be examined the less convincing the theory becomes.

"There is no evidence that Mr. Hackett's affections were engaged at all at the earlier period of their acquaintance, and there is nothing at this later period beyond the vague assertion of the deceased, who appears to have been of a somewhat abnormally jealous temperament, and whose feelings were not sufficiently aroused by anything which she saw, or fancied, to incline her to the temporary inconvenience of being without the help in the house which she liked to have.

"You have heard Miss Dorling's evidence. There are points on which it approached improbability, but it was given throughout fearlessly and without hesitation or delay. It was unshaken in cross-examination in any particular.

"Speaking from an experience of over forty years, I cannot recollect a witness by whose manner I was impressed in quite the same way.

"Her answers, without exception, were prompt and clear, and expressed her meaning with exactness. There was not a single point on which she found it subsequently necessary to modify or qualify them in any way. She made several statements which may seem improbable, but none which has been disproved.

"You have to consider whether she is of a character or temperament which could conceivably engage in a crime so openly and crudely planned as this, under that assumption, would appear to be. If you think this to be credible, you have still to face the difficulty as to how she should have had the opportunity which would only occur if she could come downstairs unseen by Miss Bickerton, a very unlikely thing under conditions which I have already discussed.

"It is possible that you may think that Miss Dorling is of a coolness and audacity to make such an attempt. You may think that it was a calculated audacity on which she relied to disarm suspicion.

"If it be so I can only say that it is probably the most nakedly audacious crime in the records of poisoning in this country.

"The weed killer is openly bought. Miss Dorling states that it was bought at her suggestion. She states herself that it was first opened—and opened by her—on the afternoon on which, we should have to believe, she walked downstairs with the probability that she would encounter Miss Bickerton at any moment, with no other object than to poison the tea which was then being prepared, which she did with a recklessly excessive use of the fatal powder, relying upon the chance that she might avoid or reduce suspicion by regaining the upper floor unseen and unheard. Well, it is for you to decide.

"Lastly, there is Miss Bickerton. In considering her position you are bound to give weight to certain differences which may or may not be conclusive, but which distinguish it from that of the other inmates of the house.

"It is an obvious platitude to say that a poisoner is not likely to act in the presence of witnesses. The evidence on which convictions are obtained—unless such crimes are to be perpetrated with impunity, and every poisoner is to go free—must almost always be of a circumstantial kind. Circumstantial evidence should be examined with great care—as all evidence should—but it is often of a more convincing character than is that which may appear to be more obvious and more direct.

"If it be an established fact—as you may agree that it is in the present case—that deliberate poisoning has occurred, and we would search for the criminal, we must look for two things, for opportunity and for motive. If we find both of these, and if we find them in what I may describe as strong combination, there is at least a probability that we need look no further, and if we can discover no alternative which approximates to a similar condition we may ask ourselves whether we have not arrived at a degree of evidence which may be reasonably accepted as proof.

"In the case of Miss Bickerton the opportunity cannot be easily questioned. She made the tea in which the poison was afterwards found, and she conveyed it to the bedroom herself. To put it on the lowest ground, it is not known that anyone else handled it at all. Apart from her own assertion of a brief interval of absence, it is not known that anyone had the slightest opportunity except herself. And there is one point to which your attention has not been directed previously, and which, if we accept Miss Dorling's evidence—and the supporting evidence of probability, in view of the amount of arsenic in the cup and its presence in the spoon—becomes a fact of a very sinister significance. The poison was not put into the pot from which others might drink—from which, for all we know, Miss Bickerton herself may have had a cup either before or after. It was put into the cup itself which was specifically prepared for Mrs. Hackett. Even Miss Dorling could not have known with an absolute certainty that Miss Bickerton had not poured out, or would not pour out, that cup for her own drinking. Miss Bickerton was the only one who controlled the destination of the poisoned cup

"Unless we absolutely discard Miss Dorling's evidence, and disbelieve that the tin of weed killer was in the scullery at all, Miss Bickerton's opportunity was abundant.

"If you should find it difficult or impossible to believe that Miss Bickerton could have poured it out without perceiving that the weed killer powder had already been inserted in the empty cup, or if you regard it as incredible that anyone should so insert it on the chance or expectation that it would be overlooked, and without certain knowledge of the destination of the cup, I am afraid you will find it necessary to go somewhat further, and to say that it is very difficult to see how anyone else could have had any opportunity at all.

"Then we come to the question of motive. It is impossible to argue that it is absent here, though it may be held that it is less than adequate—indeed, what motive could be considered adequate for such a crime? Yet, when such crimes do occur, it is at least more probable that they are the work of those who may be urged to them by some ignoble impulse of greed, or lust, or fear, than that they can be perpetrated by those who have no hope of material gain or relief to set against the fear of legal consequences and the natural instincts of their kind.

"As I have said, I do not suggest that there was any adequate motive here, or that any motive can be adequate for such a crime, but it is impossible to ignore the existence of motive, or motives, of a somewhat exceptional kind.

"There is the will, a will which ought obviously never to have been made, and which the witnesses are agreed would not have been likely to remain long unrevoked. The fact that the bulk of Mrs. Hackett's property had already been disposed of in a direction and on a security—or absence of security—which has been sufficiently indicated, without the knowledge of her husband, and at Miss Bickerton's instigation, shows how unfit she was to undertake such a responsibility, even if we accept it as a method of protecting the children's interests, which it did not do.

"It is no part of our duty here to consider the measure of responsibility which Messrs. Ashton and Cross—which Mr. Tomkinson—must bear for these precedent events, but it is mere justice to them to assume that if there had been a word or hint from either of the ladies that the will should have been so drawn that it would protect the interests of the infant children, by settling the property upon them, that they would have approved of that disposition, and that the document would have been drawn up in that way.

"But the will did not do this. It left everything absolutely and unconditionally to Anne Bickerton who would thus be freed from any responsibility of explanation as to the circumstances under which the bulk of the money had already been disposed of, and could deal with the remainder without delay or restriction—that is, if and when Mrs. Hackett should die, and conditionally upon that death occurring before the will could be altered or revoked.

"That was the position. While Mrs. Hackett lived, the will made no practical difference to anyone, and was likely to be revoked at any time. It was only if she died, and died speedily, that it was ever likely to be of a practical benefit to the one who made and carried up that poisoned cup.

"That is a fact. I do not wish you to exaggerate its significance.

"It is a fact also that Miss Bickerton was anxious to secure control of a further sum of money, and to do so quickly; not for her own use, it is true, but for the assistance of one whom, whatever their relations may have been, whether of employer or friend or otherwise, she was apparently very anxious to help.

"It has been suggested—and it has a measure of truth—that her sister's death did not, in fact, assist her to this end, but actually destroyed any prospect she may have had of obtaining the immediate sum which she was anxious to control.

"You must give such weight to that argument as you think it merits, but you will consider also whether Miss Bickerton were likely to assess such consequences with accuracy. You will remember that there is no certainty that the further loan had not been already asked and refused, and you will probably consider also that if Miss Bickerton was, in fact, the one who was guilty of this crime, it may have been—must, almost certainly, have been—done under the impulse of a sudden opportunity, rather than with the reasoned motives of a calculated murder.

"It has been suggested that Miss Bickerton was under the influence of her sister's stronger will, and that, in the visit to Mr. Tomkinson's office and in the wording of the document which was executed there, she really had very little to say.

"It may be that there is some truth in this contention, and I do not wish to overlook this possibility, but the extent and nature of the loans which Mrs. Hackett had made to Richard Thomson, without her husband's knowledge, and obviously at the request or suggestion of Miss Bickerton, may lead you to the conclusion that she was not without influence, or the knowledge of how to use it, over her sister's mind.

"Now, ladies and gentlemen, I must ask you to consider your verdict. While I have reviewed the evidence for your guidance, I wish to again emphasize that the verdict will not be mine, but yours; and while it is your duty, should you think that murder has been done, to indicate the responsible individual or individuals, should you feel able to do so, yet there is no obligation upon you to do this if there should be a reasonable doubt in your minds.

"Suspicion—even strong suspicion—is not proof.

"I want your verdict in two parts. I want first the place and the time of the death, and the cause, so far as you are able to decide it; and then I want you to deal with the question of responsibility, and if you should decide that it is a matter of manslaughter or of murder you must indicate the individual who is responsible without fear or favour, if you are able to do so. But if you do not feel a degree of certainty such as would justify the naming of any person, then you may say that it is the act of some person or persons unknown.

"Such a verdict does not put an end to the case. The police will still be free to act; and such a verdict would place upon them the duty of continuing such investigations as the case would demand."

The jury retired. The coroner left his place, adjourning the court till their return, but there was little movement from the crowded benches, where the spectators awaited the final scene of the drama. They settled down to wait. There rose a ripple of voices. Those whose conduct had been analysed and criticized by the coroner's summing-up could now hear words and phrases of freer, cruder, and sometimes more merciless comment, which were thrown up capriciously from the general murmur.

An attendant came to Mr. Duff-Preedy with a message from the coroner that if his clients would like to retire to a room which would be placed at their service he would let them know when the jury would be returning into court to deliver their verdict.

It was an offer which was not likely to be refused.

CHAPTER XIX.

"I THINK," said Mr. Duff-Preedy, "we'd better have some tea ordered in. We don't know how long we may have to wait, with that jury."

He was an expert in juries. His attention had been concentrated upon them during the summing-up, as his habit was, watching the way in which some of them received the points that the coroner made, and in the result he was in a greater uncertainty than was usual to him at this stage of a case.

"They looked to me," Miss Dorling remarked, "the sort who might wrangle all night."

She was the only one of the party who seemed entirely self-possessed, with no more than the reasonable gravity that the occasion required.

Mr. Preedy, observing her serenity, was led to observe, "It's a jury that might do almost anything in the end. You can't say the coroner wasn't fair to you, Miss Dorling, yet you've got to be prepared for anything in these cases."

"Yes," she answered, "he was quite nice to me." A slight smile at the recollection parted her lips. "You mean they might say that I poisoned Mrs. Hackett? They looked quite stupid enough for that."

She did not seem much perturbed by the risk. She may have thought that it was not very considerable.

Mr. Duff-Preedy went out to arrange for his clients (and himself) to have the meal he had proposed.

"Tony," Miss Dorling remarked, as he left the room, "I want a talk."

James looked surprised as he heard the name she had not used to him since the old days—a nickname which had been in general use among a set with which he had lost touch in recent years, and which was almost forgotten.

The half-sulky, half-worried look which he had worn since they left the court cleared somewhat as she led him out into the corridor.

Mr. Preedy, returning a minute later, found them pacing it in earnest conversation which dropped to silence as he passed.

He went in to the most miserable and most menaced of his trio of clients.

"It's no use worrying, Miss Bickerton," he said, with an attempt to be more sanguine than he really felt; "I expect it will all come right in the end. There'll be some tea here in a moment, and you'll feel better when you've had that."

Miss Bickerton turned her face to him at this remark. She had not sat down, but stood irresolutely before the empty grate, as though warming herself at a fire which was not there. It was an attitude of a characteristic futility. Her expression was that of a hunted animal that has ceased to run.

There was a weak spitefulness in her eyes as she said, "He was nasty to me. He's a very wicked man. I shouldn't wonder if he'd poisoned his sister himself one day."

The idea was new to Mr. Preedy. He was almost startled to recollect that Mr. Bradson, being an unmarried man, had lived with a sister for many years, and that she had died about two years ago, leaving him some considerable property.

She hadn't been exactly young at the time, and no one had suggested—still, it was an idea. Mr. Preedy smiled slightly at the thought. A coroner should have exceptional impunity in such escapades. His knowledge of methods would be exceptional also. It was certainly an idea!

"I don't think he's that sort, Miss Bickerton," he replied; "I really don't."

"Then he should leave other people alone."

"Well," said the solicitor, somewhat embarrassed in mind by this feminine view of the matter, "he can't help himself when a death occurs like this. It's his duty to inquire into it thoroughly. It's the law."

"Don't tell me," said Miss Bickerton. "He wouldn't do it unless he liked it. He's a wicked man."

Did he really like it? Mr. Preedy considered the point with interest. Miss Bickerton's conversation might not be highly intellectual, but he observed (as he had done before) that it was of a kind that stimulated thought. She was an original thinker.

Did the coroner, did he, did any of the legal gentlemen or the court officials among whom he consorted really like the service of the inhuman master by whom they thrived?

But Miss Bickerton was speaking again: "I don't care what he says. That fat woman won't. She's got too much sense."

Mr. Preedy concluded that she had studied the jury with more care than he would have expected. He had also observed the fat woman, but Miss Bickerton's confidence in her was something which he did not share. He was not sure that having sense would be of any great assistance to Anne Bickerton in this emergency.

"Well," he said, with relief, "here's the tea."

Mr. Hackett and Miss Dorling came in with the tea-tray, but we must be more sparing of such formal designations in the future. They had become Tony and Rose to each other during their ten minutes' conference, and James's (or Tony's) expression was more cheerful and natural than it may have been at any time since he returned from Liverpool.

He addressed his sister-in-law with an unusual geniality. "Come on, Anne, and pour out. It's no use worrying. It may be all over in an hour, and if it isn't we'll see you through. Rose feels sure that it wasn't you."

Anne looked round at him suspiciously. Was James being nasty, as usual? Doubtfully she decided that he might mean no more or less than he said. She came to the table, and sat down before a loaded tray.

But Mr. Duff-Preedy looked up in a real surprise. His glance turned to Miss Dorling.

"Sure?" he asked, with an interrogative emphasis which could not be mistaken.

Miss Dorling met his eyes with her faint, habitual smile.

"Yes," she said. "Sure—just that." He was shrewd enough to realize that she did not propose to enlighten him further—not then, anyway.

Meanwhile, Anne Bickerton put her hand to the teapot. She was one of those women to whom the pouring of tea is ceremony which approaches sacrament. Anne Bickerton in the witness-box might be an undignified figure, but Miss Bickerton pouring tea was a different matter.

A faint colour came to her cheeks, and the possibility that she might soon be standing in the criminal dock retired to its natural remoteness

"One lump or two, Mr. Duff-Preedy?" she was saying, with a recovered dignity, as an official entered and addressed that gentleman.

"The coroner wants you to come back in the court, sir."

Mr. Preedy looked his annoyance. He wanted tea himself, and he knew that his clients needed it also. Besides, he knew that a quick verdict was a bad sign. He had had some hope that the jury might fail to agree.

"They haven't been long," he said, and the man answered, "Oh, no, sir. It isn't the verdict. I think the jury want some more evidence about something."

"Well," said the solicitor stubbornly, "they'll have to wait for five minutes, whatever it is. But don't say that. Tell the coroner that Miss Bickerton is still rather unwell, and she isn't fit to come back into court till she's had some tea. She ready isn't. Of course, if it had been the verdict—"

"But it isn't Miss Bickerton they want, sir. It's the other lady."

"Well, we'll all be in court in three minutes."

Mr. Duff-Preedy folded his bread-and-butter hastily. "I shouldn't drink it while it's that hot," he remarked to James; "they've just got to wait."

Still, the circumstances were not conducive to the enjoyment of a leisurely meal. It was probably not more than three minutes before they were back in the court, to find that the jury had returned to the box, and that the coroner (who may have had his own comfort to consult also) was only just taking his seat.

"Mr. Duff-Preedy," he said, "the jury think that there is one point that has not been sufficiently cleared up. We cannot allow any doubt to remain in a case of this kind. It is an unusual procedure, but I have decided to recall Miss Dorling to the witness-box. I suppose you will have no objection to offer?"

Mr. Preedy hesitated. He thought that the coroner was maintaining his customary air of cold urbanity with some difficulty, and he wondered what the point could be which the jury considered should have been more fully investigated. Thinking rapidly, he recalled Miss Dorling's startling announcement of a few minutes ago. "Just that." If his client were being drawn into some trap which he could not guess, it was his duty to protect her from it. But was the coroner exceeding his powers in calling for more evidence after he had charged the jury, and they had retired to consider their verdict? He knew that a coroner cannot hold a second inquest on the same death on his own authority. Still, this didn't go nearly as far as that. He wished there were time to look up the point. But there might not even be any precedent if he did.

Besides, there was another consideration. What effect would it have on the jury should he object to meet their wishes?

He was rising automatically, without clearly knowing what would be the verbal outcome of these contending thoughts, which had occupied his mind no longer than it had taken his body to make that motion, when he realized that Miss Dorling had decided for him.

"Of course not," she said audibly, and left her place for the witness-box.

"Certainly not, sir," said the solicitor readily. "It is the wish of my clients to assist the court in every way."

He thought inwardly that the plural, which cost nothing, was rather neat.

CHAPTER XX.

THE British jury is a bulwark of our national liberties. Most of us know that, because we learned it at school.

But, unlike most of the "facts" with which our minds were indigestibly fed at that period, it may be partly true. The jury system is, at least, a bulwark against the new bureaucratic tyranny, and as such it is of some antiquarian interest, for few such bulwarks remain unbreached.

Still, we may recognize it for what it is, and yet observe its defects, of which some are comical enough, and others have been responsible for some of the blackest tragedies of our criminal courts.

A coroner's jury, unlike others, can render a majority verdict.

The present jury consisted of four women and eleven men.[1] The foreman was Barry Wheeler, a West Bromwich iron founder, who had inherited something of the patient and parsimonious industry of his Staffordshire father, curiously streaked with the impulsive generosity of a mother who was born about a hundred and fifty miles from Dublin, but not on the English side.

It was about twenty years ago that this maternal disposition had led him to undertake certain obligations on behalf of a relative in deeper difficulties than he had known, and these had led (as such obligations often do) to the time when Mr. Barry Wheeler had sat nervously in the waiting-room of the highly reputable firm of Collett, Bradson, and Collett, waiting to interview Mr. Bradson as to the conditions on which his cousin's creditor, now his creditor also, would allow his financial existence to continue.

Mr. Bradson had no distinct memory of that episode. It was a matter in which he had so dealt as to maintain the reputation which his firm enjoyed. He had acted without harshness, and without more

---

[1] The law relating to coroners' juries was amended in 1926, and the number of persons serving may not now be less than seven nor more than eleven.

than the severity which had been necessary to bring the matter to a conclusion satisfactory to his client.

For three years Mr. Wheeler had been a very frequent visitor to the solicitors' offices. If he had failed to come at short intervals he had received some increasingly pressing invitations to do so.

At the end of three years he had reduced his liability by about thirty percent. There had come a time when Mr. Bradson had asked him to call, and had informed him that he could arrange for the remainder of the debt to be capitalized. Mr. Wheeler's business was to be converted into a limited company. Mr. Bradson's client was to have some six percent first mortgage debentures. So long as the interest were regularly paid all might go smoothly in the future. So it had been done, and so it had gone.

The advice was a command, and as such Mr. Wheeler had accepted it.

Mr. Bradson would probably die without supposing that Mr. Wheeler regarded him even with a mild dislike. The very considerable total sum which he had contributed as "costs" to the coffers of Collett Bradson, and Collett surely could not cause resentment. It had been absolutely legal from first to last.

But Mr. Wheeler had not looked at matters in this reasonable way. When, at the end of his new company's first financial year, the accountant (one of the hated necessities of this new order) had asked for the account which Messrs. Collett, Bradson, and Collett had duly rendered for their professional services in forming the company, he had replied that he had burned the damned thing, with other remarks for which oblivion is the most suitable doom; and when that gentleman had traced the payments which had discharged the obligation, he had been really shocked to find that Mr. Wheeler had posted them to the bad debts account.

All this is by the way, but it will explain why Mr. Barry Wheeler looked upon the venerable figure of his Majesty's Coroner for South Staffordshire with a critical and unfriendly eye. He would have regarded Anne Bickerton's suggestion as to the fate of the late Miss Bradson with unholy joy, though (being a sensible man) he might have recognized its improbability more clearly than the lady did.

He had listened to the summing-up in a mood which was much more active to detect any possible fallacy in the coroner's reasoning than the delinquencies of those with whom he was dealing, and it was with some reluctance that he realized that the matter had been left sufficiently open for it to be difficult for him to advocate any verdict to which his conscience would assent, and yet to "do him one in the eye," which would have yielded more satisfaction than the hanging of all the poisoners that were ever born.

But it must not mistakenly be thought that his mental attitude was typical of that of jury foremen in general. On the contrary, he was prevented by this personal feeling from suffering in the way which is common to those who occupy that secret and temporary eminence.

The English character is as complex as the origin of the English race, but there is in most Englishmen a predominating likeness to the domestic sheep. They like to follow through a gap, but it is a physical fact, which many sheep must have observed with an inward terror, that one cannot follow unless another has gone before.

That has been the trouble of every one of a million foremen since the jury system began. His predecessors have officiated in secret. He is the sheep that has to go first through a gap.

Mr. Wheeler remembered that he had once been told by a friend who had been foreman of a jury which had decided the merits (or demerits) of a motor collision case at the Birmingham Assizes, that they had tried the expedient of putting their votes into a hat, and had commenced very fairly by this method, as there had been six on either side. After two hours of rather heated argument this had been converted to ten and two, and a threat to bash the two minority members if they wasted any more time had resulted in the unanimity at which an English jury so rarely fails to arrive.

It was true that he had got rather nervous when he had to get up and announce the verdict in a crowded court, and he had said, "We find for the defendant, my lord," when it was the plaintiff who should have been indicated. The jury had been filing out of the box, while the plaintiff's counsel was making some application to the judge concerning "the amount of damage that had been agreed, providing…"—when it occurred to one of them that there was something wrong. He had pulled the foreman's sleeve and made an audible protest, which had subsided before the stern "Silence there" of the learned judge. "Trying to make me look a fool over a little thing like that," the indignant foreman had concluded. "Someone'd got to lose, anyway." Which is incontestably true.

Mr. Wheeler did not intend to be guilty of a similar blunder, but he thought the device of the hat to be quite a good one.

He looked round the jury, with several of whom he had some previous acquaintance, and it occurred to him that they would not be easy to change if they had once announced their views in an open argument.

He said, as soon as they were seated, loud enough to bear down several voices which were already engaged in somewhat animated discussion, "Ladies and gentlemen, with your permission we'll begin like this. We'll all write just what we think, without signing it, and put it into a hat, and I'll read them all out, and then we'll have something to start on."

No one objected to this, and as the table round which they sat was freely supplied with writing materials, there was no difficulty about putting the plan into operation.

It took more time than might have been expected, some of the jury finding a difficulty in deciding what they did think, when required to do so in this pointed manner, and sitting blankly before their papers, on which they occasionally started a sentence, and scratched it out. But they had all finished at last, and Mr. Wheeler sat with a heap of papers before him, which he had tipped out of the hat, and which he read aloud as he opened them:

"Anne Bickerton, of course."
"Probably suicide."
"Anne Bickerton (murder)."
"I think the husband's the worst."
"Miss Dorling poisoned her."
"Anne Bickerton."
"Some accident."
"Poisoned. Anne Bickerton."
"What about the brats?"
"Murder. Person unknown."
"Poisoned by Anne Bickerton."
"Poison. One of the women."
"Someone came from the garden."
"It's only what the doctors say."
"Most likely Rose Dorling (and James Hackett knew well enough)."

Having read out these various opinions, Mr. Wheeler commenced to analyse them. He produced this result:

Murdered by Anne Bickerton	5
Rose Dorling (one not certain)	2
One of the women	1

Person unknown	2
Accident	1
Suicide	1
Total	12

In this list he included "Someone came from the garden" as "Murdered by person unknown," as that seemed to be its natural inference.

He ended by saying, "That leaves three that I hardly know how to place. There's 'It's only what the doctors say,' and—"

"So it is," said a man, sitting at the foot of the table, with black hair growing very low on his forehead, and a truculent manner. "When our Bessie was bad, Dr. Riggett said it was 'pendicitis, and when she went to the hospital they said it was green plums. They wouldn't even cut her open to see."

"You don't think she was poisoned at all?" Mr. Wheeler asked, amid a rising babel of argument.

"I don't say 'were' or 'wasn't'," the man answered. "I say the doctors don't know. She may have took rat poison as like as not."

"Very well," said the foreman diplomatically, "I'll say 'Cause of death unknown.' Then there's 'I think the husband's the worst.' Am I to put it down that he poisoned his wife?"

"You can put it as him and that cool hussy together if you like," said a thin spinster on his left.

"Very well, that makes three against Miss Dorling, and two of them bring Mr. Hackett in also, more or less. Then there's the last one. 'What about the brats?' Does this mean we're to put it down to the babies?"

"You can put that to me," said the fat woman of whom we have heard previously. "Why didn't anyone ask after the kids? When there's anything wrong at our house, I say 'If it isn't Mary, it's Alec, and if it isn't Alec, it's Tom.' It was those brats that did it all the time, more like than not."

"But they're only babies," Mr. Wheeler remarked; "the eldest's five."

"No, twelve," said a man who hadn't spoken before.

"No, it was eight and three," said another.

Voices rose again, amid which the stout woman could be heard to declare, "I don't care whether they're twelve or two. There's them as can do more harm in the cradle than a grown man," and then her voice was overborne by the surrounding babel.

Mr. Wheeler studied his papers for a time, and then brought his knuckles down on the table to aid his lungs as he shouted:
"Ladies and gentlemen, please! The list now reads:

Murdered by Anne Bickerton	5
Rose Dorling and Mr. Hackett	2
Rose Dorling alone	1
One of the women	1
Person unknown	2
Something to do with the children	1
Accident	1
Suicide	1
Death from an unknown cause (possibly rat poison)	1
Total:	15

"Now I think we'd better all vote again. I want you all to vote as you think, but you'll remember this. We've got to get somewhere, or we'll be stuck here for a good while. There's five for Anne Bickerton now, and only three for Rose Dorling. If we get one or two more for her it'll be more hinder than help. If any of you really think it was the babies, you can put that down if you like."

We must be fair to Mr. Barry Wheeler. His own vote was one of the five that had been given against Miss Bickerton. He believed her to have committed the crime, and if he tried to influence the votes of others in that direction he was doing no more or less than the coroner had done before him, though his was a cruder, and perhaps more effectual, diplomacy.

Mr. Wheeler tabulated the votes for a second time. The hint he had given had aided the influence—perhaps in some cases the sub-conscious influence—of the gentle pressure of the coroner's summing-up upon the various indecisions which had been exposed by the first vote. Finding themselves in a hopeless minority, they had gravitated toward one of the major groups, and had selected the same for that necessary refuge. The list now read:

Murdered by Anne Bickerton	8
Rose Dorling alone	1
Rose Dorling and Mr. Hackett	1
Person unknown	1
Suicide	1

Something to do with the children   3

The silent advocate of suicide held his ground, but the list was otherwise simplified, except for the fact that the papers that suggested the possibility of Mrs. Hackett's children having some part in the matter had been increased to three.

It was here that Mr. Wheeler saw his opportunity to give the coroner the "one in the eye" which his heart desired.

He said, "Ladies and gentlemen, I don't say that those of us who think the children may have had some part in this trouble are right, and I don't say they're wrong, but I do say we ought to have had more evidence on this point, and it's got to be cleared up now. I vote that we send a note to the coroner and say that we'd like some evidence from Miss Dorling to clear it up."

There was a murmur of several assenting voices, and none was raised in opposition to this interesting diversion. The note went.

CHAPTER XXI.

"MISS DORLING," the coroner said, "the jury have raised a question concerning the children which were in your charge on the afternoon of August the 8th. You have already stated that their ages are five and three, and that they were playing in an adjoining garden with a neighbour's child until you fetched them in from the rain. That is what I have on my notes. But the jury—very rightly—wish to explore every possible—" he appeared to be about to say "avenue," this being the year in which politicians and journalists explored avenues continually, but checked himself, and said, "explanation; and I should be glad if you would reply to one or two further questions on this point.

"In the first place, did you give the ages of the children from your own knowledge, or is it of the nature of hearsay, in which case it may be well for Mr. Hackett to confirm or correct it."

"I had the children's ages from their mother in writing before my first interview. They have also told me themselves. My experience is that a child always knows its own age."

"Boys or girls?"

"The elder is a boy, the younger a girl."

"What are their dispositions?"

"They are lively children, but quite good. The elder—Jim—is rather advanced for his age. Most people would think him to be a year older than he is."

"Can you say definitely, from your own knowledge or observation, that it is impossible that these children, or either of them, could have been the cause of the poison being introduced to the teacup?"

"I can give the facts as I know them. I did not see anything of the children while I was outside, after I had sent them to play in the next garden, until I went upstairs when I saw that the rain was coming. When I went up the tin of weed killer was on the copper, which is rather high. Neither of the children is tall enough to have taken

117

any of the powder out or to have done anything with it while it stood there, though they might have reached sufficiently to upset it.

"I met Miss Bickerton coming down to make the tea as I went up, and she was bringing it up as I came down, so that whatever happened must have been during the time that I was upstairs.

"When I went down it was raining hard. I found the children at the far end of the orchard, taking shelter. There is a place there where an old summer-house stands under a bank of ivy that has overgrown it. It gives very good shelter, and they were both quite dry.

"Had they been to the house while I was upstairs, I do not see how it is possible that they could have avoided getting very wet—at any rate, while they were returning to the orchard."

"Did you ask them whether they had been near the house during the afternoon when this question arose?"

"Yes. I asked them together and separately."

"And they denied it?"

"Yes. Both."

"Did you ask them whether they had seen anyone near the house?"

"Yes. They both said they had not left the orchard all the afternoon."

"Well," said the coroner, turning to the jury, "you will probably agree that that disposes of the children. It was not, perhaps, a very reasonable supposition to entertain, but you have acted quite rightly in clearing it up, as it came into your minds.

"The value of circumstantial evidence depends largely upon the elimination of any alternative possibility, however slight."

The jury retired again.

CHAPTER XXII.

MR DUFF-PREEDY and his clients returned to their interrupted tea.

The solicitor was not hopefully impressed by this intervening episode.

"Of course," he said to James Hackett, as they walked back to their room, the two ladies being somewhat in front, "it was a silly point to raise. It wasn't likely that a child would come specially from its play in the next garden to poison a cup of its mother's tea which it had no reason to suppose would be there, by means of weed killer of the existence of which it had now been informed; but it shows that the jury are a queer lot, which isn't very surprising to anyone who's been watching them and who knows what juries are; but it looks rather as though most of them had agreed on a verdict to which some wouldn't consent till this question about the children was out of the way. Well, it's out of the way now, and they'll be expected to fall in with the rest."

"What do you expect?"

"I don't expect, but I just hope for a verdict of murder by someone unknown, or else that they'll disagree. I'm afraid there may be a verdict of murder that goes further."

"You mean against one of the ladies?"

"I mean against Miss Bickerton. There might be some who'd go against Miss Dorling, but they'd never all agree on that after the evidence she's just given. You see, they'd say that she wouldn't be so definite that the children couldn't have done it if she wanted to save herself."

"Or to save Miss Bickerton, they might say."

"Yes, in a way. But why should she, from their point of view? They'll just take it that she's telling the truth, or perhaps that she feels sure that Miss Bickerton is guilty, and doesn't intend to shield her."

"Then you think they'll bring a verdict of wilful murder against Anne? It seems a wicked thing and a useless one, because, even if she were guilty, it could never be proved."

"I don't say they will, but I say it's a likely thing, and we ought to prepare her for it. As to it not being possible to prove it, you mustn't rely too much on that. Under our modern way of conducting a murder trial, the amount of proof required isn't over-great, especially if it's a bad crime.

"You see, if the accused doesn't go into the witness-box the jury gets a hint that it shows he's afraid, and if he does he's practically placed in the position of having to prove his innocence, which isn't always an easy thing to do.

"They don't really bring in a verdict against the man who happens to be in the dock. They bring in a verdict against the crime."

As Mr. Duff-Preedy said this, they gained the door of the room, which the ladies had just entered before them.

He paused with his hand on the handle, for it was a subject on which he held a strong opinion, and went on.

"If you take at random half a dozen of the most famous murder trials of recent years, and read the evidence carefully, you'll probably find that not more than two were really proved—not to the degree of proof which would satisfy a bank or an insurance company in a business deal.

"Take the Crippen case. Well, we mustn't go on talking now. I'll tell you what I think of that some other time."

They went into the room together, to find that they had been away so short a time that the tea was not yet cold in the pot.

CHAPTER XXIII.

IT was not the first time that Mr. Duff-Preedy had had occasion to warn clients that the merciless hand of the law was likely to close upon them. It might be supposed that, to anyone who had listened to the coroner's summing-up, little warning would be needed, but his experience told him that those are often the most anxious who are in no danger whatever, and that those who are almost beneath its claws are often incredulous concerning the impending menace.

He addressed himself to Miss Dorling, both because he regarded her as the cooler and more reasonable of the two, and as the one who was not in any very probable jeopardy.

"I think I ought to warn you that we must be prepared for almost anything from that jury, especially after the way in which the coroner dealt with the evidence, and this last episode."

"They are rather freaks," Miss Dorling answered, taking his cue very readily. "I shouldn't wonder myself if they decide that Tony— that Mr. Hackett sent some poison by post. Just what can they do, Mr. Preedy, if they want to make as much trouble as possible?"

"They can bring in a verdict of wilful murder against anyone they please. Of course, there'd be a proper trial after that; but it would mean that anyone they named would be arrested on the coroner's warrant."

"How soon?"

"Well, at once, if it were anyone in the court at the time."

"I suppose we could leave now if we pleased?"

"Perhaps you could; but I wouldn't even say that. Certainly it wouldn't be wise to try. Inspector Taverton's prowling round like a tiger at feeding time."

"Does the coroner always order an arrest on such a verdict?"

"Practically so. There are circumstances under which he may refuse to accept it. Probably he might do so if they brought in a verdict that he'd done it himself, but, speaking seriously, yes, always."

"I wish they would," Miss Dorling answered. "It would be worth all the worry we've had to see his face. I suppose you can't get bail till the real trial comes?"

"Not in a murder case. You might if they were to bring in a verdict of manslaughter, which they're not likely to do."

"Well," she answered, keeping her tone as light as possible, for she saw the effect which the conversation was having upon her less resolute companion, "if I'm going to be arrested, I don't know that I shall mind overmuch. I've always hated a dull life. I only hope I get three blankets at night. There'll be a row if I don't."

"You know it's not you, it's me, that he wants to get," Miss Bickerton's frightened voice interrupted.

"It isn't what the coroner wants that matters: it's what the jury decides," Miss Dorling answered, in a less flippant tone. "It may be any of us, or none, as far as I can make out from what Mr. Preedy says, and he knows better than we do. Can't you give us any good tips, Mr. Preedy, to meet such an emergency. I suppose your clients get arrested about as often as not."

"Not quite that," Mr. Preedy considered. "It's not quite that bad, but it happens often enough, and a good many of them deserve it rather less than the average. There's one thing I might mention. It's just as well not to have any large sum of money on you, or anything of a confidential kind, because the police will turn it over, and it's easier to let it get into their hands than to get it back."

"It's as well to know, but they'll draw a blank here. I've got nothing but about eighteen pence, which they can have if they want, and a handkerchief—they'd hardly take that, would they?—and a return ticket to Solihull. I must have thought I'd get back tonight, or I shouldn't have booked return (though it does save eight pence), but I shouldn't have been so careful of what I brought if I'd felt as sure as I thought I did."

"It isn't you he's trying to get," Miss Bickerton said again, "you all know it's me. He's a very wicked man. No, I haven't got anything; of course I haven't. They won't *let* him do a thing like that. I know that stout woman won't."

There was a knock at the door, and the officer entered again, to say that the jury were returning to court to deliver their verdict.

Mr. Duff-Preedy considered Miss Bickerton's condition. He judged hysteria to be near the surface, and he must avoid a scene in court if he could.

He said, "I don't think Miss Bickerton's really fit to come back. Will you stay with her, Miss Dorling, and we'll let you know what's happening as soon as we can?"

Miss Dorling looked her hesitation. It was evident that she would rather have gone back to the court, but after a moment she gave way.

"Very well, we'll stay here. It won't be long." The two men left the room together.

It was ten minutes later when they returned. As they approached the door they heard a sound of loud sobbing from Miss Bickerton. It was evident that she was telling some narrative, or making a confession to her companion, which broke off as they entered.

It was James Hackett who spoke. "I'm very sorry, Anne, but they've made up their minds that you murdered Belle. Of course, you've nothing really to fear. We'll all see you through."

He had scarcely said this when Inspector Taverton entered the room without the ceremony of knocking.

Miss Bickerton was pulling wildly at the neck of her dress. She brought out a handful of letters, which she held out to Rose. The Inspector saw it, and came forward quickly to intercept them, but he failed to cover the last yard before they were in Miss Dorling's hand.

She stepped back quickly.

"You must give me those, miss," he said, politely enough, but with an official curtness which he did not doubt would have the desired effect.

"No one's to have them," Miss Bickerton called out in a voice that rose almost to a scream. "You'd better burn them than that. No one's to see them at all."

"Why?" said Miss Dorling to the Inspector.

"Because I'm arresting Miss Bickerton for her sister's murder. I must see those letters."

"I don't quite see the connexion," Rose answered, with her usual coolness.

"Perhaps not, Miss Dorling, but that's for me to say. I'm a police officer, and I must ask you not to obstruct me in my duty."

"I don't think I'm obstructing you in your duty at all. Am I, Mr. Preedy? You hadn't arrested Miss Bickerton when she gave me these letters, and anyway they're private papers of hers, and it's not likely I should hand them over for you to read."

The Inspector looked at the solicitor in hope, if not expectation, of his support; but Mr. Preedy temporized. Like most solicitors, he liked to keep on good terms with the police, and he knew also that he was technically an "officer of the court," and that it would be an irregularity for him to do anything to defeat "the ends of justice." He cursed inwardly at the folly which would not take a hint when he gave it.

What he said was, "I don't see how you can press it, Inspector. Not now, anyway. You see, you haven't arrested anyone. If you arrest Miss Bickerton now, as I've no doubt you will, you can't say that the warrant covers letters that she hasn't got at the time. Suppose I look them over, and see if there's really anything that bears on the case?"

But Miss Bickerton called out again at that, "No one's to see those letters. Promise you won't let anyone, Miss Dorling. I want them burned." She looked at the empty grate, as though in the vain hope that a fire would appear for her purpose.

"I don't think I could agree to that, sir," the Inspector answered civilly, but evidently as determined in his own way as were the others in theirs; "I quite expect those letters will be needed in evidence, and it's my duty to take possession of them."

Miss Dorling took up the answer. "You can't know what there is in letters that you haven't seen, and I don't see that they're anything to do with you. They're Miss Bickerton's letters, and if she thinks they'll help her defence, or if she wants them destroyed, that's for her to judge."

Inspector Taverton's temper showed signs of giving way.

"No, Miss Dorling, it isn't. When we arrest someone on a charge like this we think we're the best judges of that."

"Probably you do; but Miss Bickerton might think differently."

"It doesn't matter what Miss Bickerton thinks. I represent the law—"

"But suppose you misrepresent it?" Miss Dorling asked. "How am I to know?"

"Because it's for me to say, miss, not for you. I know what my duty is."

"I don't know whether you do or not; but I know that I'm not going to hand over these letters to anyone without Miss Bickerton's authority. I don't believe you've got any right to ask."

"I'm not asking. I'm telling you you've got to part with those letters, and you're doing Miss Bickerton no good by the way you're acting. It looks as though there's a good bit there that she doesn't want us to see."

"I don't suppose she wants anyone to see them. They're private letters, Inspector. Can't you understand that? I can't see why you want them at all. You oughtn't to arrest Miss Bickerton unless you've got proof, and if you have you don't want more. It looks as though you arrest people on the chance of finding something out of which you can make a case."

"It's not me," the Inspector answered, with better reason than grammar; "it's the coroner's jury that's done that."

"Then they didn't do it because of some letters they'd never heard of. Hasn't Miss Bickerton as much right to do what she likes with her own letters as anyone else in the world? I thought English people were always innocent till they'd been properly tried. Isn't that so, Mr. Preedy?"

Mr. Preedy hesitated. He knew that that was no more than a schoolbook tale. He had not sufficient knowledge of history to be sure that it never had been true, but he knew that it wasn't now. His only thought was whether the letters really might compromise his client's defence. If they would, it might be well to back Miss Dorling up, as far as he could. If they wouldn't, it was best to hand them over at once. The question of Miss Bickerton's feelings did not enter his mind. People who come in conflict with the law, under whatever circumstances, must expect its dissecting knife to expose their most secret things, and the only point which interests the lawyers on either side is how far these things may affect the issue of the case. Possibly there may be a day of a higher civilization and a better code, but it is an indecency of today which is so obvious that it is universally disregarded.

But Mr. Preedy had considered by now that the letters were almost certainly from Richard Thomson, and that they might be of a gravely prejudicial character. That was a real risk; on the other hand, they might be helpful, in which case he might even make a virtue of letting the police have them when he had looked them over. He did not think the Inspector was sufficiently sure of his ground to try violent methods if he should fail to obtain his support.

He said, "I'm sorry, Inspector, that Miss Dorling feels so strongly, but I don't see how you can say more now. I've no doubt you'll get all you want in the end."

The Inspector felt that, for the moment at least, he was beaten, but he was a stubborn man, and he made one more effort.

"I must warn you for the last time, Miss Dorling, that you're obstructing the law, and it's a serious thing to do. It's my duty to take possession of those letters, and I ask you for the last time to hand them over. You're not so clear yourself in this matter that you can afford to get into trouble in this way."

Miss Dorling smiled. It may have been at the consciousness of victory, for she recognized the tone of retreat which underlay the threatening quality of the words, or it may have been at the retort which came to her lips.

"I don't know what you mean by that, Inspector, unless it's that you know Miss Bickerton's innocent, and that you ought to be arresting me. If you do, I'll not say you're as far wrong as the jury think. If you'd got to arrest one of us, and thought I was the one to choose, I shouldn't say that you were far wrong."

BOOK TWO

THE TRIAL

CHAPTER XXIV.

INSPECTOR TAVERTON sat in the Commissioner's office.

"It may be best, as you say, sir," he admitted doubtfully, "but I'd rather have had an open verdict, and had more time than we've got now. I tried to pull Russell-Welch up, but he'd gone too far. He's sure that it's the Bickerton woman, and he likes to do the scoring himself."

"Well, said the Commissioner, "if he feels sure, there's not much doubt about that. He's a safe man, and he's usually good for a verdict if he's briefed in a case that he's gone through from the first. Do you mean that you're not sure yourself?"

"It sounds a queer thing to say, but I'm not sure whether I'm sure or not. When I take the case against her by itself, it's about as strong a one as you could wish to have.

"But when I think of the other woman, well, I feel there's something I don't know—something I haven't got at yet, that I ought to find out, and it's an uncomfortable feeling. It's as though something might be sprung on us at any minute which would upset everything."

"Then it's just as well that it's on the coroner's warrant, if you feel like that. I suppose the two women couldn't have been in it together? You told me that they weren't on good terms."

"That was so. There's no chance of that, and no sense in it either. It isn't the kind of thing that two women would plot who'd only met a week before. They were on bad terms right enough. Just contempt on one side, and spite on the other. And then, when the case against Miss Bickerton came out strong, the other woman turned round, and they were as thick as thieves. It's Miss Dorling I can't make out, think as I will. I've never been cheeked by any woman as coolly as I was by her over the letters. I don't suppose we shall ever see them now, unless Duff-Preedy thinks they'll do some good to his side."

"We can subpœna her to produce them."

"Yes, and she'll say they're burned, or bring out half that don't matter, as like as not."

"You wouldn't trust her on oath?"

"I don't even know that. She's one of the best witnesses I ever heard. She quite got over old Bradson. He was suspicious at first, and then he was eating out of her hand. She as good as told me that if I'd got to make a fool of myself over someone, I'd have done better to have arrested her."

The Commissioner pondered. Like his subordinate, he had an instinctive feeling that something was wrong. Yet Bradson had a good reputation. So had Russell-Welch. And it was the jury's verdict as well.

He said again, "I'm glad we're going on a coroner's warrant; but I don't want any fluke, all the same. It always reacts on us, and we've had one too many this year already. You must do your best to pull it off. If it looks as though anything's wrong we can have a reprieve, of course. But you must try hard for the verdict. I suppose this Thomson can't be in it at all?"

"No, sir, I don't see how he could. He didn't leave Shrewsbury all that week. The police there are just sure about that. They were watching him, for their own reasons, all the while. They'd have arrested him sooner than they did, but I asked them to wait till it was too late for Miss Bickerton to know before she got to the court. He saw her off in the train, and they arrested him outside the station that evening. Of course, that's why I wanted the letters. If there were any Bywaters business that would give us a walkover, and no need to worry at all. But I suppose that's hopeless now."

The Commissioner said, "Well, if you can't bring him in there's no use worrying. Probably he's nothing to do with it directly. I doubt whether he's the plotting sort. Just a handsome sot, who found the till opened too easily for his own good. How long have you got?"

"About three weeks. It ought to have gone to Stafford, but the Assizes there are just over, and it's been arranged to take it at Birmingham. It's the most convenient way, and Duff-Preedy raised no objection. Ackling would have been the judge in any case. He offered to go back to Stafford to try it, so that she shouldn't be kept in jail for three or four months."

A glance of understanding passed between the two men.

"Yes. He doesn't miss many of these cases. It's a queer taste," the Commissioner remarked, more to himself than to his subordinate, and the Inspector made no reply.

CHAPTER XXV.

"THEN YOU want me to take the case?" asked Mr. Duff-Preedy, tipping himself back on his swivel chair in a way he had at such conferences, so that his clients were in a frequent state of mental agitation lest he should fall backward into the grate, which he never did. "Am I to look to you or her for the costs? I suppose that will depend on what happens to the will in the end, but I shall have to have something substantial for counsels' fees. We shall need two good men, and they won't work for nothing in these cases, as I expect you know."

James's face was expressionless as he asked, "Who should you recommend?"

"Well, I suppose it's natural to think of Porter-Weston first. Russell-Welch would have been the man, but he's against us, and we've got to do the best we can with what's left."

"You think Porter-Weston's good?"

"He's got about the biggest reputation for this kind of case of any man at the Bar. He was in the Tavistock case, and he defended Brewster, and the Warburtons, and Piercy and Cobb."

James thought for a few moments. "They were all hanged, weren't they?"

"Yes, I think so—except Mrs. Warburton. She's in for life."

"I suppose they were all guilty?"

"Oh, yes—except, perhaps, Cobb. There's always been a doubt about him."

"We won't have Porter-Weston," James said with decision.

Mr. Preedy did not protest. He had his own opinion of Porter-Weston, but it was the correct thing to have him in a case of this kind, and he had thought it right to make the suggestion.

"What would he have cost, anyway?" James inquired.

"Well, he's fairly reasonable, if you put it in the right way. He likes to be in these cases, but it wouldn't do for it to be said that his price had come down.

"Say five hundred pounds, and refreshers. Altogether you ought to have a thousand pounds on the table to start—and then there may be the appeal."

"Well, he won't get it from me."

"There's one or two good men that you can get for less than him," the solicitor remarked, unperturbed by his client's tone. It often took a little time to make them see reason when the cost of litigation was the topic. But a great deal can be done by steady persistence, and talking of large sums in a casual tone, till your client thinks that he ought to be ashamed not to have more of such amounts to hand over.

Anyway, a good sum must be found somehow. It wasn't like a civil action, where you could mark a brief high, and your clerk could give the barrister's clerk the straight tip that that was only for if he won, and you would be taxing costs against the other side. You can't tax costs against the Crown. You've got to milk the prisoner's friends while you can, or you just draw a blank—and no one wants to do that, whether he be a lawyer or a sweep. Besides, why should you? There's always the Press.

"I don't see why it need cost you anything, if you'd rather it didn't. Why not approach one of the newspaper combines? They'll finance it for a few interviews, and an undertaking from Miss Bickerton that she'll write her life for them if she gets off."

"I don't think she'd like that, and I'm sure I shouldn't."

"That's only because you haven't thought it out. They'll get what their readers want, one way or another. And, you know, she wouldn't really write it herself. What's their staff for?

"It only means that you can be paid for it and correct the proofs; or get nothing, and let them print what they like."

James, who could look sulky without any very exhausting effort, looked his sulkiest.

"They'll get some broken heads, as likely as not. Because Belle died, it's no reason to turn us all into a set of performing bears. I wouldn't do it to fill my own pocket, and I'm not going to let Anne do it to fill yours. I'll tell you what I will do, neither more nor less.

"I want you to carry this through for Anne, and I want you to be well paid. There's about eighty-three pounds in the bank, and I shall want all of that before I get any more. Besides that I've got two hundred put away which an uncle left me three years ago. We'd agreed to touch that, so that we'd always have it at a last pinch, but the pinch has come in a way we couldn't have guessed, and I don't

131

think I could please Belle better than by letting it go to help Anne now."

"You've made up your mind it isn't she?" the solicitor interposed, being somewhat less than confident on this point.

"Yes, I have—"

"Then you know something that you haven't told me, and you can't expect me to do any good for her unless you and Miss Dorling are quite frank. As to the two hundred pounds, it will be useful, of course. You'd better let me have a cheque for it now if you can. But I must tell you plainly that it won't carry you far in a case of this kind."

"It'll carry me to the winning post, or it's a non-starter," James answered stubbornly. "I know Belle used to throw money about, but I never did, and I'm not going to begin now.

"I'm going to have 'Warty' Salmon to defend this case, and you're going to have a hundred each, and it's a good fee. I don't suppose either of you'll spend a solid week on it from start to finish."

"I'm sorry," Mr. Duff-Preedy replied, with a sudden stiffening of manner. "I could not undertake the case on such terms, and I suppose I needn't tell you that Rickard Salmon—if you mean him— wouldn't take any case unless he's briefed in a proper way."

"You'll find he'll take this," James answered stubbornly. "I'm going to see him this afternoon."

"He won't see you, if you try. He'll tell you that you must approach him through a solicitor in the proper manner."

"No, he won't. He'll remember that I used to lick him at school. Besides, he'd eat his hat to be in this case. It's a fortune to him, if he gets her clear, which he's got to do, or he gets no hundred from me."

Rickard Salmon, familiarly known as "Warty" to his older friends, in memory of a blemish of his schoolboy days, was a young barrister who had already made some reputation at the Birmingham County Court. His star there had, however, been a somewhat flickering, if not a fading, light, for he had committed the blunder of being too clever for the judge on one or two occasions, on the last of which the old gentleman had shown an open resentment. A whisper among the solicitors that "Monkford doesn't cotton to Salmon" had caused his briefs to diminish in a way that would have been troublesome, had he not found himself in increasing demand as a junior in the local Assizes cases, and at other courts in the Midland Circuit.

"He might be a good junior to have," Mr. Preedy remarked, as though thinking aloud, and willing to meet his client's wishes as far as he reasonably could, "but you'll need an experienced leader to stand up to Russell-Welch—and Ackling's worse than he."

"I don't care who they are. I'll back Salmon to talk the jury over, if he's as good with his tongue as he used to be fifteen years ago. I told him once he could make a man believe he'd died the week before, if he really tried, and he set on me at once, till I almost thought that I had. You'd better leave Warty to me. I'll get him right enough, but if you want to back out of this mix-up, now's the time to say, and we'll square up for what you've done."

But Mr. Duff-Preedy made no motion to "square up." He knew well enough that he didn't want to be out of the mix-up in the least, even if he were destined to bank no more than £100, and have a free advertisement from the press that he couldn't otherwise get for a hundred times that amount.

He temporized weakly: "It isn't only the money. I can't act unless you're frank, and you've known something that I haven't ever since you talked to Miss Dorling outside the room."

"That's right enough," said James, "but it's just a question of what the girders'll stand. I've got to boss this contract. You'll see that when you know more. But I'll ask Rose to meet you and Warty together, and we'll have a straight talk."

CHAPTER XXVI.

"WARTY" SALMON'S chambers consisted of a single room overlooking the gardens of St. Philip's, which he shared with another barrister, who, having a good head and a slow tongue, specialized in the giving of "counsel's opinion" on questions of company law, for which he was assured of a comfortable, though not a princely income.

This gentleman was engaged in a timid argument with his more volatile companion concerning an episode of an hour ago, when a brief had been brought for Mr. Salmon by a clerk from one of the more conservative firms of solicitors in the city, who had previously ignored his existence.

Mr. Salmon had returned the brief, after a somewhat severe mental struggle, with a message that he regretted that he was too busy to take it on. The knowledge that he had acted with a doubtful wisdom made him the more emphatic in the indignation with which he defended the decision that he had made.

"I don't care if they're the best firm in the world. I'm not going to take a brief marked five and two in a case like that. If they'd sent it to Mitchell they wouldn't have dared to mark it at less than twenty or twenty-five."

"I don't even know that," his companion answered mildly. "You know they always pay on the nail, and you're sure of what it really means. They're not like Lethbridge and Clarke. You know you never get much out of them, unless you happen to win."

"I don't care, Exell; I won't take a brief marked like that. I daren't let it be seen."

"It wouldn't have done you any harm, coming from them. It's their Quaker way. They'll never send you another now."

"I don't know that. But it'll do them good to get it back, anyway. Come in."

The door opened, and James entered the room.

"Hullo, Warty; looking as young as ever," he remarked genially, as he shook hands, and was introduced to the other occupant of the room.

"Don't remember Swot Exell? Well, he remembers you. Used to be in the same form as me, and then went up, out of sight.

"Of course, we've heard of this trouble of yours. Everyone has. It's damned bad luck for you. I suppose there's no doubt they've salted the right bird?"

"No, I don't think they have. Anne was a pest to me. There was always trouble when she came, and she made trouble till she left between Belle and me, but I don't think she'd have done that, whatever mess she was in."

"Well, I offered Exell five to one that it wasn't the lady help, but he wouldn't bet. I suppose you'll tell me that I'd have lost if he had. But it's a stiff thing to believe, if she's the girl that I've met at tennis two or three times. She's got one of the best drives I ever saw in a girl; if she were equally good at the net—"

"No, I'm not going to say it's her. I'm only saying it's not Anne, and I'm going to see her through."

"Well, that ought to help her a lot, if the jury know you believe she's straight—unless they think you wanted to get rid of your wife, and feel rather grateful than not. You never know what a jury will think for certain, not if you've talked at them like I have for ten years. But it's good of you to stand by her after that dirty work over the will. There aren't many that would—and her blueing most of the cash too! I suppose you'll have Porter-Weston; everyone does for those cases. Don't let him skin you too close. He'll do it for two hundred and fifty if you stand out. That's between ourselves, as a friend."

"Never mind about him. I came to ask you to take it on."

Mr. Rickard Salmon stared at his friend in a genuine surprise.

"Oh, I say, I couldn't do that! I'd do junior, of course, and glad of the chance. But you've got to get a big name. The public expects that, and the press. You see, Hackett, a murder trial's like a funeral in the slums. You mustn't try having only one coach. You'd get mobbed. It's got to be properly staged."

"I don't care a straw how it's staged," James answered, with the sullen note in his voice which came when he had made his mind up and didn't mean to be talked over. "I don't want it staged. I want it won. And I'll tell you this: I'm not going to be skinned by Porter-Weston or anyone else. There's a hundred quid for you, and a hundred for Duff-Preedy, to pick up when you've got her clear, and there's not a penny more that I'll pay, first or last, and I told Preedy that about two hours ago."

"Well, I'd like to be in it, of course; but you know we can't fix up anything like this. I've got to have a brief in the proper way. But you'll find that Preedy won't be willing to brief me to lead. I'll be glad to come into this on any floor that I can. But you've got to do it through him."

"Look here, Warty, it's no use talking that rot to me. You'll get the brief from Preedy all right, and you'll find it's solo for you. But I've come to you as a friend. I know you don't need the cash, and I know you'll be glad to be in this. You mightn't get such a chance for ten years. But that doesn't matter either way. I've come to you because I want Anne out of the mess, and I think you can do it if anyone can."

Mr. Salmon looked more serious than he had done previously.

"Of course, I'll do it if you feel like that. I'd be glad, in any case. It's a big chance, as you say. But I'll do the best I can, apart from that. You'd better sit down now, and tell me all that you can— Swot doesn't hear anything if you tell him to go on with his work— and then we'll have a proper conference afterwards, when I've got the brief."

CHAPTER XXVII.

"How do you do, Miss Dorling?" said "Warty" Salmon. "I think we've met once or twice before, haven't we? I hope you won't mind my not having a coat. It's so deuced hot in this office."

"Yes, I think I've seen you at Edgbaston. I don't mind in the least," Miss Dorling answered. She had entered in advance of James and Duff-Preedy, for the conference which had now been arranged with the etiquette which the occasion required; Mr. Exell having retired to a neighbouring *café*, as he was accustomed to do when the resources of the chambers were strained to such an extent.

The weather had turned hot again, and Mr. Salmon's rejection of his upper garments may be taken to indicate the decision and enterprise with which he was accustomed to face the emergencies of civilized life.

The room had two windows, which were wide and low, and the lower halves had been pushed up, so that when he observed that his three visitors would exhaust the supply of chairs (omitting the one which had given way last week), he had no difficulty in finding a resting place on one of the sills, remarking that they must try not to give him any sudden shock, unless they wished to see him disappear into Temple Row. He was not usually so informal in his receptions, but these were friends, and it certainly *was* a hot day.

James, remembering Mr. Duff-Preedy's feats of agility with his office chair, was led to wonder whether legal gentlemen gain some recondite advantage from the practice of such precarious balancing.

Mr. Preedy opened the conversation by remarking that he expected Mr. Salmon had received the brief safely. He was sorry to have to ask for a conference within twenty-four hours, but time was short.

"Yes, I've swallowed that," Mr. Salmon answered briskly. "It took some swallowing too, here and there. I expect the jury'll say the same, unless we can cook it a bit better before it's served. There's one or two points we'd better clear up first. What about

137

those letters, Miss Dorling? I hope you've brought them. Though I expect they're just the usual stuff a man writes when he's fooling a woman. They're not likely to be any help to us."

"I cannot show you those. Miss Bickerton gave them into my charge particularly so that they should not be seen."

"Oh, but, Miss Dorling! We don't stand on such points as that in these cases, you know. If we don't look at them the police will, and we'd better be first, and know just where we are."

"You think I might be obliged to produce them, without regard to her wishes?"

"Of course I do. No judge would listen for a moment to what she wished, if he thought they might be anything to do with the case. It wouldn't be right if he did."

"Well, I don't agree," Miss Dorling answered. "If they've got proof they don't want any more; and if they haven't she oughtn't to be where she is. Anyway, she oughtn't to be made to show her private letters to see whether they'll do her any harm. I shall burn them tonight."

"I suppose you look at it like that because you think she's innocent, and you're taking her part," Mr. Preedy interposed, in an effort to reason with this difficult young woman. "But suppose it was someone who had poisoned your own sister, and you felt sure she was guilty, you'd feel differently then. We've got to look at it reasonably. After all, the law—"

"No, I don't think I should," Miss Dorling answered confidently. "I don't think I should, even then. But if so it would only show that when I was angry I didn't mind doing dirty things. But it's no use saying any more about that. I wouldn't say Miss Bickerton's got much brains, but she wasn't silly enough to give those letters to a man."

"So that's that," said Mr. Salmon, who didn't waste time on a lost point. "You must expect a warm time if you have to tell that to Ackling in the witness-box, but that's your lookout, Miss Dorling. It may be as well for us. Not having seen the letters, I can't say. No one could. But there's something more important than that. Mr. Preedy thinks you know more than you told the court, and that the case really hinges on that. It's a bit awkward if you've got to alter your evidence now, but the case couldn't be much worse than it is, unless you could produce a photograph of Miss Bickerton filling the spoon. So let's hear the tale."

"I don't want to alter anything I've said," Miss Dorling answered. "There was one thing I didn't say, which you might think that I should. I don't want to mention it now, unless I have your word that it goes no further without my consent. You'll understand when I've said what it is. But it was knowing that I hadn't mentioned it that made me tell the Inspector that if he'd made up his mind to arrest someone I was the one he ought to have chosen."

"I shall not promise that," Mr. Salmon answered definitely. "Not unless it incriminates you, and I don't know that I ought even then. If I'm defending Miss Bickerton she must come first, and I must have a free hand. If you think you can do it better I'll retire at once. There's no need to make the case worse. It's bad enough as it is."

"You know I can't do that, Mr. Salmon. I'm a games-mistress, not a barrister, and the time's too short to change. I don't want to be awkward, but what you've said about the letters has really made me hesitate about this other matter more than I did before. Only, I don't want to keep anything back from you. Mr. Hackett knows already, and he feels just as I do. I'm willing that it should be that either he or I can give consent for this to be used. Will that do?"

"That so, James? Well, go ahead. You can call it a deal. I suppose you don't really want to hang her, or you wouldn't be here."

"Well, it was this. When I came downstairs after the talk with Mrs. Hackett I passed the window at the turn of the stairs. It's a broad window, all across the half-landing, and it gives a good view of the back of the house, and the path that leads to the other garden, where the children were.

"I thought I saw Jim—the elder of the two children—going along the path away from the kitchen towards the other garden. He was going fairly fast, but close under the laurels, as though he didn't want to be seen, or it might be to get what shelter he could from the rain.

"I stopped, and watched him for a moment. It seemed such a silly thing to do, instead of coming in from the rain."

"That certainly alters it all," said Mr. Preedy; "but why on earth didn't you say this before?"

"Wait a moment, Preedy. Go on, Miss Dorling," Mr. Salmon interposed, with an expressionless face.

"In a sense, there's no more to tell, except what I've said already. I didn't take much notice of it at the time. There was no reason why I should. When there was the question about the tea the next day I asked him, of course, but he said he hadn't been in the garden of The Firs at all till I fetched him in."

"But you said at the inquest that the children were both dry?"

139

"So they were, or so I thought at the time. Indeed, I'm sure still."

Mr. Preedy would have spoken again, but Mr. Salmon checked him quickly. "Leave this to me, Preedy, please. Will you tell us just why you didn't mention this at the inquest?"

"I should have thought you could see. If I'd made a mistake it would have been like accusing the child of causing his mother's death. Even if he denied it (as he does) and nothing more could be said, people might talk against him all his life. He would be the boy that had poisoned his mother. And suppose he *had* done some mischief, and we let him know what it had caused? The boy was broken down enough when he heard she had died, without that."

"Yes. Go on."

"Besides, whether I was right or wrong, it doesn't explain anything, when you come to think. The only chance he'd have to do anything was while Miss Bickerton was out of the kitchen, and I don't believe he could have reached the tin; and I believe that she'd have seen if there'd been anything put into the empty cup; and there was his being dry; and he's not a boy to tell untruths…and I thought it was best to keep him out of that court."

"But it may not have been him at all. It may have been some other boy."

"Well, I thought it was Jim. And what other boy should it be? It didn't seem a likely tale that any child should appear in that way and do such a thing. If it had been another boy they'd either think it was Jim, and perhaps make him wretched all his life for nothing, or they wouldn't believe me at all. That was how it seemed to me, and I think it does still, but James and I agreed that you ought to know."

"Well," said Mr. Salmon, "you've given me something more to think about." His voice was as expressionless as his face. He seemed to have acquired a gravity which made him a different man from him of the quick-talking friendliness of their first reception.

He rose from the window, putting on his coat. He held out a parting hand. "I'll let Mr. Preedy know if I want to see you again." They went out.

They had not gone five yards down the passage when he appeared at the door.

"One moment, Preedy. What about arranging for me to see Miss Bickerton?"

Mr. Preedy went back alone. Mr. Salmon stepped back for him to enter, and closed the door.

"I don't know what you think, Salmon," the solicitor said, "but it seems to me that we've got to make Miss Dorling tell her tale to the court, and we ought to get the boy too. There's more in this than we've found out yet."

"Use *that*?" Mr. Salmon asked, staring incredulously at the solicitor. "It's about the thinnest tale I've ever heard; and I've heard some in the last ten years. Even Miss Dorling could see that it won't hold water, and she had the wit to tell us its weak points, instead of waiting for them to be told to her.

"I'll tell you this if she goes into the witness-box with that tale she won't help Miss Bickerton, without hanging herself. And I'm more than half-inclined to think that that's what ought to happen."

"You mean that she poisoned Mrs. Hackett, and wants to think of something which will get Miss Bickerton off without confessing herself?"

"Yes. I'm inclined to think that she's about the coolest, cleverest criminal that I've seen for a good while. She's got Hackett's wife out of the way, and she's got round him with this talk of putting the child first. But it's no good having her in the box with that tale, unless we *mean* her to break down and to end in the dock."

"Then what line can you take?" Mr. Preedy asked anxiously. He had really thought that Miss Bickerton was more probably guilty than not, but if Mr. Salmon were right he saw that they must make somewhat more than the usual conventional efforts on her behalf.

"Oh, we may pull it off. We must confuse the jury with doubts and hints of suicide, and rile Ackling as a last chance."

"I don't quite see what you mean. Ackling'll be quite bad enough without that."

"That's what I *do* mean—just get him a bit worse than usual, and he may set the jury's backs up. He's done that before now. Or put his foot in it in the summing-up, and give us a chance on appeal—though he's fairly downy about that, since the Croft and Benson case. Still, we'll pull through somehow. We've got a fortnight yet. I must see Miss Bickerton. If only she were a better witness than she seems to be!"

The legal gentlemen shook hands again, and Mr. Preedy descended to his waiting clients, a very thoughtful man.

CHAPTER XXVIII.

"TONY," Miss Dorling remarked, as they stood waiting for Mr. Preedy in Temple Row, "I wasn't far wrong, was I?"

"I didn't think Warty'd be such a fool."

"You didn't call him a fool an hour ago, and you don't really think he's a fool now. But I'd bet anything you like that he's telling Mr. Preedy now that he doesn't believe a word I said, and level money that it's made him think I'm the criminal."

James said again, "I didn't think he'd be such a fool"—and then to the solicitor, who joined them at the moment, "Miss Dorling thinks that Salmon didn't believe her."

"Well, it's this way," Duff-Preedy answered. "When a man's been talking to juries year by year he gets to know just what they'll swallow and what they won't. That's, of course, if he's a good man. He doesn't really think whether a thing's true or not. He just thinks that one will go down and another won't, and if it won't it's his business to throw it out of his brief.

"I'm not saying whether he believes you or not, but he just thinks it's too dangerous to try. Certainly so, with Ackling on the bench."

"Then what does he propose?"

"He will see Miss Bickerton at Winson Green tomorrow, and discuss it with her. I don't think he'll decide anything further till after that. But I suppose he'll go on the lack of any absolute proof, and possibilities of suicide or accident, or someone else having done it. It's wonderful how probable—or improbable—anything becomes when he's talked about it for a couple of hours."

"Then you think," said Rose, "he'll get her off in his own way?"

The solicitor looked as cheerful as he could, as he answered, "Oh, yes. We mustn't doubt that." And then with a feeling that candour might be best, "But I'm not going to tell you that I'm as sure as I'd like to be. It's a bit of a knockout to me that Salmon's taken this as he has. I knew it sounded a bit queer, especially as you hadn't mentioned it before, but I thought he'd snatch at it with both hands, and dish it so that a jury'd suck it up like milk. So he would have done if he'd taken it on at all. But I expect he knows best."

"He doesn't know half as much as he's got to learn," James remarked darkly. "He always used to think too much of himself till he'd been kicked, and he doesn't seem to have changed."

"Look here, Tony," Rose remarked, surveying her sullen champion with amused eyes, "it's no use sulking like that. I want to go somewhere and talk. What about Pattison's?"

"I don't know that it's over-wise for you to be seen together," the solicitor interposed. "I was about to offer you a lift in my car, Mr. Hackett, if you're going back to The Firs. It's only round at the garage."

"Well," said Rose, "I've got time. I'll come back with you if you like."

The solicitor did not approve. "I should think that would be more foolish still. The less you are seen about together the better it will be."

"Better for what?" she answered. "It won't be better for Miss Bickerton; and it seems to me that our first job is to get her out of the mess. I don't want to be rude, Mr. Preedy, but it seems to me that no one in the law ever likes anything done in a straightforward way and they're a lot sillier than they think. If the tale I've told Mr. Salmon isn't good enough, we've got to have something better ready for Monday week. Tony, come in here. I want to talk sense."

"Suppose," said the solicitor, "I'm back here with the car in about half an hour? I don't think I should get anything ready for Monday week that won't stand turning inside out if I were you, Miss Dorling. You've seen Russell-Welch, but you haven't met Ackling yet. He'd give you a short cut to the dock if he thought you were trying any woman's tricks on him."

"Oh, you men!" said Miss Dorling. She seemed amused.

Mr. Duff-Preedy went off to get a hurried cup of tea by himself, and to fetch his car out as promptly as he could. He meant to give James a plain warning on the way back. He had decided that Rickard Salmon had summed that young woman up more promptly and accurately than he had been able to do.

CHAPTER XXIX.

"TONY, I want an ice. I could do with a large one if you've got any money left. But if not I'll have a small one, and pay myself. I expect Mr. Preedy would say I ought to pay anyway, or perhaps he'd get counsel's opinion before he'd open his mouth. They are funny."

James Hackett grinned. "I think I've got a bob left for that." Rose always could raise his spirits, however down he was feeling. Perhaps, he thought it was because she didn't seem to notice, and declined to sink with him. But this *had* been rather a facer this afternoon.

"Tony, I want the children."

James looked puzzled.

"Well," he grinned, "they're not a bad pair. Do you want them for a gift or at a valuation?"

"I want them on loan for a week. I'm going to Weston, and I want to take them with me."

"I suppose you think you'll get something more out of Jim?"

"I'm going to try."

"Well, I'll tell you straight that you'll draw a blank. Jim says that he never came back into our garden at all till you fetched him in, and, if he says that, it's true. I'm not going to have him worried over that again. He's too young; and I don't want anything said that'll give him any idea how his mother died. For that matter, Baby says the same. They were playing under the ivy in the orchard all afternoon."

"I don't disbelieve him at all; and I don't intend him to be drawn into this. I've shown that, haven't I? And I don't mean him to know where his aunt is. But I want them both for a week. And if you've got it, I shall want ten pounds—or fifteen, if you can. I've had a term doing nothing, and I haven't got much left. Of course, if you're hard up with this trouble over the will there's nothing for it but to bilk the landlady, and if it's got to be done I'm always game in a good cause, but I'd rather not. I'd probably get run in, and our names are in the papers quite enough as it is."

"I've had to pay some accounts since Belle died, but I'm still in credit at the bank. You can have twenty pounds if you're serious, but—"

"Of course I'm serious, and it's the only way to arrange it. The Mercers may be going to ask me to stay with them from tomorrow, but so far the invitation hasn't arrived. Even I haven't got cheek enough to walk in and say that I've come to stay. I might have the children at The Firs. That would be the simple, sensible way, and you could avoid contamination by going back to the Mercers' yourself. But Duff-Preedy would have a fit. If he died in it, it would be manslaughter against me, and I like more variety in my troubles. But I don't want to take your last bean. I shall have to see if my own bank will spring a fiver or two. You never know but they may."

"Rose, if I show you something, you won't tell?"

"Not if I promise. Not even to this old man Ackling that they all seem so scared of."

James looked round. No one was observing the alcove in which they sat. He took a slip of paper from his pocket and handed it to the girl.

She looked at a cheque, payable to James Bruton Hackett and signed by the Lepard-Watts Construction Co. It was for £3,000.

"Do they send them out for those amounts by mistake?" she suggested hopefully.

"Not in my direction. But I wanted you to know that you can have the twenty, and I shan't miss it. There's plenty more coming."

"Have you joined the firm?"

"No. I'll tell you just how it is, but it's between ourselves for the present. For the past year I've been trying to land a big contract from the Brazilian Government. There was only our firm in it, and Lakin Brothers, but they had the pull, and we didn't think we'd much chance. Well, I worked at it on the terms that made me look such a fool in the court, but they promised me two percent, if I could pull it off.

"When I went to Liverpool it was to see one of the Brazilian Government's engineers, and I learned that we were practically sure to get it. Lakin's had made up their minds that the game was won, and had got a bit slack. That was where my chance came. I wanted to stay in Liverpool a few days and make extra sure, but it made no difference in the end. I got a letter the first evening after that ghastly inquest to say that it was coming to us."

"Is it a very big thing?"

"It's about half a million. My commission will be ten thousand, and perhaps a bit more. This is just a cheque on account. It isn't only that. I've got the offer of a job on the work. It means going out there in about three months, and big pay for about two years, and that I can get almost anything I like after that if it comes out well."

"And the dark mystery?"

"Oh—that. It's only that I didn't want the lawyers to know."

The obstinate look came back to his face which Rose knew very well, but refused to take seriously.

"Why not? You seem to have come by it honestly enough."

"Because they wouldn't rest, with this trial on, till they'd got the lot. Even Warty Salmon'd begin to think in thousands. Duff-Preedy'd have to get some of it, or he'd dream he'd been struck off the rolls.

Rose laughed. "They're not that bad."

"No," said James, "they're worse."

"Well, have it your own way. I won't tell. There he is now, hooting outside, only anxious to get you clear of danger as quick as he can. Don't you think you're rather ungrateful to think about money when you're being mothered like that? Do be serious if you can. He'll be absolutely ill if he sees us laughing here. Especially after Mr. Salmon has explained how many kinds of criminal I probably am. I'll write to Weston tonight. I've got the refusal of the rooms I want till first post tomorrow. I want the children to be at New Street at 10:15 on Saturday. Yes, in the morning, of course. It's platform six. Don't forget the time. No. You can go out first. I'll sit here a few minutes longer. I've had enough of Duff-Preedy for to-day. Don't forget the bill."

"I'm sure Salmon's right about that girl," Mr. Duff-Preedy remarked, as he pulled up in a traffic jam. "She's best left. I don't say she's done anything wrong, and I don't say she hasn't, but she's too cocksure of herself. She'll come a cropper in the end, and trip you up too if you don't watch."

James said nothing to this. At the back of his mind there was a little, lurking idea that if she were asked to go to Brazil in a year's time she might be the sort that would come to him without letting it depend upon a neighbour's estimate of the state of Brazilian education. It was a thought too shy to risk being snubbed by articulating itself, even in his own mind; but it was there, all the same.

Mr. Duff-Preedy, looking sideways at his silent client, thought that he had never seen him look sulkier.

He wondered whether Mr. Hackett were taking any notice of what he said. But James heard every word.

It was because he heard that he kept his mouth closed, and that Mr. Duff-Preedy learned nothing of the Weston plan.

CHAPTER XXX.

"WELL, sir," said Inspector Taverton, "you know I wanted more time."

He sat in the deep, upholstered chair that stood at the side of Mr. Russell-Welch's desk, in his luxurious chambers that overlooked the Embankment.

The K.C. was slow to answer. At last he said, "It's nothing more than a guess, but I don't say you were wrong. Not as things are looking now."

It was a notable admission from such a source, and the Chief Inspector was gratified accordingly.

Mr. Russell-Welch went on, "But for all that I don't say that we've got the wrong one. There's the will, and a good deal besides that points the same way. But you've been thinking these things over that I've only just heard. You'd better tell me what your theory is now, and if we've made a mistake we can't face it too soon. It's a coroner's warrant, and we can just say that the police have been making more inquiries and enter a *nolle prosequi* when the court opens on Monday.

"You'll get the credit that way, and when the others turn up to give evidence you can run them in."

"Yes, sir. That sounds right enough, but I don't say we've jailed the wrong one, and I don't think we have. But the way the other two are going on shows that there's more in it than we thought. Even their own lawyers can't keep them apart, not even till the trial's over, try as they will.

"And then Miss Dorling takes the children off to the sea, as though she were their mother already. It sounds crazy when you think how they're placed, but then they wouldn't have plotted to get his wife out of the way unless they were a bit crazed. You don't expect that class of murderer to have overmuch judgment—or self-control."

"But you said you still think it's Miss Bickerton?"

"So I do. I reckon it was all three; but she stole a march on the other two by getting the new will signed the day before. She reckoned they wouldn't dare to make any fuss, and the money'd be hers, and she could help Thomson out of his hole. That was all *she* cared for. When a woman's in love as she was a sister doesn't count very high."

The K.C. looked doubtful. "It's ingenious, Taverton, and I don't say you're wrong, but it's an unlikely thing, all the same. I can't see how they'd get together at first."

"I know it's got one or two fences to clear, but something queer *did* happen. There's no getting over that. And if you think it out you'll find it doesn't make nearly as many difficulties as it clears away. As to how it began, Miss Bickerton might have overheard the other two. They might not even have known she knew, but she thinks she'll turn it to her own gain and gets the new will signed. Then she poisons her sister, knowing the others have plotted to do it and won't squeal. Or she just gives Miss Dorling the chance she needs to put it into the cup, and she carries it upstairs. You can make out a lot of ways it might have happened if you start by reckoning that they're all in it up to the neck, and that's just what I think they are.

"There's one thing you can't get over. They neither of them liked Miss Bickerton. They showed that in more ways than one. And yet Miss Dorling backs her up over the letters, and he gets his own lawyer to defend her—and that in spite of the will!

"They must know she's innocent, in which case they know who did it—and wouldn't have to look far. Or else they know that they've got to hang together if they don't want to hang separately."

"Well," said Mr. Russell-Welch, "as far as I can make out what you mean, you think they're all in it, and we ought to hang the three.

"We may get the other two, or we mayn't, but our first job is to get the rope round the neck of the one we've caught."

"It's just that I'm not easy about," the Inspector insisted. "If they've made up their minds to get her off I'm wondering whether they couldn't fake their evidence so that the jury would give her the benefit of the doubt. It's bound to mean something when the husband comes forward and says he's made up his mind she didn't do it, and he's going to see her through. And you can't cross-examine, because they'll be your own witnesses."

The K.C. turned a humorous glance upon Inspector Taverton as he replied: "But that's just where you're wrong, Inspector. I'm not going to call either of them, and that's just where our young friend

149

Salmon will find himself in the soup. He'll have to call them himself, and he'll have to put Miss Bickerton in the box—it's his only chance—and I shall be able to cross-examine or not, just as I please. And that's where he'll come unstuck."

The Inspector stared in some astonishment at this unexpected suggestion.

"But we've got to prove the case, sir," he said doubtfully. "Without Miss Dorling's evidence—"

"That's just it, Inspector. Without Miss Dorling's evidence it's a perfect case. Perfect. And when they wake up to that they can call her and Mr. Hackett—I shan't call him either—if they dare.

"All I want is the two doctors and the two analysts, to prove the cause of death and the time.

"Then I put you in the box to prove the finding of the weed killer on the scullery shelf.

"The doctors prove that the poison was in the cup which Miss Bickerton identified to them as the one she took up with the tea in it.

"Then I put Tomkinson in the box to prove the loans to Thomson and the will.

"There you have it. Motive, opportunity, identification of the method by the prisoner herself: it's as near confession as you can get, unless she pleads guilty straight out.

"That's our case. We'll leave explaining to them."

The Inspector went out with an increased respect for the intellect on which the Crown depended for the hunting down of the evil-doers whom it was his duty to beat out of the thickets in which they lurked.

CHAPTER XXXI.

DEAR TONY,

I'm sending you this by an indirect route, because I prefer that my letters shall be first read by those to whom they are written, and the police appear to feel differently.

Anyway, there's a flat-footed individual who follows me about like a dog, and it's lucky for him that I've got the children, or he'd have done some long walks.

I went into the post-office here yesterday, just to see, and bought two postal orders, which I posted outside while he was gazing at vacancy from the farther kerb. He found his way into the post-office about two minutes later.

The envelope contained nothing but a bill for a tennis-racket, and the postal orders that paid it, which I had crossed, lest he should be led into temptation, so he was welcome to open that; but this letter's different.

I'm getting someone here to post it for me, and it will be delivered by hand through a friend in Birmingham, so I think we shall have frustrated their knavish tricks on this occasion.

Only, don't say you've burnt it when you get in the witness-box next time, and then pull it out. It's not the sort of thing to do twice. It really isn't.

Now for business. I'm not sure yet, but I *think* I'm on the track of what happened, and it may be something that we can't possibly use, unless it should be absolutely necessary to get Miss Bickerton out of jail or to save her life. But I can say this, if it's what I think, it's nothing to do with Jim, as we've both felt sure all along.

I'm coming back on Saturday afternoon. I suppose that will be time, as there's no sign that Mr. Salmon will ever want to see him again.

Of course, I've got to be at the court, as I'm "bound over," and I suppose they'll want me to say what I've said once all over again, but if Mr. Salmon's given me up I don't see that I shall be needed before Monday for that.

But this is serious. Don't faint. I want to bring the children straight back to The Firs, and come with them myself, and stay over the weekend.

You'd better just tell the woman you've got there now to make the best preparations she can, and clear out yourself, to avoid contaminations.

You can tell Duff-Preedy if you like. As Inspector Taverton will probably know within half an hour after I arrive, it seems fair. But don't let him persuade you to make any objection, because it's serious, and I should come, all the same. So it's flight for you, unless you want a worse scandal than ever.

Don't reply, unless it's something that you want Taverton to read, which he certainly would.

Shall reach The Firs about 6:30.

Yours sincerely,

ROSE

P.S.—Yes. It was out of your £20 that I paid the racket bill. But I shall have a good deal to give back to you, all the same.

CHAPTER XXXII.

"I DON'T say she's a wrong 'un. You ought to know her better than I. And I certainly don't say she's the criminal; so it's no use pulling off your coat, as you look as though you're pining to do."

This was from Mr. Rickard Salmon. The place was his own chambers, where we met him before, and the time was Saturday afternoon.

Mr. Duff-Preedy was there with his client for a final conference, and the absence of Miss Dorling enabled Mr. Salmon to retain the dignity of his swivel chair.

"I don't feel at all sure that there's been a crime at all," he went on, "and I feel almost as sure as I should like that Miss Bickerton's innocent, though she's about the most muddle-headed female that I ever had the misfortune to represent

"It isn't that she speaks first and thinks afterwards. All witnesses do that, more or less. It is that she never thinks at all, unless she's mentally kicked. What I'm to do with her fluttering about in the witness-box like a shot bird heaven only knows! I don't, anyway.

"But what I do say is this: Miss Dorling's tale either goes too far, or it doesn't go far enough. She's in a nasty position herself. It's no use squirming like that; you know it just as well as I do. And if Miss Bickerton wasn't where she is the chances are about twenty to one that she'd be there. What I say is that the tale wouldn't do a scrap of good, and if I'm wrong about that I still think that it couldn't pull Miss Bickerton out without the other one falling in, and you don't seem to want that. So there you are. I suppose you haven't thought that if you all start saying silly things to help the one that's in the worst mess at the moment it may end up that you'll be all in it together? Well, I have."

"If you didn't talk so much," said James, "you might tell us more."

"Then I'll tell you this, in a word. When I heard that you'd sent your kids down to Weston with Miss Dorling I thought you were sure to end at Winson Green, one way or other, because there's an asylum there as well as a jail. But I wasn't sure that it could do Miss Bickerton any harm, so I said no more, especially as Preedy told me that you're so gone on her that you get wild if her name's mentioned. But when he phoned me this morning that you're having her at The Firs for the weekend I looked further ahead, and I said, 'It's Broadmoor for him.' Didn't I, Preedy?"

"If you call all that chatter a 'word' it's no wonder you never stop," James answered. "I've had all this over once before, and that was once too often. It's no use rotting me about nothing. She didn't ask: she just wrote she was coming, and I was to clear out. She wouldn't do that without some good reason."

"Well, you've got a hosepipe, haven't you? If she means to break her own neck that's no reason that she should get yours in the same rope. Can't you think how it will sound on Monday? 'When were you last at The Firs, Miss Dorling?' 'Oh, I'm staying there now'. Your wife's dead, her sister's in jail, and Miss Dorling's mistress at The Firs. And this, very likely, after she's had a warm time explaining why a games-mistress suddenly turns into a 'lady help,' and finds herself quite unexpectedly in the house of the man she always wanted to marry, and then thinks that she'll turn gardener and *must* have some weed killer for the paths, and then some of it gets upstairs—no one knows how, but it was Miss Dorling who opened the tin.

"Well, when she's finished explaining that she'll probably have another ten minutes explaining why she burns letters that the police want to see, and then—well, I'll tell you this: I'll bet you that hundred quid that you've promised to hand over, at four to one, that I'll have Miss Dorling arrested, and Miss Bickerton out of the dock before five on Monday afternoon, if that's what you're driving at, which it must be, unless you've gone clean off it, as I think you have."

"Can't you ever listen to anyone but yourself?" said the exasperated James. "I'll tell you what, Warty, you're going the way to get a thick ear from me, and it wouldn't be the first, as we both know. Can't you hear when I tell you that it's all Miss Dorling's doing, not mine? Can't you see that she's trying to get to the bottom of the whole thing, and probably will while you're gassing away as though you'd never stop?"

"Tony," his friend answered, in a quieter and more serious voice, "if you really thought that Miss Dorling was trying the Sherlock Holmes stunt, couldn't you have told her that this is a matter of life and death? It isn't a parlour game.

"What on earth do you suppose she could find out in an empty house about something that happened a month ago?

"If you thought there was any way that weed killer could walk upstairs, you should have looked for yourself; you shouldn't have left it to her.

"Of course, if she's going on that line, she may turn up and say she saw a mouse in the night and tried to catch it by the tail, and it went under a board, and the board was loose, and she lifted it up and there was another tin of weed killer that your wife must have had hidden all the time. But you must remember that the police haven't any imaginations at all. They'd just set to work in their flatfooted way to find where she bought the tin yesterday or the day before; and if you married her after that it would be when she came out of jail, and she'd look a bit older than she does now."

"I'm not going to marry her or anyone else, and each time you open your mouth you talk worse nonsense than you did before. If you've anything worthwhile to say you'd better drop Miss Dorling and go ahead. She was the only one of us who didn't look a fool at the inquest, and she may be again. Anyway, she can come to The Firs if she wants, and I hope she makes you both look as silly as you're trying to make me."

"Very well. We'll say no more about that. It's about your own evidence on Monday that I want to talk. Apart from anything that they get out of you that I have to put back, so to speak, there are just one or two points about which I want to be clear. You've got to say that you're absolutely sure that Miss Bickerton was too much attached to your wife to make it possible that she should be guilty. You can say you don't like her, and she doesn't like you. That'll make your confidence in her all the better for us. You can say that your wife and she were both incompetent about money, but you're sure that neither of them was thinking of anything but the children. Just a groundless jealousy and dislike of Miss Dorling. I don't see how you can put it better than that. If you make it clear that you don't really mind about the will, it'll help us again.

"Then you've got to say that your wife often threatened to commit suicide, and that you'd been frightened about it more than once before.

"I'm not asking you to say anything that isn't true, but to be quite clear about what is. And don't be in a hurry to say any of these things, as though you've been told to. I'll see that you don't get out of the witness-box till they've come out. Just leave them to take their time. And now, if you don't mind, I want to talk to Preedy alone. All you've got to do is to see that you don't meet Miss Dorling again till you get to the court...and you won't then if I can keep you apart."

CHAPTER XXXIII.

MR JUSTICE ACKLING had a wide knowledge of law, and a passion for the conviction and punishment of the unfortunates who were brought before him.

It would not be exactly an injustice, but it would be an inaccuracy of diagnosis, to suggest that he was indifferent as to the guilt or innocence of those whom he tried and sentenced. There had been two or three instances when he had been convinced of the innocence of a prisoner, and had been firm and decisive in cutting short the case, and directing the jury to return a verdict of not guilty. He had acted as a poultry-keeper would do who observed that one of his hens was being pecked through having got, by some unlikely accident, into the wrong pen. He fetched it out at once.

But as a rule he went on the assumption that the dock was the place for criminals, and he relied upon the police to see that a selected criminal filled it as surely as that his man-servant (he was an unmarried man) would put tea, and not cocoa or coffee, into his morning teapot.

He was a man of very orderly habits. A criminal court has the same characteristics. There will be a jury in the box, reporters in their own place, and many lawyers in theirs, with a background of witnesses and spectators, whose first duty is to be very respectful indeed, and a few policemen round the door. That, with some trimmings, is what he knew he would find awaiting him when he made his important entry, and the assembly would rise, as though to greet a god.

There is also the dock, and in due course the police will insert a criminal, and the performance will commence. The criminal will naturally wriggle. If he be a murderer he may wriggle very hard indeed. He may have paid expert wrigglers to assist his efforts. But it will be the duty, and perhaps the pleasure, of Mr. Justice Ackling to see that he doesn't wriggle free.

You can trust him for that. There was a time when he might have been a little overanxious lest the jury should make a mistake, a little overemphatic in his summing-up, and so have given a loophole for an appeal, and in the end a prisoner might have wriggled clear. But not now. He had learned to draw in the line with a steady hand. He had even learned a certain suavity of language, and to keep the predatory look out of his eyes, as he sat, like a waiting hawk, watching every motion of the destined victim, lest it should escape his claws at the last.

There must always be such men. Human nature has not changed since Jeffreys lost his soul in his sadistic orgy of blood. It is to the honour of our English judges that, though there may be one such in every generation, he will stand out conspicuously among colleagues who are as able as himself, but who are kindly, patient, and humane. Unfortunately, if he have sufficient ability to sustain his part without conspicuous scandal, he will be protected by the foolish and cowardly custom which forbids the open criticism of an English judge till he be dead and incapable of any further wrong.

There was probably not one man in ten thousand who could have made a complete and accurate list of the High Court judges who were then in commission, but everyone knew Mr. Justice Ackling, and the sinister reputation which had gathered round his name.

Against such a man it might appear that Anne Bickerton had as much chance of escape as has a rabbit whose leg is fast in the snare, and who sees the poacher coming through the wood.

Anne Bickerton was still young. She was twenty-six. She was not ugly or even plain. Yet she was one of those who pass through life unnoticed, like a shadow that is indistinct on a dull day. She was of a mental and physical futility the tragedy of which is too common and too commonplace to inspire poetry or to engage the novelist's art.

It is tragedy to one poet that great deeds are forgotten, and heroic names grow dim.

> O fading honours of the dead!
> O high ambition, lowly laid!

So he sang; and another sees the tragedy of the heroism that is baffled or still-born:

> Dust of the battle o'erwhelmed them and hid.
> Fame never found them for aught that they did.

Wounded and spent to the lazar they drew,
Lining the road where the legions went through.

These things are of the futility of life itself, of which the meaning is difficult to tell and the end hidden; but there is a deeper tragedy in the lives of those who are futile without failure, who will never meet a wind that is too strong, or be drowned by any turn of tide, for they will never leave the shore. They "play for safety" from birth; they hide deep in the crowd; they tremble lest the chance of a moment's forgetfulness should bring some passing publicity, some trivial penalty, upon them. They would be agonized to walk abroad in an unusual colour or a coat of a new cut. Far from resenting the pressure of the social order that brands and limits and constrains, they would willingly be held in a yet closer bondage, if they could thereby gain a more complete obscurity, a greater restriction of opportunities either to risk or decide.

And sometimes there is tragedy of another kind when one of these is dragged out, not by his own act, but by the caprice or malice of circumstance, to an arena that he has not sought, and to a fight which he has not the skill or the valour or the will to wage.

So our thoughts may wander while the slow and pompous formalities are gone through by which provincial Assizes are opened; but we must listen now, though the dock stands empty, for the judge is charging the grand jury, and he has mentioned a familiar name.

"There is one other murder case on this calendar with which you will not be troubled—the case of Anne Bickerton, who stands committed on a coroner's warrant for the murder by poison of her married sister, Mrs. Arabella Hackett. It appears from the depositions in this case—which has already been the subject of a somewhat long inquiry by the South Staffordshire coroner—that the deceased woman died of acute arsenical poison, and that such poison was found in the dregs of a cup of tea which had been made and administered by the accused."

The case of Anne Bickerton did not come first, being preceded by that of a tramp who was accused of firing the ricks of farmers from whom he had begged unsuccessfully, and who resented that form of argument. The trial was of importance to him, and he must have regarded the heavy sentence he received with some interest, though he may not have been surprised, and it would be difficult to argue that he did not deserve it; but the crowded court was indifferent. They were waiting for other fare, and would have been somewhat startled had the man himself displayed any emotion concerning

159

a sentence in which they were so little interested. They stirred when he disappeared down the dock stairs, and began to lean together and to whisper discreetly in the short interval during which papers rustled, and counsel in the last case left their seats, and those who were to take part in that which was coming became alert and ready.

The name of Anne Bickerton was called, and the accused woman came into the dock with a wardress on either side.

She stood with a hand on the rail, looking somewhat vaguely round while the indictment was read, and took no notice when she was asked the formal question, did she plead guilty or not guilty, till it was repeated, and Mr. Salmon turned round to prompt her.

"Not guilty, of course. I didn't understand. I've done nothing at all."

She was aware that the judge's hawk-like eyes were upon her in shrewd and pitiless scrutiny, and she met them well enough, for she felt no cause for shame, but only a weak indignation, and a puzzled wonder that she should have fallen to so strange an evil.

"Not guilty," said the associate, entering the plea in a very neat and rapid hand.

"I am for the Crown, my lord," said Mr. Russell-Welch, half rising and giving the quarter-bow that implied that if he were not exactly a judge there was very little to choose between them, apart from the fact that Mr. Justice Ackling's salary was about a sixth of the K.C.'s income.

"And I, my lord," said Mr. Reginald Swayboat, with the three-quarters rise and the half-bow which were more suitable from a younger counsel who had not yet taken silk, and whose income was not more than twice that of a High Court judge.

For here there is the public purse into which to dip, and it is considered suitable that two of the cleverest counsel at the Bar should unite their ingenuity to contrive a case against the prisoner, though it might be thought that only one should have been employed, to present the facts as impartially as he could, and to give his aid to judge and jury to search the truth of the case, without regard of whether it should end in a verdict of conviction or release.

"I am for the prisoner, my lord," says Mr. Rickard Salmon. He rises from his place scarcely more that the K.C. had done, and if he is nervous he gives no sign, unless it be in a slight brusqueness of manner.

The judge pauses, pen in hand. "Mr—?" he says interrogatively.

"Mr. Rickard Salmon, my lord."

"Eh—yes," says the judge. He looks at the prisoner's advocate in a slightly puzzled way which is not complimentary.

But Mr. Russell-Welch has now risen completely, brief in hand, though he does not need it. He has adjusted his gown to his satisfaction, given a rapid glance along the jury-box that seems to each of its occupants to catch his eyes in turn, cleared his throat, and commenced to open the case.

Rose Dorling sat rather far back, but high enough to have a good view of the principal actors in the opening drama. She had had no intimation that the prosecution would require her evidence; neither had she heard anything from the defence since the interview in Mr. Salmon's office.

She came to the court alone, and without knowing whether she would be required to occupy the position of a principal witness or was to be ignored or discredited. She had observed Mr. Duff-Preedy looking in her direction and then whispering to Mr. Salmon. Inspector Taverton had gone through a similar performance with Mr. Russell-Welch. She had no doubt that both counsel had been interested to know that she was in court, but they made no effort to communicate with her.

She listened to the slow, ponderous sentences in which the K.C. set out the case, wondering a little that he should state it with such skilful inequity, and then realizing that it was precisely for that that he was employed and paid—not to state anything which he knew to be false, or which he did not hope to prove, but to present his facts, to introduce emphasis, to arrange his high lights, so that the case should appear as conclusive against the prisoner as was possible for any verbal skill to contrive it.

Then, as she listened, she experienced a new wonder in the fact that she was not mentioned—or barely mentioned at all. She had expected to have to sit quietly, as though indifferent or unaware, while he discussed the way in which she had entered the house and, perhaps, jeered or sneered at the explanation she had given. In the same way, there was little mention of James. They were just faintly sketched in, as the casual background of a sordid crime.

"The appropriation—I will not say the misappropriation—of this large sum." It was on that he was dwelling. And on the will. And then the sudden severity of illness, the doctors' inquiry, the poisoned cup, the weed killer that the Inspector found on the shelf, the post-mortem, with its conclusive evidence of the cause of death.

"Subject to any explanation that the prisoner may be able to offer, to which you will, of course, give the consideration that it may appear to merit," he concluded, with a glance that swept the jury from side to side, "I suggest that it is seldom that so base and callous a crime can be brought home with such conclusive force. Its motive laid bare, its opportunity revealed, its method exposed, the prisoner's admission extending to the very act of administration of the poisoned cup." He dropped his voice abruptly, as he called his first witness, Dr. Riggett.

Mr. Salmon had listened to the opening speech with an impassive countenance, only tapping his teeth with his pencil as it proceeded, which was a way he had when a case developed in an unexpected way. He glanced at Duff-Preedy with lifted eye-brows and a slight, humorous smile as the K.C. concluded, and then turned swiftly toward the dock to check an exclamation from Miss Bickerton, whose self-control had given way before that final indictment. "He's a very wicked—" she began, in a shrill and trembling voice, but Mr. Salmon was able to supplement the wardresses' efforts successfully.

"Just keep quiet, Miss Bickerton," he said soothingly. "We've got our turn coming. They won't have it all their own way. But you must let me do the talking, please."

He turned to Mr. Swayboat, a gentleman of an unnatural dignity and self-importance, and glanced up at the K.C. with the whispered comment, "Playing ostrich, is he? It's said to be a silly game."

Mr. Swayboat looked as though he failed to understand, as perhaps he did.

But Dr. Riggett was now giving his evidence, and Mr. Salmon settled down to listen for any admission which might be ultimately helpful, or any inaccuracy or inconsistency which would enable him to discredit the doctor later, should it seem advantageous to do so.

Miss Dorling began to feel bored. It seemed a waste of time to go on, with such elaboration of detail, over ground which had been trodden before, and about which there was no mystery and no dispute. It seemed to her that they would take all day in the weary proving of that which was already admitted, and which might have been stated in ten minutes in words to which all could have agreed, and which would have enabled them to concentrate immediately on the real issues of the case.

But that is not the legal method, which plods heavily over the undisputed ground, which plods on with laborious care till the ground fails beneath its feet; and then it does not pause or turn—the deadly guessing commences. So, at least, it seemed to her; but women have had little to do with the making of English law—at least, since Saxon times—and they may naturally fail in the respect with which it is regarded by its actual parents.

Dr. Riggett was succeeded by Dr. Elgood. They said what they had said before, and Mr. Salmon, having referred to the inquest report, asked them each such questions as to Mrs. Hackett's mental and physical condition at the time as he thought would produce the answers that he wanted to have.

There was no one in all the crowded court who was seeking the simple truth, except the jury, whose attention wandered as the dull medical evidence droned along. The judge was not seeking the truth, because he was not conscious that there was any truth to be sought. He was trying a murderess now, as he had been trying an incendiary before. All he had to do was to see that she did not escape the rope, and to that end he sat alert and hawk-like, watching that Russell-Welch should not fail to twist it, strand by strand, till it was fit to tighten about its victim's neck.

The doctors went their way, and Mr. Glasbrook and Sir Lionel Tipshift followed. The cause of death was made clear.

Those who had expected a keen legal duel as to quantities and times and theories of effects were disappointed, for Mr. Salmon asked little or nothing, letting the proof pile up; and those who watched were disposed to disparage him for his silence. They did not doubt the woman's guilt, but it seemed unfair that she should not have a more argumentative advocate. They liked a noisy crossing of swords before the inevitable verdict came. It was a rule of the game.

But Mr. Salmon knew that, were he to intervene, he would merely emphasize the certainty of the time at which the poison had been swallowed on the jury's minds, only impress upon them the connexion between the excessive dose in the cup, and the amount of poison in the victim's body.

In fact, his silence had somewhat disconcerted his opponent, who had been betrayed by his own subtlety, for Mr. Russell-Welch had passed over those points somewhat lightly, thinking thereby to encourage his adversary to ask such questions as would recoil to his own undoing.

He looked speculatively at Mr. Salmon's indifferent face, and decided that he had been saved by his own stupidity.

He remarked to Mr. Swayboat as they rose together, for it was now the luncheon adjournment, "There's not much fun to be got out of this, with a cock that won't fight."

"Perhaps he feels a bit out of his class," Mr. Swayboat replied complacently. "He made some silly remark to me, and he may have thought that I snubbed him because I didn't answer, but there was really nothing to say."

"That's about it," said Mr. Russell-Welch; "but you mustn't take him too cheaply. He's made a bit of a name on this circuit. You'd better take Taverton on after lunch: I shall be late getting back."

That was the etiquette of the case. He must let his junior do some of the examining, but not of any witnesses of the first importance. Those he was expected to take himself.

Rose sat for a moment amid a throng that stirred and livened as the judge withdrew. Fragments of sentences came to her, as they had done more than once already during the morning, though lower toned than now.

"You could tell that at a glance." "It's the criminal type of face." "Doesn't care even now." "I don't believe it's her: it'll come out yet." "Only wants to save her own neck." "That was what I said to Bill from the first." "They say the other's worse than this. A hard face. The sort that'd poison her own child." "It must be a dreadful death."

She rose and made her way to the door.

"Shall I be able to get back, if I go out, officer?" she said to a policeman there.

"I wouldn't say that, miss. Oh, one of the witnesses. Yes, you come to this door, and I'll see you get back to your seat."

She went out, and into the open air. She did not feel hungry, but she wanted light and air, and the friendly noises of the familiar street.

She wondered whether she could have spoken to Anne and whether she ought to have tried to do so. It must be dreadful for her. But perhaps it was best not. She did not want to draw attention to herself, and there was no knowing what Anne Bickerton might do or say. Perhaps by tonight she would have something that it would be worthwhile to tell.

Yet she went to have some lunch at last, thinking it foolish to abstain. Being slowly served she was somewhat late in returning, and found the door closed and blocked with a pressing crowd. She forced her way in sufficiently to see that her seat was filled. Every seat was filled. The friendly policeman was at the farther side of the court, and did not see her. She was of the temper that is disposed to step aside when others push, and she withdrew to the corridor. Very likely, she would not be needed here this afternoon. She could read the report in the evening paper. She knew that the case was not expected to finish till tomorrow, and perhaps not then. She was standing uncertainly in the main hall when she heard her name called aloud. One usher after another took up the cry. Everyone looked round as though expecting the unknown owner of the name to make some dramatic advent among them. She made her way toward the court in which the trial was held, and soon stood facing one of the vociferators, to whom she said, "I suppose I am wanted in the court."

"If you're Rose Dorling you certainly are. The court's been waiting ten minutes, and he's not a judge that stands that."

"More like three!" she suggested, with a smile, as the crowd jammed itself to right and left to make a narrow way for them to squeeze through. But the man seemed too nervous to answer now that they were within the court, and in no mood to respond to the lightness of her own tone.

It occurred to her that if a judge becomes pettish and ill-tempered the fault is at least as much with those who act with such timid obsequiousness as with the one who surrenders to such an atmosphere.

It was perhaps unfortunate that the legal wigs and gowns, which have an undeniably daunting influence upon many, both men and women, had on her mind only an effect of the ridiculous, so that she found it difficult to treat the men so garbed with more seriousness than had they been performing children.

She had to remind herself of the terrible reality of power, benevolent or sinister, which lies behind the conventional mummeries and trickeries of Bench and Bar.

She was in the witness-box, and the eyes of the judge, bright and hawk-like in the fleshless face, were fixed steadily upon her.

"Why were you not in the court?"

"I could not get back to my place when I returned from lunch, so I waited outside."

The judge's glance swept over the crowded court.

"Where were you sitting?"

She looked at the place. "It was in the fourth row from the top: the end seat on the left." All eyes were turned upon the seat, which was now occupied by a shabby little man with a head which was brightly bald. He looked so uncomfortable in this unexpected publicity that she felt obliged to add, "It may have been my own fault. I was a little late in returning."

The judge took no notice of that. He said sharply, glancing down to the well of the court, that there must be better order in future: places must be kept for the Crown witnesses. Miss Dorling was not quite clear in her own mind that she could be properly so described, but she had sufficient sense not to raise the issue.

He turned to her again. "Then you haven't heard the evidence that has just been given by Inspector Taverton?"

"No. I haven't heard anything since lunch."

"He has accused you of withholding letters which were in the possession of the prisoner at the time of her arrest, and which he required you to surrender in the course of his duty."

"Then he has said what is untrue."

The judge looked slightly taken aback for a moment by the cool explicitness of this denial, and then said sharply, "What is untrue?"

"The letters were not in Miss Bickerton's possession at the time of her arrest."

Mr. Salmon had watched this exchange with a pleasure which was not easily concealed. He had no brief to protect Miss Dorling, nor any intention of exerting himself to do so, but he had not forgotten his programme of riling the judge. He jumped up quickly.

"With all respect to the court, I suggest, my lord, that Inspector Taverton didn't say that they were."

The judge looked at Mr. Salmon for one angry instant, and then ignored him, to turn his attention to the witness.

"Inspector Taverton said that when he entered the room to arrest the prisoner she passed some letters over to you, which he told you that you must not attempt to retain, and that you refused to surrender them."

"That is quite true."

"Then why did you deny it a moment ago?"

"I did not. You said that the Inspector had stated that the letters were in Miss Bickerton's possession at the time of her arrest, and I said that it was untrue, as it was."

"Don't quibble with me. You will recollect that you are not talking to the Inspector now."

"I was not quibbling. I think there is an important difference. I had not heard the Inspector's evidence, and could not know that you had quoted him inaccurately."

The words were said quietly, without rudeness of tone or manner, as explanation only; but the reporters' pencils were busy. They knew, as the lawyers knew, that Ackling was being rebuked with a coolness that Russell-Welch himself might have hesitated to attempt, and in a way in which he had not been faced by any witness in the fifteen years during which he had sat as a High Court judge.

There was a breathless silence in the court, as the astonished judge paused to pick his words, and, perhaps, to recover his self-control; and Rose Dorling, with a little smile on her lips, faced the cold anger of his eyes.

"Miss Dorling," he said at last—and there was an icy menace in his voice as the slow words came. "You may not be aware that there is such an offence as contempt of court, for which the penalty may be instant and severe. There is also such a thing as obstructing the ends of justice, by which you may become an accessory after the event to whatever crime may have been committed, for which heavy penalties have also been provided."

But the witness declined either to be ruffled or to withdraw from the position that she had taken.

"I don't think I have been an accessory to any crime. I thought the Inspector was in the wrong. I think so still."

"You were not asked what you thought. You will produce the letters here tomorrow morning, or you must expect that the consequences will be serious for yourself."

"The letters are burned."

The judge looked at the witness in a moment of ominous silence, stroking his chin with a skinny hand, as he would do while he considered a prisoner's protest or weighed his doom.

Miss Dorling, feeling some confidence in her own position, was yet aware of the peril in which she stood, and realized that it might be better that the next move should be hers.

She went on, "I acted on good legal advice—that of Mr. Duff-Preedy—in declining to hand over the letters to the Inspector. I had no reason to suppose that they had any connexion with this case. Miss Bickerton wished them to be burned unread, being private letters to her."

While she said this Mr. Duff-Preedy had been whispering rapidly to Mr. Salmon, who saw that he must interpose again, if not on Miss Dorling's behalf (and he was forming an opinion that she might be well able to look after herself), then upon that of the solicitor, and he rose accordingly.

"I understand that Mr. Preedy recommended that the letters should be shown to the Inspector, which he thought that it would be in Miss Bickerton's interest to do, but his legal advice was that there was no obligation upon Miss Dorling to do so. I submit that Mr. Duff-Preedy was in the right, and that the Inspector was in the wrong."

"I am surprised, Mr. Salmon, to hear such a plea put forward, or that such advice should have been given. It is the duty of every citizen to assist the law."

"It is a point which I am prepared to argue," Mr. Salmon replied, "should you wish me to do so. But I would submit, in the first place, that it is no part of the duty of a private citizen to give way to illegal threats, or of a police officer to use them."

"We have had no evidence of any illegal threats being used." The judge turned again to Miss Dorling without waiting for a reply, and continued. "You have brought upon yourself the severe censure of the court, and may account yourself fortunate if you escape a further penalty. You appear to have forgotten that the first duty of any citizen is to the State, and that private friendships must be a secondary consideration. Stand down."

Miss Dorling stood down, with several things in her mind which she would have liked to say, and Mr. Tomkinson entered the witness-box.

Mr. Tomkinson had an uncomfortable half-hour. The questions of Mr. Russell-Welch were not always easy to answer, and one or two which the judge interposed were even less so. The transactions which he had carried through on Mrs. Hackett's behalf did not sound very creditable in the light of the events which had followed, and no one was concerned to put the best construction upon them. He had reason to anticipate that he might be dealt with even more inconsiderately when Mr. Salmon rose to cross-examine, but he had a different experience.

He was led skilfully and easily to assert the solid and old-established stability of the firm of Tucker and Thomson, Ltd., the natural readiness which there would be to grant substantial credit to one who was a director and a large shareholder in such a firm, and—with emphasis—the apparent health and good mental and physical condition of Mrs. Hackett on the afternoon that the will was executed.

He left the box in better spirits than he had entered it, and as he did so Mr. Russell-Welch rose.

"That, my lord," he said, "is my case."

He sat down, and there was a stir of expectancy as Mr. Salmon rose to address the court.

CHAPTER XXXIV.

THERE was probably no one in that crowded court, and few, if any, among the many millions that waited the diligence of the journalist and the broadcaster with an equal keenness, who did not confidently anticipate that there would still be two or three days of witness-baiting and forensic effort before the inevitable verdict came. It was obvious—too obvious for discussion—that Mr. Salmon must put his client and Mr. Hackett and Miss Dorling in the witness-box, and endeavour, from what remained of their tattered evidence after Mr. Russell-Welch had torn and trampled upon it, to construct some theory, however weak or wild, on which he could solicit the jury to give his client the benefit of such doubt as he would have struggled to excite among them.

It might be an effort that was foredoomed to failure, but it was one which it was his duty to make, and without it he would have no case at all.

Mr. Russell-Welch did not doubt it. He had left Mr. Salmon to call those witnesses so that he should have the advantage of cross-examining them. It was with little more than a perfunctory interest that he settled down to listen to the opening of the defence, the lines of which he could anticipate so exactly, and which it would be so easy to overcome. His time for thought and decision would be at a later hour, when he might either content himself with the securing of his single victim or endeavour to entice the others to the same pen, if he could do so without too great a risk that the first one would escape in the process.

But this apathetic ease of mind was jarred to a sudden wakefulness as he listened to Mr. Salmon's opening words.

"Ladies and gentlemen," the counsel for the defence began, in a quietly conversational tone, "you have heard the case for the prosecution. Certain things which do not directly concern my client, and which I am not endeavouring to dispute, have been proved, and certain things which do concern her have been implied or asserted, but have not been proved at all.

"It is a fact of which you were probably aware before you heard it stated here that the death of Mrs. Hackett was the subject of a somewhat long inquiry in the coroner's court.

"It would be an affectation to suppose that none of you read reports of those proceedings, or that you all came here in absolute ignorance of the nature of the case which you would be required to try.

"But, as I am sure you will be told by his lordship at the proper time, it is your duty to decide this case, not upon hearsay talk, nor upon condensed and half-forgotten newspaper reports, but upon the sworn evidence which has been brought before you here.

"The question which you are asked to decide is of the gravest possible character. It is a matter of life and death. It is a decision which, should it be against my client, may bring her to a dishonourable death, and shame and misery upon those who are nearest to her.

"Surely, if you are summoned here, if you are obliged to take this terrible responsibility which none can share, you are entitled to have the true facts—and the full facts—as they are known to the prosecution, brought before you without omission. And I must suggest to you that it is precisely that which they have failed—and deliberately failed—to do. I say that there are facts, undisputed facts, vitally important facts, which are known to the prosecution, and which they have deliberately withheld. They may suppose that I shall endeavour to fill the gaps—to call the witnesses that they should have called, to supply the information that they have withheld; but, if so, they are entirely mistaken in an assumption that they had no right to make. I shall do nothing to fill the gaps they have left. I shall call no witnesses at all.

"If they suppose it to be my duty to do so, if they think that they can gain some tactical advantage by forcing me into such a position, they are lacking not only in respect to yourselves, but in a knowledge of the fundamental principles of English law.

"Even on the meagre facts that have been disclosed, and on which you are asked to make the terrible and improbable assumption that Miss Bickerton poisoned an only sister to whom she was devotedly attached, it must have been evident to you that there are other possibilities. There is the possibility of suicide. Surely, when such a death occurs, the first question must be to decide between the natural and arithmetical probability of suicide and the unnatural improbability of murder. I say that it is the duty of the Crown, not to endeavour at all costs to build up a case against a selected victim, but to search out the truth with an open, impartial mind.

"I go further than that. I say that the ultimate authority, like the ultimate responsibility, must be yours alone. I say that no prosecution have the right, even though they may have honestly persuaded their own minds of the guilt of the accused, to select—and not to select only, but to select and to suppress—such facts as will assist or embarrass the view of the case which they are asking you to adopt. I say that you have a right to expect that the Crown will supply you with every relevant fact.

"I say—and I am prepared to demonstrate without direct reference to anything which has not been given in evidence here—that the prosecution have deliberately closed a case which is incomplete in anticipation that I should complete it for them, which I must decline to do. Let me give you one simple illustration where a dozen are equally available.

"You have heard from Inspector Taverton that he found a tin of weed killer on the pantry shelf. So no doubt he did. Is it of no importance, of no interest to you, to know how that tin came to be there on that day, and whether Miss Bickerton had any responsibility or none, even any knowledge or none of its being there? Can my learned friend deny that there is a witness now in this court who could have told you that Miss Bickerton had no responsibility for it?"

He paused, and glanced down at the burly form of Mr. Russell-Welch, but that gentleman made no response. His mind was busily considering how he could deal most effectually with so unexpected an attack, and till it was made up he would show no sign.

Mr. Salmon paused for a moment, to give its full significance to the K.C.'s silence, and then resumed with a reversion to the quiet manner in which he had commenced, and from which, as he was moved by his own argument, he had somewhat emerged to a louder voice and a more passionate emphasis.

"It is only during comparatively recent years that it has been legally possible to call a defendant in a criminal action to give evidence on his own behalf.

"Since that disability has been removed a custom has grown up of reflecting upon a defendant who does not accept the opportunity, as though it were an admission of guilt, so that a man who, from whatever reason, does not wish to give evidence on his own behalf may be almost forced to do so through fear of the prejudice that may otherwise be created against him.

"It is a practice that may be thought by some of us to be grossly unfair, and to make a use of the permission to go into the witness-box which is directly contrary to the spirit which underlay that reform; but, however that may be, if there be any attempt to raise such prejudice against my client in the present case I have two replies to make.

"First, that she has already faced that ordeal, voluntarily and when she need not have done so, in her anxiety—an anxiety which appears to have been shared by all the inmates of the house in which this tragic death has occurred—to give all the help she could in discovering its cause; and, second, that if that refusal can be open to any adverse construction must we not, by a parity of reasoning, conclude that the prosecution have omitted the calling of the other witnesses, of Miss Dorling and Mr. Hackett, who are present in court today, because they have decided that their evidence would be disadvantageous to the case which they have presented?

"No one can suggest that they are not relevant and important witnesses. You have seen Miss Dorling yourselves—you have heard her give evidence at the direction of the learned judge—and you will have been able to form your own opinions as to whether it would have been helpful to you to have had her account of the events of the two fatal days during the whole of which she was Miss Bickerton's companion in the house of illness and death. You must draw your own conclusions as to the motives of the prosecution in withholding that evidence from you. You must decide for yourselves whether you are prepared to condemn your fellow woman on evidence which the prosecution have edited and faked—"

"Stop a moment, Mr. Salmon," the judge interposed. "I am allowing much for the impetuosity—and perhaps for the inexperience—of youth, but I cannot pass such an expression as that. You must not say that evidence has been faked, unless you are calling your own evidence to support that allegation."

"I will withdraw the expression, my lord. I will readily withdraw it. I will describe it as 'selected evidence.'

"It is in protest against such selection that I am doing what I believe to be no more than my simple duty in refusing to allow my client or her witnesses—I say again that it is my decision, not hers—to assist the prosecution out of the position that they have deliberately taken up. That it is my simple duty to expose nakedly to the jury, and to the wider tribunal of our fellow citizens, the method by which...."

James Hackett, listening to the flow of eloquence and studying with some acuteness the faces of the jury, that he might judge its effect upon their variously bewildered minds, was aware of a light touch on his arm, and a voice that whispered, "I want you to come out."

Miss Dorling, who had occupied a seat near to his own—it had been hurriedly cleared when the judge's censure had fallen upon the ushers of the court—was halfway to the door when he looked round.

He did not want to leave. He liked listening to Warty Salmon, though he had known him too long to be much impressed by his eloquence, and had he had an opportunity of refusal he would probably have kept his seat. But Miss Dorling had been too adroit to give him such an occasion while he was in a position in which it would have been difficult to have attacked him with a detailed persuasion.

Waiting in the corridor, she was not surprised to see him follow her through the door, nor to observe that he was of a sulkiness of aspect which was too characteristic of his normal behaviour, and for which she was inwardly convinced that she would be the only permanent cure.

"Tony," she said, in a low voice, for there were too many people round, and curious eyes upon them, for any open conversation, "I've got to talk, and we can't here. Come outside."

Not waiting for his reply, she turned, and, leading the way out of the court, said no more till they were seated opposite to each other in a *café* on the other side of the street.

"It won't end tonight?"

"End tonight!" he exclaimed, with a grin in which his previous aspect faded, not to be resumed that night—nor, perhaps, for a longer period. "You don't know Warty. He hasn't *begun*. He won't stop tonight till he finds the court's empty, and they're switching off the lights; and then I suppose the other bounder'll have a turn tomorrow, and then, for all I know, he'll tune up again. And then Ackling has his, and then they put the jury into a room by themselves to finish fighting it out. 'Noises off stage,' and that sort of business, you know. Finish tonight? They'd keep on for a week if the fixture card wasn't full up, and they know they're out on tour, with a date at Warwick to follow."

"Well, you can't say I haven't left you alone till it was quite clear that the case is over as far as our being called goes. You could have said that you hadn't seen me for more than a week, except when I was having that little chat with the judge."

"Duff-Preedy said that if you'd been a man you'd be in jail now."

"I thought I should as it was. And the worst of it is that I didn't say any of the things I ought to have done. I've been thinking of *them* ever since."

"Perhaps it's just as well," James replied. "You said quite enough. Look here."

He picked up an evening paper from the next table, and read the headlines:

SCENE IN COURT THIS AFTERNOON

MISS DORLING AND THE JUDGE

"If you left that paper alone, and ordered tea—"

"Of course I will if you want it. But I don't want to be away very long. I want to hear Salmon winding up—"

"Well, according to you, that won't be till about midnight. But if it's much sooner, I've got to break the news that you won't be back there tonight. I want you to get a taxi and take me to Morville Road."

"Morville Road?"

"Yes. It's about three miles from here, or perhaps four, and runs parallel with the Holyhead Road for some distance, and then bends away."

"I think I know which you mean. Why do you want us to go there?"

"Because I made an appointment last night. I think it's important, or I shouldn't have fetched you out like this, but I can't tell till we go."

"It's about this case?"

"Yes, of course. There's a Mr. Repton lives there, at Upley Park. Used to be M. P. once for the Cannock Division—so your new maid tells me—and retired about ten years ago, so he must be rather a fossil now. I expect you've heard of him."

"Never in this life."

"Well, he's there all the same. He wants to see us—or rather you—at six-thirty. I'm an extra. You can go alone if you like."

"Considering that I shouldn't have the least notion of why I'd gone—"

"Well, he'd tell you that. But I'll own I should like to come; and the invitation was really to me."

"We'll go together, of course. And here's the tea coming at last."

CHAPTER XXXV.

"IF there's still time," said Rose, "when you think you've eaten enough buns, I should like to drive to The Firs first. We needn't go into the house, but there's something there that I should like you to see."

"I've had exactly one bun, if that's what you call the things, while you've cleared the dish," said the indignant James. "You must have eaten five."

"I dare say I have. I think the old judge gave me an appetite. I felt absolutely ill at midday. I know you've only had one. That's why I thought you might like to have some more. But if you won't, we'll go now."

The Holyhead Road between West Bromwich and Birmingham may not be the flattest, drabbest, and ugliest road in England. The competition for that singularity is keen, and gets keener continually. But it requires more than ordinary imagination to conceive how, in these particulars, any road could be worse. Yet it may be said for it that it is fairly straight, fairly well kept, fairly wide, and not abnormally crowded, so that it was not many minutes before the taxi drew up at the gate of The Firs, and the mystified James was told that he had better pay off the driver, unless he had already cashed the Lepard-Watts Company's cheque and wanted to clear the way for the next.

"But I thought we'd got to go into Morville Road?"

"So we have, and so we will, more or less. But I shouldn't think if I were you. Not just yet. You may have to do a good deal of that before midnight, and you can't do better than save up now."

Miss Dorling's spirits had been remarkably good since her little skirmish with the judge, and it might not be entirely wrong to suppose that she felt a certain immodest satisfaction at the sight of her own name on the placards of the evening papers.

But even she could not easily resist the depressing influence of the scene as she led the way up the paths, now covered with brown

176

and shrivelled weeds, where she had sprinkled death so few weeks ago. The house itself was a dying thing, of a kind which was no longer built in that neighbourhood, and of an age that made the cost of keeping it in habitable repair as much as would have paid the rent of a younger structure. Its gardens had once been beautiful, with an elaboration which is no longer in vogue, and which would be difficult to maintain at a time when so much of the wealth and labour of the land is poured out in the abortive production of motor vehicles, in the attention they require, and in the upkeep of the roads which they traverse.

It had still much of a tangled, weed-choked beauty, through which they passed to reach a gap in the fence that led to the next garden, which was of an even wilder character. In this the children had been allowed to wander as in the other, their parents owning both, and the chance of the second house ever being let again being small enough.

They went on through a fallen gate to an orchard of ancient trees, many of which were dead, or decayed and barren. The wasps rose angrily as they trod in a place of fallen plums and remembered that there had been a plan to pick them a few weeks ago. But the trees were bare now. Only a few apple trees were still loaded with the ripening fruit.

There had been an ivy-covered wall at the lower end of the orchard, and since the gardeners had ceased their work this ivy had crept along the ground, up the dying trees, and forward again until it lay knee-deep from side to side for half the orchard's length.

In one place the ivy had gathered upon an old summer-house with a weight which the rotting wood was unequal to bear, and it was here that Rose paused, pulling back some of the overgrowth, and showing a cavity, ivy-roofed, dark, and long, which they must explore on hands and knees, unless they were to break it down as they advanced.

"I've promised Jim I won't do more harm than we can help, but I thought I'd better show you this first. It's a pirates' den. We needn't disturb the store. It's the battery at the entrance that I want you to see."

The battery had been built with an earth mound at the side of the entrance, leaving a somewhat narrow space for crawling in beside it. It was garrisoned with toy soldiers, who appeared to have deserted in considerable numbers from the Coldstream Guards; but there was, of course, the alternative possibility that a consignment of the uniforms of that regiment might have fallen into their pirate hands. Its ordnance consisted of about a dozen guns, of some variety of size and pattern, constructed of hollow straws or reeds, on wooden carriages that had been rather cleverly carved.

"I didn't think Jim could have done these," his father remarked.

"I don't know that he did, but it's the ammunition I wanted you to see."

Beside the guns there were little heaps of tiny stones, which had probably been picked up from a gravelled path, and two little toy tubs, such as might have come from a dolls' house, each of which was filled with a black powder.

Rose stirred one of them slightly with a stick. It was only black on the surface.

"That's how arsenic goes," she said, "when it's exposed to the air."

"You mean that's some of the weed killer powder?"

"Yes. There's no doubt about that."

They had drawn back now from the low entrance, and stood erect again.

James began to move rapidly back to the house, without further words.

"Where are you going now?" she called after him, making no motion to follow.

"I'm going to ask Jim, of course. I don't see that it proves anything; but he's got to tell me the truth."

"He won't tell you anything worth hearing. It was something Beryl said that put me on the right track."

"I don't care. I've got to have the truth, whatever it is."

He came back uncertainly.

"Tony, don't look so frightened. I don't think Jim's said anything that isn't true, or only what he felt that he couldn't help. If you think he had anything to do with his mother's death, I can tell you at once that you're quite wrong. If you go to him in that mood you'll scare the child in a way that you'll be sorry for after."

"You're quite sure it wasn't him? I don't mean on purpose, of course."

"It wasn't him at all, or in any way."

"Very well," said James, with a sigh of relief. "Then it doesn't much matter what the explanation is, but I suppose you've got one coming. I hate melodrama. I wish you'd say what it is straight out."

"I can't do that, because I don't know myself yet, though I think we both shall before long."

"Very well. What do we do next?"

"We jump off a wall."

"Go ahead then. It's your deal. I shouldn't know which to choose."

Rose said no more, but led the way to the bottom of the orchard, and to a corner where the ivy covered wall was not more than four feet high; but looking over this they saw that there was a drop of seven or eight feet on the other side, into a shrubbery beyond which there were glimpses, between tree and bush, of well-kept grounds of a considerable area.

"Looks a bit used," James remarked, surveying the hard-trampled ground beneath the walls. There was a short ladder lying near.

"There seem to be better arrangements for coming in than for going out."

"That's about it," said Rose.

James slipped down the ivy-covered wall without difficulty, and raised the ladder for his companion.

"You ought to thank someone for that."

"My dress ought, anyway."

She led the way through the shrubbery. They saw a large, square-built house of red brick faced with stone, a solid, ugly structure, at the farther side of a wide stretch of park-like lawn.

"Burglary next?" James inquired hopefully, observing that he was being led to this residence.

"Not exactly. This is Upley Park—a silly name, it's no more than a large garden. It must be half a mile round by the road, so I thought we'd come the shorter way. It must be six-thirty by now."

With no more words, they made their way round to the front of the house, and pulled at a clanging iron bell, to be admitted by a manservant, with a stiff formality, into a house that was furnished with the soft, yet solid, comfort and vulgarity of the later Victorian period.

James produced a card. "I think," he said, "we have an appointment with Mr—"

"Repton," said Rose.

The man looked doubtful. "I have instructions to admit Miss Dorling."

"That is my name," said Rose. "It was I who spoke to Mr. Repton, but it was understood that Mr. Hackett would be here."

"Yes, miss. Would you please step this way, sir?" He showed James into a waiting-room, and would have led Rose on alone, but she stopped at the door.

179

"I don't think you understand that we are together."

"My instructions are that Mr. Repton will see you, miss."

"I think I'll wait here," she said, entering the room with James.
The man went reluctantly, with James's card in his hand.

CHAPTER XXXVI.

"NOT exactly cordial?"

"Not to you, certainly. But we must remember that he doesn't know you are here."

"What sort of man is he?"

"I don't know, except that he must be old and that he's a conceited man in a fright. I could tell that from his voice. I've only spoken to him on the phone."

The footman came back. "Will you step this way, please?"

They crossed the hall to enter a soft-carpeted library, not large, but richly furnished, its walls covered by books well shelved and affluently bound. An old man, very tall and thin, with a small, round bald head, rose from a deeply cushioned chair by the fireside—there was a fire in the grate, though it had not been a cold day—and greeted them with a distant dignity, though they saw that the hand shook with which he indicated chairs for their use, at some space from his own.

"Good evening, Miss—Dorling," he said, and then with a glance at the card in his hand, "Er—Mr. Hackett. Please take seats."

His tone indicated a pause of doubt before he used the "Mr.," a condescension in offering chairs. Yet he was clearly perturbed in mind, and he sat for perhaps a minute in an awkward silence, and then said:

"I have read the account in the evening paper so far as it goes. I suppose it is not over now?"

He looked as though there might be relief in the news that the trial was already concluded.

James was silent, leaving Rose to handle an interview which she had arranged and which he did not understand.

She said, "I don't think the trial will be over before tomorrow."

"It was wrong of Bradson—very wrong. I used to know him at school."

Rose wondered whether Mr. Bradson's conduct was still supposed to be influenced by that ancient intimacy, but the remark did not require reply. No doubt patience and silence would produce something of greater interest. So it did.

He turned his glance to James, to say with a half-condescending, half-apologetic formality:

"Of course, I am deeply regretful for your wife's death—deeply regretful. But I am sure that you will make allowance for a natural resentment—really a very natural resentment—and that there was no intention as against her—no intention at all."

It sounded to James as though he were apologizing for the accidental death of a dog; and being exasperated also by the fact that he could not tell what the man was talking about, he said brusquely: "I don't know what you mean, but if you can tell us who did it you'd better say straight out, and we shall begin to know where we are."

The old man flushed with a weak annoyance at the tone in which he was addressed, and his hand trembled more visibly, as he turned to Rose to say:

"I supposed that you would have told Mr. Hackett before he came."

"But," said Rose, "I couldn't do that. I don't know myself."

Mr. Repton's face showed his bewilderment, as he answered: "But you said on the telephone—"

"What I said on the telephone was exactly true. It couldn't have made you think I knew, unless you knew already yourself."

"You mean it was all a trick?" His voice rose in a shrill, resentful anger, his dignity broken down by the confused emotions that the idea brought to his mind. "Then I can tell you that I know no more than you. I know nothing at all. I must ask you to leave my house."

He rose, and they rose also, but Rose said: "We will go if you are not afraid to let us, but I must tell you first that I used no trick. I asked a question that caused you to think I knew for certain what I had only guessed. It was a question that it should not have been necessary to ask after what I had said before."

The old man made no answer. He pulled the bell.

Rose sat down. "But I don't think this conversation is quite finished," she said quietly.

The footman opened the door.

"William, show these persons out." His voice trembled with the senile passion that still shook him as he spoke.

James crossed the room to where a telephone instrument stood on a side table. He took off the receiver, but kept his finger upon the hook, so that no connexion was made.

"Put me through to the police station," he said, and had the pleasure of seeing Mr. Repton sink back into his chair, as though his legs were too unsteady to support him further.

"Wait a moment, Tony," Rose said; "I'm sure Mr. Repton will prefer to tell us alone."

James put the instrument down, and came back to his chair.

"There's going to be some straight talk here," he said. "Do you want your man to wait?"

"You can go, William, till I ring."

The man went, though probably not very far.

"Now," said James, "you'll just tell us all you know, and as quick as you can, or you'll tell the police in half an hour's time, whichever you like; but I don't leave this room till I know."

The old man appeared incapable of immediate speech, and Rose interposed again.

"There may be a better way. Do you mind if I see Peter alone?"

She took his silence for consent, and pulled the bell-handle that was on her side of the grate.

William appeared very quickly.

She said, "William, your master wishes me to see Peter alone."

The man stood in some hesitation as Mr. Repton said: "You're not going to tell the police? You'll promise that?"

Dignity and bluster were gone together, and there was a pathetic anxiety and weakness in the trembling voice.

"We will do the best we can if you leave it to us; but we cannot promise anything now."

She got up without further words and followed William from the room.

For twenty minutes the two men sat opposite to each other without speech, in a room the silence of which was only broken by the steady ticking of the glass-shaded gilt clock on the mantelpiece, and the occasional sound of a falling cinder.

Then Rose came back, leading a reluctant boy of about nine years, whose flushed and frightened face had a curious likeness to that of his grandfather, giving the same impression of rebellious resentment only restrained by fear.

"Tony," she said, "I'm going to tell you and Peter's grandfather just what happened—I think his grandfather knows most of it already—but I shall only talk of the facts, not—the consequences. We can do that after we've sent Peter away.

"It seems that Peter is at school during terms, and only here in the holidays. Both his parents are dead. When he is at home he has been in the habit, during the past year, of going into your gardens and playing with Jim and Beryl. I think Mrs. Hackett must have known of this, and had not forbidden it; but Anne found the children together, and told Peter that he must not come again unless he brought a note from his grandfather, giving his permission.

"Peter resented this, and did not attempt to get the permission, because he felt sure it would be refused. He tells me that his grandfather never allows him to see any other children in the neighbourhood. It may be that Anne understood this, and resented it on your behalf.

"Anyway, Peter did not stop coming into the orchard. He made Jim promise that he wouldn't tell, and Jim did not think this was very wrong, because he thought his mother did not mind, and it was only his Aunt Anne being cross. No doubt the children all liked playing together.

"Naturally, being forbidden, Peter took a pleasure in trying to come into your own garden without detection. On the afternoon of which we are thinking he came several times—'scouting,' he calls it—while I was using the watering-can, and entered the scullery each time without being detected.

"Jim and Beryl stayed in the pirates' den, and each time he took something back to them out of the scullery to show that he had been there.

"The last time, as I was not in the garden, he was able to watch Anne making the tea, and when she went out he slipped in, clambered up on the side of the copper, and put some of the weed killer into an empty blacking-tin, which he had brought with him.

"As he got down he heard Anne returning, and seeing the cup of tea on the side table, he hurriedly put some of the powder into it, using the spoon from the cup.

"He says that he supposed that she had made it for her own drinking, and that he wished to 'give her a nasty taste.' The only point of difference from the facts as we know them already is that he says the tea was already made. It seems that his only reason was a spiteful feeling that he would like to play a trick on her for having forbidden him to come into the garden. I don't think he had any thought of any serious consequence.

"Jim was in an awkward position, as he had promised Peter not to tell, and you know that Beryl follows anything that Jim does or says. And, of course, Jim had no idea of the reason we had for asking, but when he found that I seriously wanted to know he asked me not to ask him again till after we had come home. I suppose he wanted to see Peter and tell him that he couldn't keep it secret longer, but when they were showing me the pirates' den yesterday Beryl said something about Peter, and so I got on the right track. Is that right, Peter Is that what happened?"

The boy looked half resentful and half ashamed, but did not answer at first, and only nodded sullenly when the question was asked again.

"You can go now, Peter."

He slipped quickly away, and James stepped to the telephone.

"Double-o five eight Central," he said impatiently, and in a few seconds, "I want to speak to Mr. Salmon. Oh, that you, Preedy? Just back? How did it go? No, I didn't suppose it would. That's what *you* think. I think he's the biggest fathead I ever met. Well, he'd better come here at once. Of course you don't. I'm just going to tell you. Upley Park, Morville Road. A man named Repton lives here. Not half a mile, but it wouldn't matter if it were. Of course not. Not at this time of night. He'll be sorry if he doesn't. Rose has found out the whole thing. We should have got at it before if he hadn't been such a thundering fool the first time he saw her. Oh, that you, Warty? Well, I shan't say a word more. No. We'll tell you when you get here. Repton, Upley Park, Morville Road. You can do it in ten minutes, if you open out, and damn the police. And, I say, bring a late-edition paper. I want to see what really happened after we left, not what you fellows tell me. Not a...I think they've cut us off, and a good thing too. These lawyers wouldn't stop talking for a week."

CHAPTER XXXVII.

IT was a fortunate chance which had caught the two lawyers together; they had turned into Salmon's room to discuss the position, before Preedy returned to West Bromwich. As the barrister's car was waiting below, it was a very short time before they were standing in Mr. Repton's library and being introduced to the old gentleman, of whom Salmon, used to the rapid assessing of witnesses, thought, "Looks like a pricked bladder," as he gave a hard grip to a trembling hand.

The barrister sat down rather wearily. He had spoken for over two hours, and with little of notes or preparation, for it was only during the earlier part of the day that he had decided the line which he would take, and he had made, as he was pleasantly aware, a speech which must increase his own reputation, whatever the result of the trial might be. If he had got her off—and he was hopeful even of that—he had secured a reputation that would make success seem easy for the future years. He had made his career safe.

After such an effort he was accustomed to find that his brain continued to work actively, but that his body was exhausted as from prolonged physical exertion. So he felt now. He was glad of the soft comfort of the chair into which he sank, though his mind was alert and keen to deal with whatever near factor in the problem might be brought before him. But he did not expect much. Actually, the case was closed. It was only a matter of some more talk, and then the verdict.

Of course, you can sometimes get new evidence in on appeal, but it's got to be very much to the point, with a very good reason why it hadn't been brought in before, and after the line he had taken in refusing to produce any evidence at all—well, he didn't see how anything they were likely to have found would be of much help. Probably it would be a tale of someone who thought he had seen a lurking shadow slipping out of the garden that afternoon.

"We're wasting time, Preedy," he had said, as they left Hockley behind and came on to the level road, "and I'd much rather be going home; but we've got to hear what it is."

Now he said, "Well, James, out with it. I hope it's something worth coming to hear."

"Oh, no," said James. "It's not important at all. It's only to show you what an ass you've been. It's only that while you were braying there Miss Dorling has found out the truth. She tried to put you on the right track before, but it was like driving a pig."

Mr. Salmon looked unimpressed.

"I thought it would be something of that kind. Miss Dorling saw a shadow under the laurels, and now you've found someone who saw another under the rhododendrons. Well, if that sort of thing would ever have been any use, which I don't think it would, I can tell you that it won't now. But I hope Miss Dorling's going to tell us, and not you, for she can talk without all your loose ends, and we may get to bed before twelve."

"Go on, Rose."

Salmon listened without interruption or sign of what he thought while the tale was told to its end. Even then he was not quick to speak, and Preedy, remembering how the previous tale had been taken, was inclined to wait for a lead. But Rickard Salmon was not doubting the truth this time. His mind was busy with the problem of how to deal with the position in the most effectual manner. To get Miss Bickerton out of jail tomorrow, to score off Russell-Welch and the old judge. The hope that there would be an acquittal as the result of his own speech, of the lines of his own defence, was gone. Or was it? Could anything, in any case, be done before the verdict was given?

He saw that if he could obtain an acquittal on his own defence, and her innocence should afterward be demonstrated, it would increase his triumph. On the other hand, if she should be condemned, and he could over trump at the last moment by producing the youthful culprit, it might be an even more dramatic endorsement of the protest which he had made against the way in which the evidence had been presented.

He was not afraid that there would be any legal barrier to a satisfactory issue. The evidence was too strong. If he should make it known, by whatever channel, public opinion would insist upon Miss Bickerton's vindication and her release.

"Miss Dorling," he said at last, "I take back anything I said, whether I said it or not. I didn't think much of your tale, and I thought it was more likely to get you into the dock than to help Miss Bickerton out. I'm not sure I was wrong even now. But I'll own I ought to have thought more of what you said than I did, and James is quite right that I look a fool. But I don't suppose any of you'll mind that.

"We've got them on the hip now, and it's just a question of how best to drive it home."

"I don't quite know what being on the hip is," Miss Dorling answered, "but it sounds uncomfortable, and if so I hope you'll see that they stay there; but I don't want you to do anything that makes trouble for the boy, if you can help it. I suppose they can't do much to a child like that, especially as he only meant to be mischievous, but you know what brutes lawyers are, and the police. Or, at least, it's not exactly that, but they'll all do brutal things and say they can't help it, because it's the law. They treat the law like a god. I haven't promised Mr. Repton anything, but I told him that we should keep the police out of it as much as we could."

"A high-spirited boy, Mr. Salmon," the old man interposed, "just a high-spirited boy; and a natural resentment, a very natural resentment. I'm sure you'll see that."

Mr. Salmon looked at him coldly, and without sympathy.

"I don't see it at all. I think the boy needs to be thrashed till he can't stand, and I think you're about as bad, or you wouldn't have the infernal insolence to talk like that, knowing what he's done. As to keeping the police out of it now, I shall be glad if anyone can tell me how it's to be done.

"Of course, I should like to do what you wish, Miss Dorling. We owe you that. But it's not easy to see how.

"As to how the boy stands, I can tell you this. The law isn't quite as bad as it once was. If it had been a hundred years ago, being over seven, his neck would have been in more danger than it is now. But legally it's manslaughter, if not murder, all the same; and in England even boys of nine are not allowed to commit murder and go to bed as though nothing had happened."

"I don't see how you can call it murder. He only meant to annoy Anne by making her tea taste nasty."

"Yes, but it might be murder, all the same. It might have been less than that but for one thing that you can't get over. The boy was acting illegally at the time. He had no right to be on the premises at all. Everything he did from that point was unlawful. He went on, legally, from wrong to wrong. And that just makes the final difference. If a man does a careless thing that (but for the carelessness) he had a right to do, and he kills another in doing it, it may be no more than manslaughter, or he may even escape altogether, if the carelessness may be held to be less than criminal. But if he kills another when he's doing an illegal thing, it's just murder or manslaughter, and there's no get-out at all."

"I always thought the law was silly, but not quite as silly as that," Miss Dorling answered. "But if we're all going to pull the same way, I'll tell you just how I feel. I've not much sympathy for the boy. I think he's a selfish little cad, and his only excuse for being that is the way he's been brought up. I thought at first that we ought to try not to let him know what he had done, but I'm not so sure about that now. It might do him good if anything can. But I think we could deal with it without help, and I think it's Mr. Hackett's matter—and, perhaps, Anne's—more than it concerns all the judges who ever wore wigs. I don't expect you'll agree with me, or that many men would, but that's how I feel, and it's best said.

"But that isn't all. I think Anne comes first, and we've got to get her clear just as quick as we can, whatever happens to the boy."

"Then there's only one thing to try," Mr. Salmon answered, "and this is going to save time with the exchange."

He pulled out a telephone directory of the London district, which lay under the local ones, as he spoke, and turned the pages rapidly.

"The Home Secretary, I suppose?" Mr. Duff-Preedy inquired, possibly considering that he had been out of the conversation long enough.

"Yes, but not directly. I want to find out where he is. I want one of the permanent officials first. I'll tell you what, Preedy: if you wouldn't mind speaking to Landor while I'm on the phone and telling him to go round to the nearest place where he can fill his tank, and to get ready for a long run, it'll save time in the end. Here's the one I want—Bindon Wells."

The old man had sat without speaking, looking from face to face in a frightened, pleading way which yet suggested that a bitter resentment against these people, who made so free with his house, was not far from the surface, and would be shown if he dared. But he started at the name, and said, with a nervous rapidity: "Yes, let Sir Bindon Wells know—let Bindon know. He wouldn't let anything happen to his cousin's child."

"Are you related to Bindon Wells?" Mr. Salmon asked, with an evident interest.

"Not myself. My son's wife was his cousin."

"That's the first bit of luck we've had yet in this case."

"Is he the Home Secretary?" Miss Dorling asked.

"No. Israel Marks is Home Secretary now. Didn't you know that? But Wells is a more important man—much. It means that if we can cross the first ditch he'll probably drive us home the way that you want to go."

Mr. Repton's telephone was working without intermission during the next half-hour. At the end of that time two wives and a prospective bride (of Mr. Salmon's chauffeur) had learned that their men were having a night out, and James and Rose had communicated similar information in the directions where they might have been expected to arrive. On their part, they had learned that Mr. Israel Marks was away from home for a long weekend, and would probably be leaving Nottingham for London by an early train in the morning.

"He's at Tythby Manor," Mr. Salmon explained as he put the instrument down. "It's five or ten miles beyond Nottingham—I don't know exactly. But it's there for us. I'm not sure whether we'd better not take the boy, but perhaps he's best left. I've no doubt he'll keep."

"Aren't you going to ring him up?" said James, who had indulged in a longer silence than usual.

"And get told he can't see us tonight? Not likely. Mr. Repton's going to ring his son's cousin's boss up as soon as we've got a clear start, and just tell him it's a matter of life and death and he'd better wait up—or have a dressing gown handy.

"If he likes to ring up Bindon Wells as well and have a heart-to-heart talk, that's his matter; but I expect it'll come to much the same if he leaves it to me. Mr. Repton," he concluded, "we're going to do what we can for you, and there are just two things you can do for us. We want the best meal you can have served inside three minutes, and the loan of a few good wraps for the car."

Mr. Repton pulled the bell.

It was scarcely a quarter of an hour later that Mr. Salmon's car swung out of the gates of Upley Park, beneath a stormy twilight sky.

"No, sir, not Lichfield. It's Sutton first, and then Tamworth and Ashby. We'll be there before they've gone to bed, with any luck."

"Right you are, Landor. Wake me up when we get there."

Mr. Salmon, having completed his plans, and being a man who economized in time and energy, settled himself by the chauffeur's side, and went to sleep immediately.

After a time Mr. Duff-Preedy slept also, as was natural in one of his age after a watchful and tiring day.

James sat next to him, and Rose was at the farther side.

Swift and smooth, the car ran on through the night.

The moon was large and low in the eastern sky, from which the clouds withdrew as the night came.

The two talked now and then in low voices, not wishing, it may be, to disturb the sleepers, or to distract Landor's attention from the flying road.

The car was not meant to seat more than four, and Rose was somewhat crowded, though the men had done their best for her when they got in. But there is no record that she complained.

CHAPTER XXXVIII.

IT being contrary to English custom and law to comment publicly upon a trial during its progress, the morning newspapers contented themselves with emphatic headlines and leaded type by which to give prominence to Miss Dorling's duel with the judge, and to the unusual line adopted by the counsel for the accused. They also reported his speech with unusual fullness, and Mr. Justice Ackling, reading *The Morning Post*, with the cup of coffee and single egg which he found sufficient to keep his brain active and appease his body till the luncheon hour, was in no ignorance of the seriousness of the issues that confronted him.

It was true that he had no responsibility for the way in which Mr. Russell-Welch had presented his case, or the stage at which he had closed it. He could easily have averted from his own head any storm which might be coming by assuming a tone in the summing-up which would be inoffensive to the partisans of both sides, and would probably lead to the acquittal of the accused, without the prosecution being able to say that he had thrown them over.

But Ackling was neither a timeserver nor a coward.

He conscientiously believed that he held his office mainly to put down with a stern hand a certain section of the community which he would have designated as the "criminal classes."

He was as incapable of being deflected from the path of duty—as he saw it—as he would have been utterly incapable of accepting a bribe.

He did not consider that there was any moral justification for the protest that Mr. Salmon had made, though his acute legal mind went over every argument that could be put forward, so that he might not fail to avoid the pitfalls they might indicate. As he saw it, Mr. Russell-Welch had merely shown the ability for which he was so highly paid by the Crown in putting the defence into the most difficult position he could contrive. He would only be wrong if it should appear subsequently that Mr. Salmon had been able to handle the defence so that an acquittal would result, and then he would only be wrong because his net had been unsuccessfully cast.

It was Mr. Justice Ackling's duty—as he saw it—to give the prosecution all the help he could in his summing-up. He was not naturally addicted to presuming the innocence of accused persons, and in this case he had no doubt at all. Having read with some care, and with a mind which was very keen to analyse and to retain the essentials of such depositions, the evidence which had been given at the inquest, he had considered Miss Dorling's part in the matter, but he was not one who would allow a personal resentment to deflect his judgment, and he saw clearly that she was not of the poisoning type.

Had he first encountered her in the dock, he might have judged differently, as he would have presumed her guilt. He was subconsciously of the opinion he might even have subscribed to the explicit statement—that a judge should assume, in the absence of the strongest rebutting evidence, that anyone is a criminal who appears in a criminal dock. That is "supporting the police."

The present case was simple. Its issues were few. He had made his notes overnight. He went over them thoughtfully for half an hour after his frugal meal. Then he descended to his waiting carriage.

When he entered the court and the assembly rose to its customary obeisance he became aware, as it settled back to its seats, that there was a curious emptiness immediately before and beneath him.

He saw the prisoner in the dock as before, with her two attendant wardresses. He saw the dignified immobility of Mr. Swayboat's countenance. But Mr. Russell-Welch was not there. Neither was Mr. Salmon, nor his attendant solicitor. Looking round the court with a further inquiry, he observed the absence of Miss Dorling and of the husband of the murdered woman. These absences were emphasized by the care of the ushers, mindful of yesterday's rebuke, to keep seats empty for those who had been bound over to attend the court.

Mr. Justice Ackling misread these absences in a very natural way. He did not concern himself over Mr. Russell-Welch. After all, his part was done. He was a busy man. He might have been called away very urgently, and have left the concluding stages of the case in Mr. Swayboat's very capable hands.

But the other absences were too extraordinary in their aggregate for any casual explanation. He concluded, as did Mr. Swayboat and many others in the crowded court, that, after making his protest, Mr. Salmon had deliberately withdrawn from the case. Well, he would know how to instruct the jury under such circumstances.

The case had been brought to the threshold of his summing-up when it had been adjourned on the previous evening.

In an unaccented tone of level impartiality he proceeded to address the jury. In doing this he did not avoid the issue which Mr. Salmon had raised. He came to it explicitly and at once.

He reminded the jury, touching promptly upon the weakest point of the defence, that they were not dealing with a police prosecution, but that the accused had been committed for trial by the coroner after an inquiry which had been held by him, and as a result of the verdict of a jury who had heard the evidence of all who had been in touch with the tragedy.

"Such an inquest," he went on, "is something less than a final judicial proceeding. It is an inquiry which is conducted under different rules and to different ends. You must not admit to your minds any presumption of the prisoner's guilt because of that verdict and apart from the evidence which has been given here.

"But when you consider, as you are bound to do, the very able and somewhat dramatic protest made yesterday by the prisoner's counsel, and emphasized, as we may reasonably conclude, by his absence today, you are entitled to take into consideration the legal procedure from which this prosecution began.

"It is my duty to instruct you that there was nothing wrong in English law, and I can tell you also that there was no violation of established custom, in the course taken by the prosecution, and by their very experienced advocate, in calling only such evidence as he felt to be sufficient to prove the crime and to identify the criminal.

"Such other evidence as was at their disposal it was open to the defence to call, if they had considered that it would have been of any avail to weaken the case which had been presented to you, or to introduce an alternative possibility. It was also open to the prisoner to go into the witness-box, and to give you the advantage of hearing her sworn account of the matter.

"You are entitled to draw your own conclusions from the fact that no rebutting evidence was called, and from the nature of the protest which was made on the prisoner's behalf. But I would advise you rather to direct your minds to the positive evidence that has been presented to you."

The learned judge paused for a moment, preparing his mind for the detailed survey of the witnesses' evidence to which he had been leading, and in the momentary silence it was noticed that a telegram was handed to Mr. Swayboat, which he read with his usual impassivity.

Mr. Justice Ackling went on to analyse the case as it had been disclosed by the witnesses for the prosecution.

He dealt first with the cause of death, about which, he suggested, the jury would have little difficulty.

He came then to the manner in which the poison had been administered. Here, he concluded again, the jury might consider that the cup in which the dregs of the tea had been found was indicated beyond reasonable doubt. So far the case appeared to his mind to be exceptionally simple and clear.

They came next to the specific question which they were required to judge: if they were agreed upon the nature and method of the crime, was the woman who was now in the dock responsible for it?

They had heard the evidence of the two doctors that she had admitted making the tea and taking it up to the bedroom herself. She had actually identified the poisoned cup. Was this the frankness of innocence? If they thought that, what other ways were there of any reasonable probability—none had been suggested by the defence— by which the poison might have been introduced?

They must consider the question of motive. The absence of motive was not a sufficient defence to an accusation of this kind; and, on the other hand, it might be said that no motive could be adequate to, or explanatory of, so unnatural a crime.

Yet they knew that such crimes did occur, and it was at least more probable that they would be perpetrated by such as had something to gain or to avenge, or some fear to avoid. When they looked for motive here, what did they find? They found that a large part of the fortune of the dead woman had been transferred to another, with or without her husband's knowledge, through the prisoner's introduction.

They found that, only the day before, a will had been executed which left the whole remainder of the victim's property to the prisoner.

As to how that will had been obtained, as to the probability that it would be allowed to stand, they knew nothing beyond the evidence of Mr. Tomkinson as to the circumstances under which it had been so hurriedly drawn and completed in his own office

If they had read anything that might be considered adverse to the prisoner at some other time, evidence given in some other court in connexion with these financial transactions, they must try to put it absolutely out of their minds. It was true that there were witnesses in that court—or there had been witnesses, who ought to be present now—who might have given them further information on these matters, as might the prisoner herself, had she elected to do so—witnesses that the prosecution did not think necessary, and that the defence had refused to call.

But he must instruct them that the attitude adopted by the defence was legitimate to this extent, that they were under no obligation to assist the prosecution in any way. The prosecution must prove its case. If it had done less than that they must acquit the prisoner.

It was about half an hour since Mr. Swayboat had received his telegram, and during the last ten minutes his indecision had been outwardly observable—a circumstance so unusual that Mr. Justice Ackling's mind was diverted from its logical stream for one flippant moment, to wonder whether he were afflicted with one of those insects which are occasionally liable to take a flying leap from the persons of prisoners of the baser sort.

If we are to understand his indecision, it may be convenient to read the telegram, which he has now opened again and is holding uncertainly in his left hand, as though he were about to rise and interrupt the lucid sentences of the learned judge. It says:

> Delay conclusion trial any means till I arrive. RUSSELL WELCH.

It had been handed in at Rugby, at a time which told Mr. Swayboat, who was well acquainted with the London trains, that its sender might walk into the court at any moment and relieve him from further responsibility. But with this knowledge he was also aware that the summing-up was very near to its end. As a general may watch his own troops and those of the enemy racing from different points to the hilltop which will give victory to those of the better legs, so, and in an almost equal anxiety, had Mr. Swayboat watched the progress of the summing-up and the hands of the unhurried clock that moved, with the inevitable deliberation of the law itself, above the judge's head.

He knew, almost by heart, the concluding sentences in which Ackling would charge the jury in such a case, and he knew that another three minutes would hear the final word and see them retiring to their own room to consider their verdict.

How could he delay the trial? There were ways, no doubt. He might push past the astonished associate, swing himself over the rail, and seize the judge by the throat. Less than that might suffice.

Even an ink-well slung at the jury with the skill and force of one who still bowled occasionally for the M.C.C. would be a diversion into which the judge might pause to inquire. And, of course, he might say that the juryman who encountered the missile had been pulling faces at the judge. It would be a mere protest against contempt of court, such as a barrister is almost bound to make. He might rise and communicate the telegram to the judge, but he did not know whether his leader would approve, and he did know that Ackling hated to be interrupted at such a time and would not tolerate it for a light cause.

But he heard the penultimate words, *"beyond reasonable doubt, such as in the affairs of your own—"*

In the courage of desperation he rose abruptly, holding out the telegram as he did so.

The judge stopped.

"Yes, Mr. Swayboat?"

The tone was curt even to rudeness, contrasting with the toneless periods which had been so inopportunely interrupted.

"I think, my lord," said Mr. Swayboat, recovering his balance (so to speak) when he was once on his legs, "that it may be my duty to show you this telegram, which I received about half an hour ago."

The judge read it with attention, and then looked up with a frown.

"This doesn't tell us much, Mr. Swayboat. Do you know when he will be here?"

"No, my lord. But I should think it may be at any moment now."

"I suppose that means that you guess by the trains. You really know no more than this tells us?"

"No, my lord."

"Then I'm afraid we must go on."

The incident had caused a stir of curiosity through the court. What might the telegram be? What might it mean? Apparently they could go on guessing, for they were not to know.

Even the prisoner had raised her head, watching with more interest than she had previously shown that morning.

We have almost overlooked Miss Bickerton. That is natural enough, for she is not a very emphatic personality, and it is in the routine of an English trial to relegate the accused to a somewhat obscure position, unless he shall insist on emergence from it to give evidence or to conduct his own defence.

Miss Bickerton was of a type with which the judge was familiar by a hundred precedents. They just sit in the dock, looking at nothing in particular, or perhaps at the floor. They occasionally make a hysterical outburst, which must be promptly silenced for the decorum of the court. They often faint when the sentence is pronounced. They are not very important.

Yet they must have their feelings; and those of Miss Bickerton, vaguely raised by the eloquence of Mr. Salmon, though she had only partly understood it, on the previous day—an eloquence of which we unfortunately missed the ultimate heights when we followed Miss Dorling from the court—were now bewildered and depressed by the absence of those to whom alone she could look for any human friendliness or aid from the pit into which she had so strangely fallen.

She knew little of the etiquette of such trials. Were the others excluded from the closing stages after their part was done? Did it mean that they had abandoned her to the dreadful fate of which she feared to think?

She heard the measured sentences of the judge, but they had no emotional impact upon the stunned bewilderment of her mind. Always more sensitive to tone and manner than to actual words, she was impervious to the judge's gentle, implacable pressure upon the scale of death.

But a telegram had always meant something important in her life. Vaguely she wondered if there were some friendly intervention in the nightmare in which she moved.

She saw the frown on the judge's face, and she felt instinctively that anything which annoyed him should be good for her. With the intuition on which she must rely in the absence of any logical faculties, she knew him for the one most to be dreaded of these wig-headed men who were gathered for her destruction. But Ackling's annoyance was mainly at the brevity of the telegram. It was an economy for which Russell-Welch had been noted in the days when they had both been juniors on the same circuit. Never, in any emergency, had he been known to exceed the shilling minimum at which such communications can be sent. Always he would content himself to express as much of his meaning as he could contrive to compress into twelve words, including his own signature and the address of the one who was to receive the conundrum. If Russell-Welch had anything to say why didn't he spend a few shillings in saying it? Anyway, he couldn't stop at this stage to await the K.C.'s return.

"I am afraid we must go on."

And then he must pause again, for there was the stir of several people coming in at the door.

CHAPTER XXXIX.

THE judge paused, with his chin raised, in a way he had when he looked at the back of the court, probably because the position of his eyeglasses otherwise gave him a restricted vision. It was an attitude which lengthened the scraggy neck, and produced something of the aspect of a vulture disturbed at his carrion meal.

He saw Mr. Salmon come in, followed by Mr. Duff-Preedy, the wig and gown of the former, which he had hurriedly put on, doing something to conceal a fact which was more apparent in at least two of his companions—that they had been up all night.

Perhaps we should except Miss Dorling, whose cool neatness was preserved by a seeming miracle, but actually through the opportune assistance of Miss Barbara Marks, a youthful niece of the Home Secretary, who doesn't otherwise intrude into this narrative, about which I am sorry, for she was a nice girl, on whose black eyes and somewhat opulent beauty it would have been a pleasure to dwell.

But about Mr. James Bruton Hackett there was no doubt at all. Even the obtuse policeman of popular fiction would have said at the first glance, "There goes a man who has slept in his clothes." Mr. Justice Ackling saw it at once. He did not conclude that they had attempted the murder or abduction of Russell-Welch during the night, for he was a man of orderly and controlled imagination, but he did see that his first supposition as to the cause of the absence of these four people must be mistaken, and that there was a probability that it might have some connexion with that of the K.C. which it would be well for him to know.

He waited, in a pregnant silence, till they had taken their seats, and then addressed the prisoner's counsel.

"Mr. Salmon, I have, of course, no control over your movements, nor right to complain if you absent yourself from the court. That is a matter which lies between yourself and your client, subject to any complaint to the Bar, with which I am not concerned. Nor do

I wish to suggest that you have made any default such as would justify such a course being taken. But there is such a thing as respect for the court, and a courtesy which is due from Bar to Bench, and I think some explanation, if not apology, is due for this somewhat unceremonious entrance, which coincides with that of two of the witnesses who were bound over by the prosecution to attend the trial, and who had no right to be absent till it was over."

Mr. Salmon was tired, but in excellent spirits. He had looked round to the prisoner, even while the judge was addressing him, to give her a friendly nod, and to say in a whisper which was audible over half the court, "We'll soon have you out of this." He was prepared to argue anything at that moment, from the heights of heaven to the nether regions, but he was rather short of breath, which may explain why he got on his legs, and said no more than, "My lord, I submit that their obligation of attendance ceased when the prosecution's case closed. I am prepared to argue that if you wish me to do so."

"I dare say you are, Mr. Salmon," said the judge dryly, "but you won't now. Will you kindly address your mind to the earlier part of what I have just said."

Mr. Salmon saw his opportunity, and had regained his breath.

"My lord, I am not conscious of having shown any disrespect to the court, and I have yet to learn that my client is likely to be dissatisfied with the way in which I have defended her against a charge which may ultimately reflect no discredit upon her."

Mr. Justice Ackling stroked his chin. He weighed Mr. Salmon's words carefully in a very shrewd mind. He saw that the remark could hardly fail to have its effect on the jury. Yet he could find no breach of the etiquette of advocacy. Had he said "will"—but he had said "may."

He recognized a fighting quality in Mr. Salmon's advocacy which deserved respect and suggested caution, and he felt that there were movements behind the scenes of which it would be well for him to be more fully informed. He said:

"Very well, Mr. Salmon. If you do not feel that you have treated the court with any lack of respect we will say no more. You may be interested to know that Mr. Russell-Welch is also absent this morning. Or perhaps you are already aware of that circumstance?"

"I was not aware of it, my lord, but I cannot say that I am surprised."

"Then perhaps you can tell me the meaning of this telegram?"

Mr. Salmon considered it in a long moment of silence.

"My lord," he said at last, "I think it means that Mr. Russell-Welch underrated the intelligence of the jury."

"Will you kindly be more explicit, Mr. Salmon?"

"My lord," said Mr. Salmon, with an internal pleasure which he was only partially successful in concealing, "it is with reluctance that I make any suggestion. I am not sure that I ought to offer interpretation of the telegrams of the prosecuting counsel, but I suggest, with diffidence, that he was afraid lest the jury might have brought in a verdict against my client before he could arrive to prevent it."

"Mr. Salmon," said the judge, with the cold anger which Miss Dorling had faced so equably on the previous day, and which he found it no easy thing to meet in a similar spirit, even with all he knew to support him, "you are either playing with the court, which I should be reluctant to believe, and with which I should know how to deal, or you have information which you would do well to state in the plain words which you are quite able to use if you...."

"My lord," Mr. Salmon answered, with some reduction of his previous confidence, "I am sorry if anything which I have said has appeared to fail in respect to the court, but I am in a real difficulty, in the absence of Mr. Russell-Welch, in deciding how much I am entitled to say. I am sure you will appreciate the difference there may be between what I may reasonably suppose to be the course which he will have been instructed to take and actual knowledge, which I have not got."

"I think, Mr. Salmon, it may be best that you and Mr. Swayboat should see me together in my own room.

"As your lordship pleases," Mr. Salmon answered, and the two counsel were already rising, when the burly form of Mr. Russell-Welch was observed to be pushing itself rapidly along the gangway.

The judge settled himself back in his seat.

There was a minute of rapid whispering between Mr. Swayboat and his leader, after which the latter gentleman rose, and said: "My lord, I must apologize for any inconvenience which has been caused by my absence this morning, but I was called to London during the night, and since my return here I have been delayed by the necessity of obtaining telephoned instructions before I was able to come into court. My instructions now are to enter a *nolle prosequi*, the Crown being satisfied that it is not a case in which they ought to proceed further against the prisoner."

The judge considered this.

"Can you refer me to any instance in which such a course was taken after the case for the prosecution was closed?"

"I cannot immediately, my lord. It is a point which I have had no opportunity of looking into."

"Then I am afraid that it is a course to which I cannot give my consent. Perhaps I should tell you, Mr. Russell-Welch, that I have already dealt with the question of the propriety of the method by which you conducted the prosecution yesterday in the course of my summing-up, which has been so irregularly interrupted, and I can tell you that I see no deviation from what is either legal or customary."

Mr. Russell-Welch bowed. "I thank you, my lord. It is a vindication that I might otherwise have lacked, in view of the way in which it appears likely that this case will terminate. But the two matters are quite separate, my lord. My present instructions are that the Crown is now fully satisfied of the prisoner's innocence as a result of further facts that have come to light since yesterday, and I must retire from it in whatever way and on whatever terms your lordship may direct."

"I shall direct the jury to return a verdict of 'Not guilty.' Whatever may be thought of the way in which this trial has been prepared or conducted, it would be impossible for them to bring in any other verdict after the statement which you have now made."

The judge remembered that there were other cases to be tried. He felt some natural annoyance at the abrupt reversal of the verdict which he had too plainly indicated. The whole trial had been annoying and unsatisfactory. He remembered Miss Dorling's insolence of the previous day. She was one of those who had entered the court with Mr. Salmon ten minutes ago. He felt that she was not disconnected with these latest developments, and he felt much less than sure of the actual innocence of the prisoner. It was a case in which the majesty of the law had been treated with too little respect from first to last. The character of the defence which Mr. Salmon had set up was of the same pattern as the other incidents of the trial. He would have been a much happier man (though he would not have admitted it, even to himself) had he been pulling out the black cap which he had put in his pocket that morning, with little doubt that it would be used before he returned to his judge's lodgings at night.

But he was a sound judge and a good lawyer. He knew that there was only one possible verdict now.

The jury agreed. They had been whispering among themselves. The foreman rose at once, as the question was put.

"Not guilty," he said, in a voice that sounded clearly through the court, and had scarcely ceased when a murmur of applause broke out and a clapping of hands that drowned for a moment the angry voice of the judge threatening to clear the court.

But the threat had little terror for an audience to whom the show was over, and who were already pushing their way to the door to discuss the dramatic conclusion of this surprising trial as they joined the outer crowd, and waited on the pavement for the chance of cheering those who would appear a few minutes later, to be guided by a retinue of police to Mr. Salmon's waiting car.

CHAPTER XL.

"YOU'D better come with me to the Queen's," said Mr. Salmon, as the car slipped through the cheering crowd. "We couldn't go far crushed up like this." They had had enough of one another's company—some of them, at any rate—in that car during the night, and now there was Miss Bickerton also to be accommodated as best they could.

"I'll tell you what," he added. "I expect Miss Bickerton will be all the better for a good meal, and a bottle of wine won't do any of us any harm. We'll have that now, and then you can go home by train, Preedy, or how you will. (You won't think I'm rude, but the back axle won't stand much more of this.) And then I'll drive Mr. Hackett's party home to The Firs, and if you don't want to talk to reporters all the rest of the day, James, you'd better put a notice on the door that you've gone to bed as soon as you've got in. I don't suppose that'll be far wrong either. And now here we are, and it's a straight streak for a private room and the best lunch they can serve us."

The five people who sat down a quarter of an hour later to the excellent lunch which Mr. Salmon had ordered may be considered to have had some reason for satisfaction, and for the making of such merriment as could be expected after the physical and mental exercises that were immediately behind them, and three at least were in the mood to do so.

Of Mr. Salmon's own spirits there could be no doubt. Miss Dorling also was quietly happy and of a mind to fall in with the emotions of those around her. Mr. Hackett, who had done less than the other two to produce the position, was well content at his sister-in-law's vindication, and might take some pleasure in the thought that he had stood by her against the weight of the verdict in the coroner's court and the apparent evidence of the facts themselves. He was in congenial company and quite prepared to be festive, though he yawned occasionally.

Mr. Duff-Preedy was sleepy, and was primarily aware of this physical circumstance.

But Anne Bickerton, who might be considered the one who had most cause for satisfaction in the event, and gratitude to those to whom she owed her freedom, and perhaps her life, remained unsmiling at any jest and unresponsive to any word, looking more abjectly miserable than when she had sat in the dock awaiting a doom which might have appeared inevitable only an hour ago.

But she had escaped a danger which had seemed too dreadful, even too grotesque, for reality, and her mind came back, weakened and bewildered, to familiar things, to be aware that they had fallen around her. For when the law strikes at the innocent, with its inhuman, if necessary, cruelty, it cannot withdraw its fangs and loose an uninjured prey.

She thought of the situation which (she supposed) she had lost, of her room in Shrewsbury, to which she had expected to return in a few hours so many weeks ago, which held all her personal things— would they be there now? She thought of the man that she so foolishly and weakly loved, whom she vaguely supposed to be in jail. She thought of the treasured letters that had been burned. She was aware, without self-criticism, of a feeling of bitterness against Miss Dorling for that unavoidable sacrifice. She thought of the sister on whom she had leaned, and to whom she had been very deeply attached. She felt no friendship or fellowship with those who had brought her here. With the shallow acuteness of her mind, she was aware that they had no friendship for her, that they disregarded or even despised her.

She sat at the round table with Mr. Salmon on her left hand and Mr. Preedy on her right, Miss Dorling being next to him, and Mr. Hackett completing the circle. She looked at James and Rose, seated opposite to her, and it seemed that they shut her out, even from her sister's home.

She was not of the kind who meet adversity with a lifted head.

The waiter set down the soup, and as he did so she suddenly pushed the plate from her, with the cutlery around it, splashing half its contents on the cloth, as she exclaimed: "I don't think you ought to go on like this, as though Belle wasn't dead."

Her head sank on the table, and she sobbed aloud.

The three men looked at one another uncomfortably. The waiter went on serving as though unaware of what was happening, till Miss Dorling rose and said something to him, to which he replied, "Yes, certainly, miss. You'll find number seven's clear."

206

She went round the table, saying, "You'd better go on, but we shall be back soon."

She led Miss Bickerton from the room.

"Well," said Mr. Salmon, "we'd better do as we're told."

The three men lifted their spoons in silence. The situation seemed beyond comment.

The waiter returned and was wiping up the spilled soup.

Outside they could hear the cries of the newsboys: "Bickerton Case!" "Dramatic Collapse!" "Scenes in Court!"

"There's a big crowd outside, sir," the waiter ventured.

They rose and went to the window.

They saw a crowd that filled the station approach and Stephenson Place and the street to the left waiting patiently for them to come out.

"It's the station lift for me," said Mr. Duff-Preedy.

"I don't see why you should do that," Mr. Salmon replied. "There's an ambulance just under the statue. Why not make for that, and the crowds could walk round and admire you while you sleep?" It was evident that Mr. Salmon's spirits were not permanently blighted by the unfortunate incident which had just occurred.

"It isn't me they want," Mr. Preedy answered, with truth; "it's you and the two ladies. You could get anything you liked to ask if you'd go on the Empire stage tonight."

"Do you always have such beastly ideas when you're half-asleep?" James asked indignantly. He was not of those who appreciate publicity, and the sight of the crowd made him almost too sick to eat.

"Of course he does. You should read Freud. You'd be a god-send to that man, Preedy."

They went back to the table. If the lunch were to be a dismal affair it would not be the host's fault.

"If you see Preedy's going off, James, there's only one thing that will keep him awake. You must ask him about Crippen. He's got an idea that most murderers who get hanged are innocent men, and if they get off he usually has some doubts as to whether they ought to. He'll talk about any case for a week if he gets wound up. But Crippen's the ace of spades."

Mr. Duff-Preedy stifled a yawn at its birth, and rose hastily to the bait.

"It's easy to rag, but I've put it to you half a dozen times"— "Say twenty," Mr. Salmon interjected—"and you've never given me a convincing answer. Mr. Hackett, I'll put it to you. Of course, when

Dr. Crippen was tried, everyone knew he'd cut up his wife's body, and they thought it was a nasty thing to do, and it was quite understood that he'd got to hang, but it doesn't follow from that that he'd murdered her, or that they could prove it if he had.

"I'm not going on the question of identification, because it was common sense that it was Mrs. Crippen's body, though if anything would make you feel doubtful it would be the evidence by which they tried to prove it; and I'm not going on the cause of death, though any chemist will tell you that hyoscine couldn't possibly be found, except by a very vivid imagination, after the interval which had occurred; because she was certainly dead, and the cause of death doesn't really prove or refute anything.

"And I don't say he didn't do it. He may have confessed, for all I know, though I don't think he did.

"But what I say is that it wasn't proved, and it never *could* have been proved if he'd said that she committed suicide when she found he was going off with the other woman, and he was frightened that he'd be suspected of murder, and so did what he did as the lesser risk of the two.

"That's not only a possible, it's quite as likely a solution as that he should have taken the risk of killing her in such a way."

"I've told you twenty times," Mr. Salmon answered, for James was silent before this surprising theory, "that if that was what happened, and if he told his lawyers, they wouldn't have dared to put in such a defence. You know you wouldn't yourself. He'd have had to own that he cut up the body, and any jury would have hanged him without listening to anything else. Thorne learned that later, though if I had to bet I should put it at about twenty to one that he told the truth from first to last."

"I don't dispute any of that," Mr. Preedy answered. "I only say that when people call Crippen a murderer, they're saying something they don't know. We've just had a proof of how strong evidence can be made to look when it's all worked up to point one way. I'll tell you that, used as I am to the game, before Russell-Welch had finished I almost began to think myself that Miss Bickerton had done it, and if they'd gone for Miss Dorling they could have made it out just as strong."

His voice sank as the two ladies returned to the room.

Miss Bickerton looked somewhat happier and more alert to what was happening around her as she resumed her seat, and said: "I expect you'll think that I ought to have thanked you before now for all you've done. I didn't understand till Miss Dorling told me, and

I'm not sure that I understand now, but I'm very grateful. Of course I'm grateful. Yes, thank you, waiter, I'll take some soup. But I can't understand it now. You must have been going about all night. He was a very wicked man."

No one inquired which of Miss Bickerton's persecutors was in her mind as she pronounced this judgment.

Mr. Salmon said hastily, "We couldn't tell you all that happened last night. Not one of us, anyway. We weren't all awake at the same time. But I might tell you The Adventure of the Home Secretary Who Wasn't There, and someone else might tell you The Adventure of the Burst Tyre, or The Adventure of the Permanent Official Who Didn't Want to be Told too Much, and Miss Dorling might tell—"

"I wonder what they're going to do to that wicked boy?" Miss Bickerton interrupted. She had no intention of rudeness, but the kind of conversation in which Mr. Salmon indulged had no meaning for her. It was mere noise that filled up the intervals of sensible speech—in which estimate she may have been more nearly right than he would have been pleased to know.

He abandoned flippancy to give a serious answer.

"I've been thinking about that. Of course, Bindon Wells will do what he can to hush it up, and a word from him will go through the Home Office and Scotland Yard in less time than it takes to sign a cheque. But a lot depends on the Press. They'll be left puzzled and wondering, and if the Sunday papers get at the truth, it may be hard to let it rest where it is.

"But there's a difficulty of an opposite kind, which that doddering old grandfather hadn't the sense to see, or we mightn't be just where we are now.

"We've just seen how easy it is to get legal proof of something that didn't happen. But if any proceedings were taken against the boy we might see the difficulty of legal proof of something which everyone would know really did. You couldn't make him give evidence against himself, and without that what proof have you got? But I'll tell you one thing, James. You've got to get something in writing for the sake of your own child. If you don't you'll find that there'll be loose talk always going on about the children that did it, and it's more likely to settle on to your own Jim than anyone else. It'll be a whisper against him all his life.

"If you'll leave this to Mr. Preedy and me we'll have a written statement sworn by the old man as to what his grandson confessed, and if he objects we'll publish the whole tale now, and he can kick up any dust that he dares. It'll be a bit extra fuss now, but it'll save more in the end."

"The popular idea about Brazil," said James, "is that it is a—"

"We weren't talking about Brazil," Mr. Salmon answered, with some irritation.

"No," said James, "but I was."

"Tony was telling me quite a lot about Brazil when you interrupted," Miss Dorling explained.

"Didn't know you'd ever been there in your life."

"No, but I'm going very soon."

"Well, you needn't talk shop if you are. Miss Dorling doesn't care if it's all apes and peacocks."

"Oh, yes, I do," said Miss Dorling calmly. "It's an interesting country."

But James relapsed into a gloomy silence. The eloquence of which Miss Dorling had had the benefit was not to be continued now that the attention of the rest of the company had been directed upon it.

Mr. Salmon kept up the conversation.

"I wonder whether any of you noticed a discrepancy between the boy's account and the evidence that Miss Bickerton gave at the inquest. To some minds it would be almost enough to upset the whole tale."

"No," said Mr. Preedy honestly, "I can't say that I did."

"I suppose you mean about the cup being full?" said James.

"Yes. It's a small point. But it's not easy to get over."

"Then you don't know Anne, if you think that. Rose said the same thing to me, and I said that was just what showed me that he was telling the truth. If Anne said she filled it before she left the kitchen you can be sure she didn't, and if she said she didn't you can be sure she did."

"James," said Miss Bickerton, "was always nasty to me."

CHAPTER XLI.

MR ABRAHAM TUCKER was a spacious man, fleshy rather than fat, with a benignant manner and a large, moist hand, which he held out, so that you might shake it if you pleased, but it could not be observed that it developed any responsive activity.

He received Mr. Salmon and Mr. Hackett by appointment at the offices of Tucker and Thomson, Ltd., which for ten years past he had ceased to attend, except at the monthly meeting of the board, until the auditors' revelation of his nephew's conduct had called him back to the helm, to the serious detriment of the Society for the Preservation of Ancient Limekilns, and several similar organizations, to which he had devoted the leisure of his later years.

"The shares," he said, "as you probably know, are not freely transferable. I am offering twelve shillings per share for the four thousand which you hold, subject to one or other of the wills being proved and all fear of further complications being removed, and I think it to be a very good figure to name. Anyway it is the best I am prepared to do, and I don't see how you can get another. You can't force a transfer while my nephew lives."

"On your own accountants' figures, they must be worth about forty-five shillings," Mr. Salmon answered, "and they are all the security we hold for advances of nearly eight thousand pounds, but we will accept the offer, providing that we have also a receipt in full settlement of all claims against Mr. Richard Thomson, and that the prosecution be withdrawn, so far as it be still in your power to do so. As to the will, there will be no difficulty. Miss Bickerton has placed herself in our hands entirely."

"Well, gentlemen, you are wasting your time. I cannot make any bargain on that basis."

"But you would actually be repaid more than is due, and it is the only source from which you can obtain restitution."

"I am not prepared to discuss such a proposal."

"But you don't want one of your family landed in jail?" James broke in.

"It will make little difference, one way or other, to the dishonour which he has brought upon the firm and his family. But I have told you already that I see no occasion to discuss it with you at all."

Mr. Salmon became conciliatory.

"We don't want to force any suggestion upon you, Mr. Tucker, and I think I understand how you feel. But we've come fifty miles to get this matter settled, and we have got one or two interesting suggestions to make. I'm not an expert in company law myself, but I've had the advice of a colleague, and I think your real object is to get your nephew off the board."

"I see no reason to discuss my intentions with you."

"Then I can only say that if you go on on your present lines you won't get what you want, which you might do if you'd listen to us."

"Mr. Salmon," Mr. Tucker replied, "you may be a good lawyer yourself, but I'm afraid your friend isn't. Under the articles of this company we can require the resignation of any director who may be criminally convicted, and, I am sorry to say, there is no possible doubt of my nephew's guilt."

"I have no doubt you are right," Mr. Salmon replied very cheerfully, "but if you'll read over the articles again you may observe that there's nothing to prevent him, even if he should be sentenced to a term of imprisonment, claiming re-election when he comes out."

Mr. Tucker was obviously disconcerted by the suggestion.

"He'd never have the impudence to do that, and he wouldn't get elected if he did."

"On the contrary, he placed himself absolutely in my hands when I saw him an hour ago, and that is just what I have advised him to do. The shares we hold will be available for voting, and, with the support of his two aunts, which is already promised, he would be able to secure re-election."

Mr. Tucker rose from his seat in an anger which he controlled with difficulty.

"Mr. Salmon, if you know my nephew, you know that you are proposing the final ruin of a business which has been built up by the frugal industry of three generations. I know that he can always get round the women. I am at a loss to know why you should apply your scheming legal brain to give him further opportunities of bringing ruin on others and final retribution upon himself."

"But I am not doing so," Mr. Salmon replied with a disarming smile; "I am asking you to buy the shares."

"Then if you think you can force me to pay a blackmailing price for those shares by such a threat you were never more wrong in your life. I'll just wait till he comes out—I dare say it won't be very soon—and I'll fight you all along the line."

"Mr. Tucker, if you'll be patient for ten minutes you'll see that you're wrong on both points. I want to sell you the shares at your own price, and if you think that your nephew is likely to be sentenced to a long term of imprisonment I think I can show you that you may be wrong on that too. I'm willing to lay all my cards on the table, and I think I can give you all that you want at your own price; but anyway it can't do you any harm to look at them."

"Mr. Salmon, I've no doubt you're a much cleverer man than I am, but if I listen I tell you first that I won't agree to anything now. If I did it would be after full consideration, and through my solicitors. I'll just listen, and there it ends."

"That's quite clear," said Mr. Salmon, "and we both know where we are.

"Now you want your nephew out of the firm—I suppose anyone would—and we want just the same thing. We want to give him a new start, in a new country, where there'll be plenty of work, and not quite so easy an access to the cash-box.

"I don't think, with your help, we should have much difficulty in getting him bound over, and even if you oppose it we shall have a good try. Goodwin's coming on this circuit, and he isn't overfond of sending first offenders to jail. He isn't overhard on anyone, unless they've been robbing a church.

"We could show a good many extenuating circumstances—I'm not going over them now, unless you wish me to do so—and we shall be able to show that we have offered full restitution. Besides, there'll be a natural sympathy for his wife—"

"*Who?* I didn't know—"

"There isn't yet. But there will be. He's going to marry Miss Bickerton on Wednesday week."

"You mean she'll marry him with—"

"I mean she'll marry him while he's on bail, and if he should go to jail, which I don't expect, she'll wait for him till he comes out. She wouldn't think of this trouble making any difference. She's better than most in that way."

"But he never meant to marry her. He only made use of her for his own ends."

"No? I suppose no one really knows that, except himself. Anyway, he does now. It wouldn't make any difference legally, of course, but everyone knows what she's been through, and it mightn't make the judge any less inclined to deal with the matter in a lenient way.

"Anyhow, that's what I think.

"It's just for you to decide. You can have his resignation, with an undertaking that he won't seek re-election, and the shares at your own price; or you can fight, in your own words, 'all along the line,' and if you find he's back on the board in six months—well, it will have been your own choice."

"What guarantee should I have—?"

"We would satisfy your own solicitors."

"Well, gentlemen, I'm much obliged to you for calling."

Mr. Abraham Tucker rose and held out a passive hand.

CHAPTER XLII.

"THAT'S a good thing settled," Mr. Salmon remarked cheerfully, as his car ran out of Shrewsbury on the Shifnal road.

"You think it's settled?"

"Yes, of course. Only he wouldn't trust us not to have some trick up our sleeves. He's a cautious bounder. And he was kicking himself all the time that he hadn't offered ten shillings instead of twelve for the shares. I shouldn't wonder if he tries that on yet. But leave Preedy to deal with him."

"I'm sailing in about eight weeks, and I should like to feel that it's all settled before I leave."

"Well, we ought to manage that. I'll bet ten to one that you'll have Mr. and Mrs. Richard Thomson on board, and I hope they won't be a bigger nuisance than you expect."

"I've told that young man," James said confidently, "that if there's any trouble out there I'll thrash him till he can't stand. But he's a decent sort in his own way. His aunts let him run too loose. I'm not worrying about that. The danger is that Anne'll forget that she's of age, or turn up at the wrong church."

"By the way, what are you going to do with the kids?"

"Rose is going to take charge of them at The Firs for a time after I've gone. I can't take them out, till I see what the place is like, and it's better than leaving them with strangers. After that—well, I don't know."

"Don't you really?" said Mr. Salmon. "Well, I think I do."

www.ingramcontent.com/pod-product-compliance
Lightning Source LLC
Chambersburg PA
CBHW032001240626
47153CB00003B/1076